THE DEAD ONE STINKS

By

DON THOMPSON

Copyright 2012

ISBN-13: 978-0615973425

ISBN-10: 0615973426

Table of Contents

The Dead One Stinks

1 BUMPER LOHMAN

I'm afraid it happened again to the big nobody Managing Partner over at Fenton, Pettigrew and Cohenstein, the big Chicago law firm. I always forget his name. Lohman. It's Bumper Lohman.

Fenton, Pettigrew represents large and wealthy clients. It is an amalgam of an old line waspy outfit once called Fenton, Pettigrew, Sidley and Lord, after long gone partners, and a hard charging modern business getting outfit headed by Zenon Cohenstein. The Chairman of the firm is Graybourne St. Charles, but the guy with the name on the billboard is Cohenstein. Graybourne is old line and a descendant of a prior firm Chairman. Cohenstein is a descendant of a push cart immigrant. Normally these two would not have any contact with each other. However, business makes for strange bedfellows. Fenton, Pettigrew was headed downhill to eventual elimination or absorption by another firm. Cohenstein could make use of its name and reputation. Hence F, P & C. To St. Charles, though, it was simply Fenton, Pettigrew. Never Cohenstein.

The firm had been growing even though in the midst of a recession and now had about 375 lawyers, exclusive of a breed known as contract lawyers. These were lawyers hired at lower rates to do things like reviewing documents. There were about 50 equity partners who controlled the firm and who were the real owners. They elected a Management Committee which was headed by St. Charles as Chairman. The Management Committee consisted of the partners with the highest billings. Lohman was a member of the Management Committee and he had the lowest billings of the group, although more than any of the non-Management Committee partners. Besides the equity partners there were about 100 other partners who really were not owners. Their pay

1

was determined by the profits of the firm, though. They were called income partners. Below the partners there were other lawyers called associates.

A lot of modern law firms were larger, but not many were more profitable. F, P & C relied on higher prices and something called leverage for its high partner incomes. Here you should note that lawyers do not use vulgar words like "prices" and "sales" and "selling" as they do not want you to think that they are associated with those things. But they are, just like all business people. Anyway, all big firms used leverage. Fenton, Pettigrew used more. Leverage involves how the firm's work was billed. Lawyers in large firms generally charge for their services by billing for the time devoted to the clients' affairs. If the subordinate lawyers' time can be billed out at more than the cost of those lawyers then there is excess money for the senior lawyers. For instance, an associate at F, P & C averaged 2200 billable hours per year. That is not all the hours they worked, but that is the amount of their working time that was billed. The average associate billing rate was $350 per hour. That is $770,000 per year. First year associates started at about $180,000, including year-end bonuses, and the average associate earned about $275,000. Other costs for each associate averaged $200,000 per year. That leaves a $295,000 profit on each. Deduct some for non-paying clients and there still was a good profit. Only the equity partners generally shared these profits. The income partners were paid more than the associates, but they billed at higher rates and merely got more, but not all, of the profits they produced. The equity partners fed on them too. The key to the equity partners' high incomes was the ability of their clients to pay the firm high rates and the firm then getting the work done for less – leverage. The billing rates of the equity partners themselves were much higher than those of the associates or income partners.

The firm was located in the middle of downtown Chicago in an 85 floor tower called One Swifton Plaza. This was named after The Swifton

Bank, one of the largest in the county. The Bank occupied the bottom floors and also floors at the top for its upper management and its dining club. The Bank was part of a huge group of companies and other investments controlled by the Swifton family whose wealth originated in meat packing and farm implement machinery. Its main company was The Swifton Corporation, a large conglomerate which had some of its offices in the building.

Fenton, Pettigrew occupied 15 floors in the middle of the building from 40 to 55. They had offices in New York, Los Angeles, Shanghai and a suburb of Chicago named Highland Park, but the main office was in Chicago. The main entrance on the 40th floor had an impressive reception room. It was three stories high surrounded by balconies and contained one of the most prestigious private art collections in the city. The works were expensive and talked about. An impressive stair case served the three floors and conference rooms surrounded the reception room on each floor on the other sides of the balconies. The firm had its own internal elevator, used mostly by the equity partners.

On the top floor of the firm offices St. Charles and Cohenstein each had suites at opposite ends. Each suite consisted of a secretarial and reception area, a large conference room and its own private office. Lohman's office was on the fourth floor of the firm, the 44th floor of the building. He had a large office and, because he was the Managing Partner, a large conference room attached. His office overlooked the building's plaza to the North. And across the street was another plaza belonging to another very large bank building. Swifton's was taller.

Lohman theoretically did not make the important decisions as Managing Partner. Technically the Management Committee ran the firm and he merely carried out the Committee's decisions. As a practical matter though the Committee just decided what they wanted to. Cohenstein decided most of the sales questions and the Committee went along with him after toning him down. Everything else, especially the hard stuff, they left to Lohman. Note again my reference to "sales". Lawyers do not know this word. They call it "marketing".

The firm had a business office headed by Geeley McDade whose title was Business Manager. This office handled most of the non-legal matters. Lohman's main task was to keep up on what was going on, to supervise the whole process and, above all, to handle any problems. The Management Committee members did not deal with problems. They did not even determine what their lackey should do about them. They just demanded that Lohman fix them. The Prima Donna does not clean up the theater after her performance has caused half the audience to puke in their seats. Naturally, when the problems were fixed, the other Management Committee members, and especially St. Charles, took credit for it.

As I said, Lohman was a nobody. In any group he was in very few of those present were aware that he was there. He was not a big talker and when he did talk he was brief and to the point. He used simple nouns and verbs and few adjectives and adverbs. The words he did use were simple and of established meaning. Because of his brevity a lot of people did not know he had spoken. Consequently they were unaware of what he had said or that he had said anything or that he was there. Most people prefer speakers who are more verbose and who, besides greater quantity, use words of less precise meaning. That way they can imagine the speaker is saying what they want to hear. They think such speakers are profound. They don't understand what these speakers say any more than they understand what Lohman says because nothing much is actually said, but they think the speakers are masterful and significant, whereas they do not think of or notice Lohman at all. Lohman actually preferred to escape the notice of these people.

So they did not pay much heed to Lohman. Except when the shit hit the fan. Lohman fixed the problems and that is why he was around. And he stuck his nose in the day to day details of firm management and made things work. Of course an additional reason he was around was the fact that he had a large clientele.

His qualities, or lack thereof depending on your viewpoint, are what appealed to his clients and were why he had such a large client base. He had come from a modest background and had developed a fairly large firm of his own before merging it into F, P & C. His clients were mostly businesses doing five million to several hundred million in sales each year and most were owned outright or controlled by one or a few owners. Only a few were publicly held with a lot of owners, but even these were controlled by a few owners of large percentages. The people controlling these companies were mostly as level headed as Lohman and appreciated his simple and plain approach to things. Plain and simple is best. It is also cheaper. Lohman considered minimizing client costs (the bill) to be one of the goals of law practice. Most lawyers were Hell bent on maximizing the bill.

Lohman lived in a large old house about two miles north of Swifton Plaza on a street named Dearborn in an area called the Gold Coast. He was married to Gloria Lohman and their kids had grown up and married and gone. Just the two of them lived in the house, along with a huge Great Dane called Louie. Louie was the friendliest dog in the neighborhood and one of Lohman's favorite activities was taking him for a walk and meeting people as a result of Louie's friendly approaches. Sometimes Louie was too friendly such as when one day the most distinguished Rev. Pratton Cuthbert came walking down Dearborn with his poodle towards Lohman and Louie. Cuthbert was the pastor of the Gold Coast's Episcopal snobbery, St. Tom's of Christ. As they got close Louie went over towards the poodle for a sniffing match. In the process he got between the pastor and the poodle. His tail was wagging furiously. Louie was a big Great Dane and his tail was like a bull whip. In this case the pastor got whipped. Fortunately the matter was resolved through prayer.

So there you have Bumper Lohman. No big deal. Louie might be big, though.

The Dead One Stinks

2 SATURDAY, OCTOBER 8, 2011

Lawyers in large firms work on Saturdays. They work all the time. They are supposed to produce billable hours. If they are awake they are supposed to be working. Except for the equity partners. On Saturday morning, October 8, 2011, a young lawyer named John Sweeney was engaged in a conference with a young child star named Trisha DeLang. She was in films, on the stage, and was a recording artist. She was all over the popular media and she was a teen idol. She was hot. Oddly enough she was a hit with the kids' parents too. She had a wholesome all-American image and advocated all the things parents wanted their kids to do and be. Actually she was a potty mouth and kind of a trash basket. She and Sweeney were going over one of her potential endorsement contracts. Sweeney was still an associate, but he was bringing in a lot of clients in the show business, sports and allied areas and he was going to be made a partner soon. He was outspoken, spontaneous and disrespectful and show business is not respectable. So ordinarily he wouldn't be allowed in the halls of F, P & C, but he had the business.

Sweeney was working on the matter with Sean Featherbottom. Sean was the young associate who was involved in that unfortunate incident earlier in the year involving the demise of one of the equity partners. You will recall I told you about that earlier. Sean was of blue collar origin and gay. However, he was fairly new and few of the equity partners were concerned or knew about him. So long as he produced the hours he could ride under the radar. Sweeney didn't care about blue collar. In fact people of his age had never heard the term. As for gay – that was part of show business. Half of show business is gay or doesn't care what they poke it in. Sweeney also, like most business getters, needed someone to do the work and he knew Sean was one of the best at that.

The Dead One Stinks

Trisha was not an accidental star. She may have been talented, but she was also a granddaughter of Edgar Ivan O'Brien, the wealthiest man in Chicago, rumored to be worth $25 billion. With his connections she went to the top quick.

The conference involved Trisha, Sweeney, Featherbottom and several of Trisha's agents and lawyers from the ad agency for the products that were to be endorsed. Since Sweeney was not a partner he needed one to supervise his work. Lohman filled that role, but he did not generally appear at conferences with Sweeney's clients, both to avoid giving the client the impression that Sweeney was not in charge, and because he knew from experience that Sweeney was competent.

After the conference Sweeney and Sean went to the john to relieve themselves. Male lawyers in firms are like women in restaurants. They all go the john together. But the reason is different. They go together because they all are in the same meeting when it breaks. Sweeney and Sean were talking about Trisha and her trashy ways as they walked up to adjacent urinals and began to relieve themselves. There was a sickening stench in the room. One of the stalls was occupied and Sweeney looked over at it. He motioned over at it with his head and said, "Man! Smells like an onion farted. Shitted, Man." They zipped up, washed up and walked out. Sean went one way and Sweeney headed the other way to find Lohman who he had to talk to about something that came up at the conference. He didn't have to go far, because Lohman was coming down the hall to use the john himself. Sweeney just followed him and started talking to him while he was standing at one of the urinals.

Sweeney paused and then said, "Hey Man! You smell that? Christ Man, what did that guy eat?" He motioned to the stall. "He's still there." Then he shouted out to the stall "What did you eat Guy?" There was no answer. Then he went over and knocked on the stall door. There was no response. This is not what you or I would do, but Sweeney would do it.

The Dead One Stinks

Lohman was curious and he also was accustomed to having to cover up for Sweeney. He went over to the stall. It was the disabled person stall. Lohman knocked on the door himself and said, "Hello. Are you all right in there?" There was no answer. He knocked again. No answer again, so he pushed on the stall door. It was not locked. It opened and some paper fell down from the door. Apparently paper that had been wedged in between the door and its frame and was keeping the door shut.

The sight was not pretty. Sitting on the toilet was none other than what looked like Edgar Ivan O'Brien. He was fully clothed. The guy customarily dressed in a way that covered much of him up, but Lohman could recognize him since he was a client of the firm and Lohman had dealt with him occasionally. He was dead – or at least looked it. The skin that was exposed was discolored and puffy. And he stank. O'Brien customarily used a wheel chair but it was not in the stall with him. Lohman looked around the stall and he didn't see anything out of the ordinary. Nothing else was in the stall. He did notice that one corner of the toilet paper was tucked under, but he had seen this at other times and other places in firm toilets. He had asked the cleaning crew about it and they denied doing it. Lohman touched the one area of O'Brien that wasn't covered by something, his forehead. It was cold. Lohman said, "I think he's dead."

Sweeney was right behind Lohman. He looked over Lohman's shoulder. "Oh crap Man! It's O'Brien. I think he shit himself to death!"

"Apparently not," said Lohman. "His pants are still on. I wonder how long he's been here."

"Yeah, well," said Sweeney, "I was taking a dump in here yesterday. He wasn't here then. I used this stall. It was the only one open. If it'd smelled like this I would've puked instead of dumped."

"When was that?" asked Lohman. "Was he in here around then?"

9

"No Man," said Sweeney. "At least I didn't see him. It was around 11." He looked at his smart phone and fiddled with it. "Here. I keep my original time records on here. When I start something and when I finish." He fiddled with his phone. "It was right after I finished going over Trisha's contract for today. 11 a.m. That's when I finished. Then I came here." He held the phone up to Lohman, who looked at it to be courteous.

Lohman sighed and said, "I'd better get the police. You stay here and keep people out of here. And I'll send housekeeping in to lock up. Stay here till they get here and then see that all they do is lock up and don't touch anything. And don't you do it either."

"Hey Dude," said Sweeney, "I ain't gonna touch him."

"Or anything else," reminded Lohman.

Lohman went back to his office.

So Lohman was going to call the police. Why? Anyone else on the Management Committee, except perhaps Cohenstein, would have said get him out of there. They would have called an ambulance and sent him off to a hospital and maintained that he was dying, but not dead. Cohenstein would have immediately started thinking of how the firm could get good publicity out of the matter. Lohman just knew that when you find a dead body you should call the cops. He also knew that attempts to cover things up often failed because of witnesses and he knew that his partners would try to do such a thing if they got a chance. And he could imagine what the resultant publicity would be like. So he was going to call the cops

Lohman went back to his office to do just that. He went in the reception area where his secretary was. Her name was Tina Goblat. Tete is what everyone called her. She was kind of big. Not fat. Big boned, big muscled and tall big. She had wrists like a line backer's ankles. She spoke like a punch drunk boxer turned Mafia hit man and called everyone Hon.

If she didn't like someone or didn't like what they were doing she just stared them straight in the eye until they ran off with their tails between their legs. If the Bears had her they would have won the Super Bowl. When she spoke everyone listened. No one dared disobey. She was married to a little shrimp and she often showed up on Monday mornings with cuts and bruises. No one could understand this, but no one was going to ask about them.

Lohman said, "O'Brien's dead. He's in the disabled stall in the men's room on 43. I have to get the police. Call reception and warn them and call housekeeping and get the place locked up so no one can get in. Call reception on 43 too. Sweeney's in there now to keep everyone out. Make sure housekeeping just locks up and doesn't go in there or touch anything. But tell them Sweeney is in there.

Tete said, "Right Hon. But why bother. Half the people around here wouldn't get caught dead alone in a room with Sweeney and the other half couldn't stand to be alone with O'Brien. Boy what a creep he is – was."

"Well in this case," said Lohman, "it's O'Brien who is caught dead." Then he went on into his office to call the cops. He told them he would meet them on the 43rd floor. Visitors to the firm were ordinarily told to enter on 40 where the main reception area was, but each floor had a smaller reception area with its own receptionist. Firm personnel and regular visitors usually went direct to the separate floors. In this case, Lohman did not want the police coming through the main waiting and conference room area.

Lohman went down to 43. Sweeney was still there in the hall and Lohman asked him if anyone had come in. Sweeney said no one had, but that he had kept a few people out and when questioned about he had said it was on Lohman's orders. Lohman asked, "Did you tell them why?"

"No Man," said Sweeney. "They could smell the stuff out here and I told them there was a plumbing emergency."

Soon some patrolmen showed up and Lohman showed them to the men's room. It was locked, but Lohman had a master key for every lock in the firm. All the doors that were lockable opened with codes too, but Lohman was part of the creaky joint crowd that liked keys rather than codes. The officers asked Lohman what happened and he told them and they said they would have to call the homicide detectives. They asked him to remain available and they proceeded to secure the area.

Lohman went back to his office again. Here he began calling for St. Charles and Cohenstein. They were not immediately available and he left messages for them to contact him as soon as possible about an emergency matter. He also told Tete to keep trying to get them and tell them what happened and that they needed to meet. He then instructed her to remind them to contact the family and inform them. They were the contact partners. If she couldn't find them soon he told her to let him know and he would find out who could tell the family. He also told her to get McDade, the Business Manager, and fill him in and to have him contact the public relations outfit the firm used and to get the word out through the firm quick. He told Tete to tell McDade the facts and to leave it up to him what to tell people in the firm, just so long as he instructed them to stay away from the area and above all to keep the matter confidential. Lawyers are obligated to keep client matters confidential. In addition to that, those who are up to no good always hide behind the cloak of confidentiality. Therefore the people in the firm should be able to keep from spreading it around too much. At any rate, Lohman knew he had a gossip problem coming on and he had to take steps to control it.

3 THE STINKER

Edgar Ivan O'Brien, as I told you, was one of the world's rich guys. Certainly he was the richest guy in Chicago. He was an eccentric 82 year old and usually used a self-propelled wheel chair to get around, although he could walk and get around by himself a bit. He had been treated for throat cancer and talked through one of those electronic machines called an electro larynx. Always being interested in new products, he was using a hands free device being developed by a medical device company he controlled. He dressed and bathed himself although he could have used more bathing judging from the smell of him sometimes. Usually he was driven around by his chauffeur. But sometimes he just took cabs and put his wheel chair in the trunk since he could get in and out of a car. He had a beard and mustache and long hair and would have been called a mess if he wasn't wealthy. He was fond of sun glasses, large hats and head and throat scarves. He often wore gloves. He usually wore the complete get up even if he was inside. He had a pen with a big diamond on its head sticking out of his chest pocket and he often pulled a small rock out of his side pocket to fiddle with. The rock was smoothly rounded and irregularly shaped and looked like something that was pulled out of a creek. There was nothing special about it except that it had what everyone assumed was a ruby set in its center. Actually it was red glass, but everyone assumed it was a ruby because of O'Brien's wealth. It was his good luck charm he said. He didn't bother to correct those who called the glass a ruby in his presence. He had a big bag on the back of his wheel chair in which he carried things.

Edgar liked girls. He had three ex-wives and currently was working on a 22 year old girlfriend who he called his assistant. Moronika Headpin was her name. The whole family was worried about what kind of cut she was going to get. As to what he was doing with her, the whole family also knew that he took regular shots of testosterone. Edgar didn't seem to spend too much time with Moronika, even when she was at his house, but that probably suited her as well. According to Edgar the only two parts of a relationship that are important are the introduction and the orgasm.

Edgar lived by himself in a huge house on the lakefront in the suburb immediately north of Chicago called Evanston. Sometimes Moronika stayed overnight with him. Sometimes some of his family members stayed in the house too, as they were often coming and going, either on personal matters or business. Other than that, only two servants lived there, the chauffeur and his wife.

Eccentric is a word used for weirdos who are rich. Edgar was a weirdo who was rich. He was often crabby and critical of those around him and he often did not speak much, although he would usually greet those he met. He often fell asleep, even while talking to someone, although sometimes he only pretended to do this to get rid of the people. Around good looking young women though, his whole personality changed. He was very nice and outgoing. In fact you could say for a stinking guy in a wheel chair he was charming.

Edgar's full name was Edgar Ivan O'Brien. EIO, although his parents never heard of MacDonald and his farm. He was known as The Lion O'Brien. The spelling of "Lion" was up to the listener.

The Lion controlled a lot of companies and oil and gas interests. He also controlled what he claimed was a separate county which he called the Plutonian Principality. It was a small island in the Caribbean Sea between the Dominican Republic and Puerto Rico. Some geological quirk had caused it to rise from the sea while one of his oil exploration ventures was working there and he subsequently occupied the whole place. There was no oil and gas there, but he had found the world's biggest deposit of gold and quickly began mining it. Both the Dominican Republic and Puerto Rico claimed the place as theirs. While they haggled over it

O'Brien set up his own national government for the place. Of course he controlled it.

He controlled a lot of companies through a holding company called Champion Holdings, Inc. He did not get too involved in the companies Champion controlled, but he watched over Champion itself like a hawk. There were other companies he owned directly or through other holding companies. He also owned the oil and gas interests and a lot of real estate, both urban and farm. He owned a large company named O'Brien Financial, Inc. which was supposedly an investment bank and also a hedge fund group called O'Brien Hedge Funds, LLC. Always he was doing deals and buying and selling companies and other things.

The Lion was a client of Fenton, Pettigrew. Big time. The partners responsible for the account were St. Charles and Cohenstein. The Lion's companies were also major clients. The Swiftons' companies, including the Swifton Bank, were major clients of F P & C too and The Bank and other Swifton companies did a lot of business with Champion and the other O'Brien interests.

The firm was handling numerous matters for O'Brien. Among other things the Securities and Exchange Commission was after him for artificially pumping up the earnings of one of his companies indirectly without disclosing that to investors. The company whose earnings were goosed, according to the SEC, was Champion Foods, Inc. According to the SEC Champion lent $50,000,000 which it had borrowed from Swifton Bank secured by its plants to a company called US Financial, Inc. Swifton Bank lent the money to Champion at 8 percent interest. Champion lent it to US Financial at 12 percent. After a year everybody paid everyone back and Champion made a nice profit. Without the profit from the loan Champion would have had a bad year. The next year Champion was doing fine and making a big profit without any finagling. US Financial however, was in the hole. This time US Financial borrowed the money from the Bank at 8 percent and lent it to Champion at 12 percent. So in the end everything came out even, except for costs. Since both US Financial and Champion used borrowed money they would have had to pay these costs anyway. So what is the big deal? According to the SEC these were not independent companies. While the O'Brien interests had no ownership interest in US Financial almost all its income came from contracts with the O'Brien companies and that gave O'Brien practical control over it. Thus, the SEC claimed, when Champion was having a bad year and needed to improve its earnings to keep its stock price up, the O'Brien interests could get US to do a deal it would otherwise not do.

The laws the SEC operated under did not make this illegal per se. However, they required publicly held companies to disclose all material information and Champion was public. The SEC was claiming that Champion should have disclosed that its profits were hiked by the loan transaction with a seemingly independent entity that was not actually independent. They were also claiming that O'Brien himself was instrumental in this and was liable as an aider and abettor. Champion and O'Brien claimed that US was independent and that, in any event, these were perfectly normal transactions.

The Lion was convinced that the SEC had an informer. He had hired all sorts of investigators to find out who it was. Fenton, Pettigrew was also working on this.

Another thing the firm was handling for O'Brien was his estate planning. This is a fancy lawyer phrase for determining what to do with your stuff when you die. For a billionaire it involved a lot of tax, corporate and wealth management considerations, as well as the considerations of who gets what. Wealth management is another term used by lawyers and those in the business of handling other peoples' money. It means handling other peoples' money. Believe it or not, none of this estate planning had been done for O'Brien. He didn't even have a will. The firm had been making proposals to him for years about it, but he wouldn't do it. He believed that if he signed documents for any such arrangements, he would die. As I told you, he was a little do do in the head. When pushed he would just say, "Fuck 'em! Let them deal with it." He meant his family and all the people who would be affected by his demise.

Interestingly enough the Plutonian Principality was involved in the estate planning. The idea was that O'Brien would renounce his US citizenship and become a Plutonian citizen and thus escape US estate tax. Congress had wised up to this trick a few years earlier and plugged the hole in the Code that allowed this, but O'Brien was skilled in lobbying Congress and F, P & C was proposing a special exemption which they thought he could get enacted.

The firm was also doing a lot of work for the gold mines in the Principality and doing a lot of work seeing how O'Brien could make money in the financial markets off of gold. O'Brien wasn't too hot on gold. He considered its price a vastly inflated bubble. He always said that if the streets were paved with it no one would want it and asked why other things like wheat were not considered money or valuable by themselves. But he recognized that there isn't enough gold to pave streets and that gold, like wheat, is worth what other people will pay for it and currently people were paying a lot for gold. So he was trying to develop a new gold–based financial product. O'Brien himself was a participant in this as well as two other things that he was trying to get started. One was selling credit default swaps on Pakistani debt. A credit default swap would say to a buyer of the Pakistani debt, if you lose money on this I will pay. I will charge you for my commitment to do this. O'Brien was also developing trade and other schools since everyone and every government seemed to want to subsidize them.

Fenton, Pettigrew was also handling a lot of buying and selling of companies, financings, litigation, real estate, employment, patent and trademark, and other miscellaneous things for the O'Brien interests.

Most were routine. One of note though involved City Hall. I have told you that O'Brien was influential with Congress, and so he was. The firm had its influential partners too. The most influential was Bungus LaRue, head of the Governmental Affairs section of the practice. Bungus was a former Congressman and a disbarred lawyer who the firm had got rebarred, if that is what you would call getting reinstated. Bungus and others were working on a deal for O'Brien involving Chicago's City Hall. The City would sell City Hall to a company controlled by O'Brien. The City would then lease it back. O'Brien's company would buy the place with a loan from the City. Then the building would be resold to hedge funds who would sell interests in the building to sucker investors who would in turn assume the loan. O'Brien would make a big profit on the resale and fees for putting the deal together and the prominent investment banking firm of Goldboi and Baggs would sell the deal to the suckers for huge fees. The rent was so high that the City, which was broke, probably couldn't pay the rent without some further deal to bail them out. More fees would be earned on that. In the meantime Goldboi and Baggs were selling the deal short so if the City couldn't pay the rent and the investment went south they would make money. No City in its right mind would do this – unless Bungus was around.

And finally, there was the family fight. The Lion had a brother named Ryan who had been the Chief Operating Officer of Champion Holdings. The Lion had recently fired Ryan. Ryan then filed a petition in the Circuit Court to have The Lion declared incompetent and to have himself appointed as guardian. Most of the family members had some kind of company job and were opposed to the petition and Ryan becoming guardian, because they thought Ryan would not act in their interests. Naturally Ryan had other lawyers representing him.

4 THE COPS

Soon the detectives came and surveyed the men's room scene. Then they went up to 44 to see Lohman. The receptionist there called Tete and told her they were coming. They were Detective Smokey Bongwad and Sargent Wilbert Gilbert. They found their way as directed to Lohman's suite. They came in and Detective Bongwad said to Tete, "Detective Bongwad. Smokey Bongwad. We're here to see Mr. Lohman."

Tete said with an air of disbelief, "Smokey Bongwad?"

He said, "Yeah. You got a problem with that?"

"No," she said, "But I should think you would."

The Sargent was more formal. "Sargent Gilbert, Wilbert."

"Bert what?" said Tete.

"Gilbert, Wilbert ," he said.

"Gilbert Wilbert?" she asked.

"No," he said, "Gilbert.

Detective Bongwad interceded. "He means Wilbert Gilbert. He's militarily oriented."

Tete asked, "Gilbert? Wilbert? Which?"

"Wilbert is the first name," said Bongwad.

Tete said, "Oh, well. I see. Well Sargent Wilbert,…."

"We use last names," he told her. "Sargent Gilbert. Gilbert, Wilbert."

"So," she asked, "You're Gilbert Wilbert?"

"No," said Bongwad. "Gilbert. His last name's Gilbert. First name is Wilbert."

"Oh, I see," said Tete. "So why are we talking about this?"

She rang Lohman and told him the detectives had arrived and he came out and greeted them. They went into his office and they told Lohman they had surveyed the scene and had ordered the body sent to the morgue where the Medical Examiner would perform an autopsy. They said they had an evidence technician coming in and in the meantime they had patrolmen keeping people out of the area. Lohman rolled his eyes. He was wondering just how long it would take this information to spread around the firm.

Bongwad told Lohman he knew who the dead guy was and asked Lohman what he knew about the matter. Lohman began by cautioning the detectives that he could not reveal client confidences and that was a matter of law and not anything of his making. "So, you can see," he said, "If anything confidential comes up I can't go into it with you. But so far as I know…… . Well, let me tell you I don't know what is involved. I just know one of our associates met me going to the men's room and we went in and he remarked on the smell and we approached the stall. When we got no answer to a question about who was in it and if they were all right I pushed on the door and it opened. It wasn't bolted from the inside. A piece of paper fell down on the floor. Apparently it had been wedged between the door and the frame to keep it closed, but I don't know that. We left the paper where it fell."

"Yes. We found it," said Bongwad.

Lohman continued. "I could see it was O'Brien. You say you know who he was. I assume you know something about his being the richest man in Chicago and in control of a lot of companies. He and his companies are our clients."

"Yes. We do. We know about that," said Gilbert.

"Well," said Lohman. He looked awful, even though I could see only parts of him under all that clothing. Mainly the top of his face. I put a finger on it and it was cold. I concluded that he was dead. The associate is John Sweeney and I told him to see no one came into the area and I came back here to call your department and to get housekeeping to lock the area. "

Lohman continued. "John said he had used the stall the day before around 11 a.m. and there was no sign of O'Brien in there then or smell. When he saw me in the hall today he had just met with one of our clients named Trisha DeLang and some other people to go over some of her matters. She's a client too. He's her lawyer. Oddly enough O'Brien is her grandfather. "

Lohman told the detectives he couldn't tell them much else about the matter.

Bongwad asked, "Is there any record of who is in the firm offices at any particular time?"

"Not really," answered Lohman. The building checks people in and gets their name and asks to see their i.d. but there is no record kept of when they leave. Our lawyers keep time records of what they are doing for which client and when. We use these for billing. We bill for time spent. However, these records are not always entirely accurate and usually do not indicate where the work was done, although sometimes that can be inferred. At any rate these records are confidential, since they involve client matters."

The Dead One Stinks

Bongwad said," Sweeney was in the john just before he got ahold of you in the hall. Did you know that?"

"No,' said Lohman simply.

"Did he have anything against O'Brien?" asked Gilbert.

"Not that I know of," said Lohman.

"What about Featherbottom?" asked Gilbert.

"What about him?" asked Lohman.

Gilbert said, "He and Sweeney were in the men's room together just before Sweeney got ahold of you. Did he have anything against O'Brien?"

"Not that I know of," said Lohman.

"How many like him do you have around here?" asked Gilbert.

"We have over 200 associates," said Lohman.

"What are associates?" asked Bongwad.

"Lawyers who aren't partners," answered Lohman.

"What I mean is….," said Gilbert - and then he flapped his left wrist.

"Oh I see," said Lohman. "You mean gay?"

"Yes," said Gilbert.

Lohman said, "I don't know. We don't keep track of that."

"So what about Sweeney?" asked Gilbert.

"You want to know if he's gay?" asked Lohman. "I don't think so."

Gilbert said, "They went to the john together didn't they?"

"I don't think that makes him gay," said Lohman. Actually Sweeney's penchant for potentially embarrassing involvement with women had cost Lohman considerable time in the past, but he didn't want to tell the cops that.

Bongwad asked, "Was Sweeney's client still there when you were in the john?"

"I don't know," said Lohman. You'll have to ask him. My guess is that she had left since their conference was over."

"Do you know if anyone had it in for O'Brien or if he had any enemies?" asked Bongwad.

"No. No, I don't know anything specific," said Lohman.

"So where were you that day?" asked Gilbert.

Lohman responded. "I had been in a conference on an acquisition for another client that morning. That's why I was on the 43rd floor. It was a client and a deal that had nothing to do with O'Brien. Earlier I had been in my office preparing for the conference and tending to my other paper work and calls. Before that I had walked in from home. I got here about 8:30."

"Did anyone else know about O'Brien in the stall? Did anyone complain about the smell? Did anyone notice it?" asked Gilbert.

"I can't tell you that. They may have, but no one mentioned it to me. I asked housekeeping about it and I was told the cleaner assigned to that wash room noticed the stall in use the night before when doing the final clean up. They thought it was in use. I forgot to ask them what they smelled. The cleaner on the morning crew thought the same. I didn't ask specifically about the smell there either. You can get them through our business office. Geeley McDade is the Business Manager. Tell Tete you want to talk to them on the way out and she'll get you in touch with them."

"Tete is the, what do you call her, outside?" asked Gilbert. "She's big."

"Yes. Just ask her," said Lohman.

They took their leave and Lohman got to work on some of his own client matters that needed attention.

5 LET'S KEEP THE BUSINESS

Graybourne St. Charles was the firm Chairman. An old line, old wealth, waspy anti-Semite, who claimed superior breeding and lineage. He had learned early on that the key elements of respectable superiority are discretion and pretense. This is why those who shoot their mothers do so discretely and then tell everyone how much they miss her. It takes kind of an idiot to do this, but Graybourne was kind of an idiot. Someone once said he was a good example of repetitive redundancy because he was a vacuous idiot. This was said to his face. He took it as a compliment. Graybourne, unlike Lohman, was an adder. He used a lot of adjectives and adverbs. He was always right and in case of conflict between what he said or thought and the facts, it was the facts he found to be in error. Graybourne was known to his friends as Graybee. To his partners he was called Grabby. To Tete he was often The Saint or Charlie. One would think from his behavior that he did not need lights due to having a halo. Cohenstein couldn't see it. Zenon Cohenstein was a little different. He was accustomed to working for a living. Together they ran the firm. They were also the two main contacts in the firm for O'Brien and the ones who got credit for all the billings to him and his controlled entities. Tete had rounded them up and they were waiting in St. Charles' office for Lohman.

St. Charles office was magnificent. It was on the 55th floor at the North East corner. Large and with a good view to the North over the Swifton Plaza and the plaza across the street and also a view to the East to Lake Michigan. St. Charles had a huge and elaborate desk with his back to the windows. Behind the desk was a pedestal upon which his cat, Pussy, was usually perched when St. Charles was not fondling her in his lap. A cat? He's the boss. Get over it. As usual when someone was summoned to an audience with St. Charles and Cohenstein, St. Charles was in his desk chair, Pussy was on the pedestal and Cohenstein was standing near the window behind St. Charles and looking out.

Unlike most occasions when Lohman went in to talk to the two about firm business, someone else was there. This was Arthur Swifton, head of the Swifton interests, another big client group. Arty and Swifty were his nicknames. He was of the St.Charles old line group and he and St. Charles were like twins mentally, although he was less reserved, practiced his dignified look less, and consequently showed the idiocy more. When Lohman came in he was a little surprised to see Arty. For a moment he thought that Tete had neglected to tell them the reason for the meeting, but he quickly realized that Arty had a reason to be in on the deal too. The Swifton Group did a ton of business with O'Brien's interests. In particular the Swifton Bank had a lot currently going on with them. F, P & C wanted to keep the business. And so did Swifton.

As Lohman entered they all greeted each other. "So we heard about O'Brien," said Cohenstein. "We've got some work to do. Who's in charge of things now?"

"Yes. Yes. Very unfortunate," said St. Charles. "A very great loss. We are in mourning. We cannot bear our sorrow. He was a great leader of the modern world. He was a positive and forwardly enhanced example for us all. Such a loss is unbearable and a great detriment to Western civilization. It is a shock beyond belief to hear of his passing."

"And right here in the office too!" said Cohenstein.

"Tell me Lohman, how did he die?" asked St. Charles. "I hear you found him. Such a monstrous and negatively affective event that must have been. "

Lohman replied, "Yes, I found him. In the disabled stall in the men's room on 43. But I don't know how he died. Maybe a heart attack. Must have been right after he got in the stall because he didn't have his pants down."

"When did this happen?" asked Cohenstein.

"I don't know that either," said Lohman. "John Sweeney, you know him, one or our associates with a lot of billings…. ."

St. Charles stiffened, rose up a bit in his chair and put his nose further in the air, which was due to his dignity training, and interjected, "We are well aware of him. I thought we had disposed of him and his ill-mannered, ill-considered, ways." He sniffed and looked aside.

"Not with his billings," said Cohenstein.

Lohman was about to say, "Please, not in front of Arty," but then he realized that Arty would not connect any of this conversation to anything involving him, such as his law firm only being concerned with how much it could get out of him.

"So was he sick?" asked Arty. "What did he have?"

"25 billion," said Cohenstein.

"No, I mean medical conditions," said Arty.

"Well just look at him," said Cohenstein. "He had everything."

Lohman said, "The body was sent to the morgue and the Medical Examiner will do an autopsy. We'll know then."

Cohenstein said," Take care of this Bumper. This is bad PR."

As I told you before, no one gave a thought to Lohman until a mess had to be cleaned up. Then they remembered him. "So what is our story?" asked Lohman. "I have put out word around the firm that he died on our premises, but we don't know why and confidential client matters are involved so no one should be talking about it. But they will and the word is probably out to the press already."

St. Charles straightened up again and put his nose higher in the air. If you don't know what to do, look dignified.

Cohenstein said, "Call the PR firm. Maybe they can help. Can we just say what happened?"

"You mean tell the truth?" asked St. Charles with wonderment.

Lohman said, "We could just say he died and the cause is yet to be determined. It happens all the time. The place is just incidental. We don't have to go into the details."

"The press will," said Cohenstein

"So when they ask we will tell them. He isn't the only person who died in a law firm," said Lohman. "What's the big deal? He probably had a heart attack."

"Here? People do not die here," said St. Charles.

"Yes they do," said Cohenstein. "So it's just normal. He was an old guy and he died. That's our story. I think we're getting spooked because of the real problem. How do we keep the business?"

"Did you tell the family?" asked Lohman.

"Of course," said St. Charles.

"So what was their reaction?" asked Lohman.

"My secretary is dealing with it," sniffed St. Charles.

Cohenstein took the lead. "Here's what we should do." He looked at St. Charles. "You and I should make a list right now of all the people we can contact and for which we are the best contacts. You make yours and I'll go back to my office and make mine then we'll talk to see who is going to talk to whom and then we'll try to contact them. Then you Lohman. You go through the records and your own memory and see which of our people are doing things for O'Brien's interests. Get them on the contact job. And see who is the main contact for each general counsel of his companies. Get them on the job. At least if they can handle it. Don't let our nerdulahs do it. Get someone else. Express our sorrow. Ask if there is anything we can do. Make clear that we are available. And who is handling his estate? Who is his trustee? The trustee of his trust or trusts. Swifty, is the Bank the trustee or executor? You know, if you are, it will be a lot easier for you to keep the business. Us too."

Lohman said, "I don't know who is in charge of his estate or trust. I know Nuftdone has been talking to him about his estate planning." Jerry Nuftdone was the head of the firm's trusts and estates department. "I'll talk to him."

The Dead One Stinks

6 THURSDAY, OCTOBER 6, 2011

The current hot matter being handled by the firm for O'Brien was the fact that his brother wanted to have him declared incompetent and take over as his guardian. His estate planning was linked to this as both matters raised the question of who was going to get what and who was going to be in charge. These were also the matters that O'Brien had most recently been in the office for.

F, P & C still had a trusts and estates practice. Most large firms were getting rid of this or trying to limit it to just extremely wealthy people like O'Brien because there was not much leverage involved. A good large lawsuit or business deal required a lot of lower level bodies to do things like look at documents and write briefs or proposals or other documents. In lawsuits and deals there were lots of juniors to produce income in excess of their costs. Not so with estate planning and probate and estate administration. However, F, P & C got around this by having everyone involved charge huge hourly rates. And why not? Their expertise in tax avoidance and controlling future generations was unrivaled.

The head of the trusts and estates practice was Jerry Nuftdone. Nuftdone was supposedly skilled in tax and business matters. According to him his sophistication, knowledge, skill, contacts and superior abilities put him on a different level than anyone else in the field. He was the one true expert in the field. He had many publications and awards to demonstrate it. The work was really done by some of the more nerdy associates and lower level partners who really did have superior skills in the area, but they couldn't sell. They also knew enough not to advise clients to do certain things. Things that would not work or were just plain against the law. Nuftdone did not. If it sounded saleable, and especially if it involved getting over on Uncle Sam, Nuftdone sold it. Fortunately his nerdy juniors had the expertise to make it work or at least to allow the client to avoid detection.

Most estate planners in large firms do not just do a job for the client and then let it be. They are constantly involved in suggesting new things to the client and yearly reviews of everything. You might ask why this is necessary if the prior work was so outstanding. The clients rarely ask. They fall for the lines that the law is changing and their lawyers have developed sophisticated new devices to avoid tax or creditors or somehow screw someone. It is true that the law sometimes changes, so there. Congress is very helpful to some of us. As for sophistication – when you hear the term, run.

Anyway, Lohman knew O'Brien was just recently in the office to see Nuftdone. He rang Nuftdone up and found him free and went to see him. Lohman usually went to see people in their offices instead of having them come to an audience with him. Lohman wanted to get out and see things and he didn't put much store on the show of having others acknowledge his superiority by having to come to see him. Nuftdone was the sort who required obeisance. At least from all his inferiors. Nuftdone thought Lohman was one. After all, just what was his expertise? He just handled a motley mixture of clients and consulted on all their affairs. In a large firm he was called a general business lawyer. To Nuftdone he was nothing but a general practitioner. He certainly was not a specialist, much less one renowned throughout the world. The fact that Lohman always came to his office confirmed to Nuftdone that Lohman accepted Nuftdone's superiority.

Lohman stopped by Nuftdone's secretary who rang in to Nuftdone and said, "Mr. Lohman's here." She listened a bit and then hung up and motioned to Lohman to go in.

Lohman entered Nufdone's office. "Hello Jerry," he said.

"Bumper," said Nuftdone by way of return greeting.

As usual he had two associates there. Nuftdone didn't do anything alone. Lohman wondered if he had them around to help him with sex. Lohman greeted the associates generally, but not by name because he couldn't remember their names. Lohman said, "I think we should talk alone." Then he nodded towards the associates who got up and left.

"So Jerry," he said. "You heard the news?"

"I certainly did," said Nuftdone. "It's a great loss." He meant to his billings.

"Yes, yes," agreed Lohman. "I'd like to know what was going on and get up to speed on what is needed here. And we need to know who is in charge now. Who is the trustee of his trust? Who is his executor? What's going to happen to his assets?"

Nuftdone looked a little uncomfortable. He was in charge of estate planning for the richest guy in Chicago. There was no estate plan. No will. No trust. No other arrangements. "Well now Bumper, I don't know," said Nuftdone.

"So is there some new selection process you are using?" asked Lohman.

Nuftdone knew he couldn't hide it. "He had no estate plan. Not even a will. We managed to get powers of attorney out of him, but that's it. As you remember, he thought he would die if he signed things like wills and trusts or designations of who would take on his death. He was superstitious about some things."

Lohman was a bit incredulous. "What have you been billing him for all these years?"

Nuftdone said, "Planning. He wouldn't do it, but he would discuss it. And we did implement many things that involved strictly income tax and asset protection that affected only him."

"Crap!" said Lohman. "So it's all up in the air to see who his administrator will be?"

"No, not at all," said Nuftdone. "It will be one of his kids. They have the right."

"Yes, but which one? Are they fighting about it? Don't they fight about everything? And will it be one who will keep the business with us?" Lohman then said, "That's another thing we have to get on. You know Graybourne and Zenon are going to be all over this."

"Of course, of course," said Nuftdone. "Don't worry though. The family bickers, but in the end they work it out and stick together, even if they would rather kill each other. They have been able to recognize so far that they are all better off with a united front."

"So what was going on the other day?" asked Lohman.

"Which day?" asked Nuftdone. "He was here yesterday and the day before. He was in here on the 6th about the guardianship and to discuss the estate planning. You've heard about the guardianship haven't you?"

"Who hasn't," said Lohman. "It all over the TV and the internet that his brother filed a guardianship petition against him. And you remember you informed me of it. I passed it on to the Management Committee."

"Yes," said Nuftdone. "As you know, I hope, he fired his brother Ryan. Anyway, as you know too, Ryan was COO of Champion Holdings. I don't know what was going on, but Ivan told me Ryan was trying to take over. So he fired him. Not long after that Ivan was served with the petition for guardianship filed by Ryan. I talked to Ivan and we thought having someone else file a cross petition just in case would be a good idea."

"In case he was incompetent?" asked Lohman.

"Just in case," said Nuftdone. "And it would slow things down and give us an additional thing to negotiate around."

"Do you think he was incompetent?" asked Lohman. "I haven't dealt with him much lately so I couldn't tell. He was always a little strange."

Nuftdone straightened up. "Of course he wasn't incompetent. I have dealt with him frequently in recent years and he's was as competent as you and I."

Lohman thought about what that meant. Maybe it meant the guy was half incompetent. Anyway he said, "When you're around someone all the time you don't notice their decline. Today they are like they were yesterday and yesterday they were like the day before. Now, while I didn't deal with him that much, I did have contact with him recently about an SEC matter. He definitely seemed less sharp than the last time I dealt with him which was some time ago."

Nuftdone said, "Well that's your impression. I am an expert in these matters and I made a careful assessment of the matter and based on my thorough review I determined that he was competent."

"What about a doctor?" asked Lohman. "It's the doctor who testifies."

"We certainly would have obtained a favorable medical report," said Nuftdone. "There are any number of doctors we use."

Lohman wondered how "we" were using the doctors, but he let it pass. "Did Ryan have a medical report? You have to have one don't you? Did any of those doctors you use examine him?"

"Oh Ryan didn't have one," said Nuftdone. He had subpoenaed Ivan's doctor and he was about to depose the doctor when all this happened – the death I mean."

"What was the doctor going to say?" asked Lohman.

"We were negotiating that," said Nuftdone. Yes, lawyers negotiate the truth.

"So who was filing the cross petition?" asked Lohman.

"That was Watta O'Brien, his daughter by his first wife, Hu Yen Fong. She was on our side," said Nuftdone.

"Well we were representing O'Brien so we couldn't represent her," said Lohman. "Who was representing her?"

"It was all in the family," said Nuftdone. "You know Fenlow Dancaway –"

"Christ!" said Lohman. "We're about to acquire his firm. We would have been on both sides. We can't represent the petitioner and the respondent."

Nuftdone said in a conciliatory manner, "But we haven't acquired them yet. We were going to ask you to delay things. Think of it. We would have had the whole ball park, both teams that way."

Lohman was not surprised. As lawyerly things go this was not too bad a scheme. This doesn't mean that he thought it was ethical or right. It just means he was thinking he would not have one more emergency, like criminal charges, to deal with. The fact that Dancaway was soon to be a member of F, P & C was not public and there was nothing in writing yet so, at least for the time being, the fix would not have been obvious and the firm could always deny there was a deal with Dancaway.

Nuftdone continued, "Neat, don't you think. So we have Watta and her lawyers in on the deal. Fenlow and Pukutania Moore of Muttwuf and Meowi. The top two in trusts and estates at that firm. We will be working with them closely in coming years. Puk. That's what we call her. Sometimes Puku."

Lohman wasn't listening too closely. "Puku?" he asked.

"Yes," said Nuftdone, "Puku. It's her nickname. Sometimes Puk. So Puk or Puku."

"Oh I see," said Lohman. "For a minute I thought you were cursing at me."

Nuftdone did not curse. Or joke. He gave Lohman a blank stare.

Lohman gave him a hint. "You said Puku. Sounds like something else."

Nuftdone gave him another blank stare. So Lohman continued. "What went on at this meeting?"

Nuftdone replied, "Well, we were down on 43 in one of the conference rooms. I had a lot of the files in there. We reserved it for two days because we had another meeting set the next day. We started about 9 a.m.. Ivan and his son Henry came in together. Henry wheeled him in. It was in that self-propelled wheel chair he uses, but Henry was pushing him. Ivan was all wrapped up. He had his hat brim turned down and he had his scarf wrapped over his hat like a babushka. Turtleneck, gloves, sun glasses. The usual outfit. I was waiting for them. We were going to discuss his estate planning and the guardianship situation. I also wanted to be informed of the IT situation so we could look into any potential tax or other strategies using the IT. That's why Henry was there. As you know he's the head of IT at Champion and all the other companies' IT guys report to him. Of all Ivan's kids Henry's the only one with a brain. The others are not so bright."

"Yeah," said Lohman. "I hear they're dodos."

"Yes," said Nuftdone. "It has always surprised me that Ivan gave them all substantial jobs in the companies. How a business can function with people like them in charge, I don't know."

Lohman thought of St. Charles. Then he thought of Nuftdone. He didn't say anything though.

"After Ivan and Henry came in Jason came in. You know him do you?"

Jason was another son of O'Brien's. Lohman nodded.

Nuftdone continued. "He came in to deliver some papers Ivan wanted and Ivan told him to stay. You know, in that weird voice his speaking device makes."

"I know," said Lohman. "It's weird."

"We had also asked all the kids to be there and they all came with their mothers. It's surprising to me how all the ex-wives always show up on his family matters. We all wanted him to take action. I've been going over various planning devices with him for years, but when we got down to effectuating anything he always told me that if he signed anything he was going to die. He was superstitious I guess you could say. Anyway, everyone was telling him to do something if only to reduce estate taxes. And I was trying to use the guardianship angle to get him to do something. In developing a scheme to handle the guardianship issues we could do the other estate planning through the back door. Now in the past he had used quite crude language in discussing his thoughts on the estate tax and his family's interests. So crude that I cannot describe it."

Lohman said, "Well, under the circumstances it is probably your duty to tell me what he said, even though it may be painful for you."

Nuftdone stiffened up and said, "He said – now these are his words – and he said it more than once. 'Fuck them.' "

"Who?" asked Lohman.

"His family," said Nuftdone. "Whenever I mentioned estate tax savings and planning for succession to his interests and control issues, that is what he would say. His view was that he would be gone so what did he care. He could be very vulgar at times with no thought or consideration for my sensibilities."

Lohman didn't give a shit for Nuftdone's sensibilities either, but he did want to avoid a huffy fit so he stuck to the point and asked, "So what happened at the meeting?"

Nuftdone replied, "We never got to the IT issues. It was just endless bickering by the family. One time Jason proclaimed that he heard that Ivan was going to disinherit him. Then they all bickered over whether that was true or not. Ivan didn't say anything until he finally said Jason was going to get plenty. Then Jason demanded to know what. I only managed to calm everyone down when I reminded them that nothing had been done."

"It sounds like them from what I hear," said Lohman. "Always fighting."

"Yes," said Nuftdone, "But they always come together in the end. Anyway, another thing they got into was the marital deduction. Everything passing to a spouse is a deduction from the estate and there is no tax on it. He wasn't married and there was a discussion of whether he should get married and they kept asking me how things could be arranged so they could get the marital deduction without the spouse really getting the money. Then they started in on Moronika, his girlfriend. Thank goodness she wasn't there. Naturally no one wanted her to be the spouse. Then they got into the Plutonian Principality thing. The idea was that it was a separate country and he could be a citizen there and not subject to US estate taxes. I had to inform them that it was not so simple and we were still working on that. Basically we didn't get anywhere."

"I can imagine," said Lohman.

Nuftdone continued. "Ivan finally told them all to be quiet in that vulgar way of his. Then we got into the guardianship proceeding. One thing we did accomplish was to get him to sign powers of attorney appointing someone to act for him if he was found to be disabled. He said he'd do it and I had some of the associates draw the papers up while we were talking. We got him to sign them during the meeting. We also had him sign a declaration that if he was found disabled he did not want Ryan to be his guardian. There he was in front of everyone with a little signing ceremony. There was nothing formal about it, but as soon as we put the papers in front of him everyone quieted down and stood around in a circle to observe. He had been fondling that little stone of his and he put back in his side pocket. He didn't have his gloves on. He often takes them off you know when he plays with the stone. Then he put the gloves back on and he pulled out that pen of his and signed the papers with the gloves on. You know, the pen he had sticking out of his chest pocket with the diamond on the end. Then I remember Henry saying he couldn't find his pen. I think he had one like Ivan's. "

"So if he is disabled – incompetent – how are any of those papers any good?" asked Lohman.

"There is a different standard for the competence to choose an agent under a power of attorney," said Nuftdone, "Or at least that is what we would claim. Also, a court is supposed to give great weight to the expressed wishes of the disabled person as to who any guardian should be."

"So who?" asked Lohman. "Who did he name as agents?"

"Naturally we got The Bank named as agent under the property power," said Nuftdone. "As for the health care power, well - he wanted Moronika." The Bank was, of course, the Swifton Bank.

Nuftdone paused. Then he said, "Talking about competence – we checked his signature too. I had several of the associates take the original documents and compare them to signatures on earlier documents we had. They were a perfect match. His signature was very distinctive. As you know, or maybe you don't, the signatures of many people deteriorate with age and the signatures of people who are suffering from Alzheimer's usually deteriorate too. That was not the case with Ivan."

"Don't you need a handwriting expert to determine that?" asked Lohman.

"Usually," admitted Nuftdone, "But in Ivan's case the similarity with earlier signatures was obvious. We were not in doubt."

Nuftdone went on, "Then we got into what to do about the guardianship. Henry and Jason started in right away on why Watta should not be the guardian. Ivan finally shut them up and said she should be the guardian because he said so. Now you know that we have Morton Wharton from the litigation department to help us on this matter. He was there too. At this point he suggested trying to settle the matter. Imagine that!"

Lohman could imagine it. It is generally advisable to settle any litigated matter. You can never tell what a court will decide, despite what you think it will, and litigation costs a fortune. The Lion had the fortune and F, P & C stood to collect more of it the more they litigated anything, but there was still the matter of doubt as to the outcome. Lohman could understand that. Nuftdone could not. What Nuftdone could understand was that his billings would suffer if the matter was resolved quickly. As for doubt as to the outcome, well, the righteous are never in doubt. Nor are lawyers who do not try cases.

Nuftdone continued, "Well they got into discussing how to settle it and finally Henry came up with an idea that they should offer Ryan one of the companies to have as his own. Just give it to him. Henry suggested that they had a variety of companies that they would like to get rid of. Ivan then got into it and said that Ryan knew what all the undesirable companies were. He used one of his vulgar terms. Jason then volunteered his company where he was Vice President in charge of Long Term Planning. You know, Champion Shipping. All sorts of new ships are coming on line these days. People started building them before the recent crash and they are just now coming on line and driving down shipping rates. But this hasn't been reflected in the financial statements yet. Jason said he wanted to go to another company anyway. He remarked that he didn't think Ryan was aware of the situation. They all agreed that we would make the offer and see what happened. For my part I informed them that this was nothing but a sign of weakness, but Ivan wanted to do it."

Lohman said, "Sounds like quite a show. So what happened then?"

Nuftdone said, "The meeting was over. We couldn't accomplish anything else. Ivan didn't want to discuss the IT matter either so they all left. First most of the family left. Then I talked to Ivan and Henry and Jason together to see if there was anything else. Henry said he had to leave because he had to get to Omaha for some other matter. I can't remember what he said it was. After that they left. They all went together. Jason wheeled Ivan out in the chair and Henry went with them. I went with too to walk them out. I was going to see them to the elevator, but Ivan motioned to the wash room and Jason took him in there. Henry went on down the hall towards the elevator and I went back to the conference room and summoned some of the associates to arrange it for the meeting the next day."

The Dead One Stinks

7 FRIDAY, OCTOBER 7, 2011

"So what was the meeting the next day about?" asked Lohman. "When was it?"

"It started about 10 and lasted till about noon," said Nuftdone. We were going to talk to all the sides in the guardianship proceeding. Ivan was there. He came in with Henry again. I was there. Two of my associates were there and one of the minor partners. Morton Wharton was there. For the litigation you know. He had five of his associates with him."

Lohman reflected that it was necessary to get Wharton, a trial lawyer, involved because Nuftdone barely knew where the court house was. Wharton did know where the courthouse was, but he didn't know anything about guardianships. Hopefully, what one lacked the other could supply. In large law firms there was a lot of lacking and a lot of supplying with the result that it takes a lot of lawyers to do anything.

Nuftdone continued, "Ryan was there with his lawyer Gordine Howe. She had two associates with her. Not very impressive," he sniffed.

"Sounds like we out associated them," said Lohman sarcastically.

Sarcasm was beyond Nuftdone. "We certainly did," he said with pride. "And Watta was there with Fenlow and Puk and several of their associates. Not as many as we had. It was in the same conference room on 43. Ivan was his usual self. He came in with a scarf over his neck and mouth. His hat brim was pulled down as usual. The dark glasses, the gloves, the diamond pen sticking out of the pocket. I said 'Hello' and he didn't even respond. As usual. Impolite."

Nuftdone went on. "We exchanged the usual pleasantries. At least to the extent you can with people like Ms. Howe. Then Wharton started talking and it is amazing how he worked things around to settlement without making it sound like we were being weak. He made it sound like we were going to do them a favor. He reviewed the matter and reminded everyone that the medical reports would show Ivan was competent and then explained that even if Ivan were found to be disabled, he had powers of attorney in place and they would prevent a guardian from being appointed. As you know, the Probate Act says they trump a guardianship. Then he explained how, even if there were a guardianship, the guardian would not be Ryan because Ivan had expressed his wishes that Ryan not be chosen. Ms. Howe argued with all this. She is such a trouble maker. Then Wharton made the offer. I thought we had the matter resolved, but Ryan just said, 'Why would I want that crap company? It's going down the tubes.' He's so crude. So evidently he did know about the state of the company. We didn't get anywhere."

"So what did The Lion say?" asked Lohman.

"Not much," said Nuftdone. "I had cautioned him in advance not to say anything and Wharton had emphasized it. You know, like the old English movies where they say 'Anything you say will be held against you.' At one point Ryan said to Ivan, 'You don't even know what you are doing here.' Ivan didn't reply and then Ryan said 'See what I mean. He's out of it.' At this stage Henry leaned over and whispered something in Ivan's ear and Ivan said 'No.'. I know Ivan was under stress because he wasn't even fiddling with his stone."

Lohman thought about what a scene it must have been. Then Nuftdone confirmed that, "It was quite a scene. All this time Henry was fiddling with his phone. It was a black thing and I remembered he had a white one the other day. He's always fiddling with a phone or some other gadget. And sometimes he pulls something out of that big wheeled bag he pulls around with him. He really is quite a sight pushing Ivan around in a wheel chair and pulling the bag behind him at the same time."

Lohman remarked, "That's the future. I've seen his act too. The kids these days – they're all fiddling with some device. And he's a so-called IT guy. He's worse."

"Yes he is," said Nuftdone. "Before we really got into the discussion he was telling everyone how he had a new experimental phone he was trying out that day. He seemed to want to impress Ivan with it. He showed it to Ivan and said something like 'Nice isn't it?' I think. Ivan just gave him a curt 'yes'."

Lohman quipped, "I'm surprised The Lion didn't say one of his more vulgar things."

"Well, I think Fenlow wanted to say something like that," said Nuftdone. "He said something about kids these days and Henry's bag and Henry got defensive and said he wasn't like all the others with their big back packs and he started describing how the bag was much more useful and so forth."

"Did anything get resolved?" asked Lohman.

"No," said Nuftdone. "Just more fighting. Along the way Howe was saying that in the end Ivan would be found incompetent and that he really needed someone competent to take care of him and someone who was able to handle the business matters to be guardian and that was Ryan. Well, I think there has always been bad blood between Ryan and Henry and Henry stood up and shouted – now you know I don't talk like this. It was Henry. The whole family can be very vulgar. Henry shouted, 'Go to Hell Donkey Dog.' That's what he said. Can you imagine? He said, 'Go to Hell donkey dog. You just want to take over the company. Dad said so.' Then Henry went over to Ivan and whispered something in his ear and Ivan said, 'Yes.' Then Ryan started in. I remember him saying something like, 'You don't even know what you're talking about, you nerdass IT.' This was very stressful," added Nuftdone. "Then Ryan said something like – Oh I find it very distasteful to talk this way, even when telling you what someone else said. Ryan said 'You should take your brain out for a walk until your psychiatrist gets back from vacation.' Can you imagine? Then Watta got into the act. She's as bad as the rest of them. I usually have to bill extra for the stress when I consult with these people. She said to Ryan, 'If I had your balls I'd be in a bull ring. And remember, it's the bull that gets killed.'"

"So," said Lohman, "I take it the whole thing went nowhere?"

"Right you are," replied Nuftdone. "They all left. Ivan and Henry and Wharton and I all watched them leave and then I walked out with Henry who was following Ivan down the hall. Ivan was puttering along and Henry followed right behind him fiddling with his smart phone. Then Henry came up to Ivan and started pushing Ivan and while he was pulling that big bag of his. And Ivan of course had that even bigger bag on the back of his wheel chair. I walked them down the hall towards the elevator and they went into the wash room and I came back to the conference room to talk to Wharton who was still there about what might be our next moves. We didn't come up with much except to continue with our preparations for the court matters. So I went back to my office. As I was walking on the balcony around the reception room I saw Ivan leaving down on 40."

"What about Henry? Was he with The Lion?" asked Lohman.

"I don't know where he was," said Nuftdone. "He probably left earlier."

8 A LOT OF HANDS TO HOLD ANOTHER LOT OF HANDS

That afternoon another meeting had been called in St. Charles' office to follow up on ways to keep the business. St. Charles and Cohenstein wanted Lohman there. Since one of the biggest problems was that no executor or trustee had been designated to handle The Lion's affairs, Lohman had told Nuftdone to be there. Lohman had been going over the status of his own clients' matters. As the time for the conference approached he left his office and headed down the hall towards the elevator. He met Sweeney coming the other way in the hall.

"Hey!" said Sweeney.

Lohman knew enough by now to respond, "Hey."

"Hey Bumps Dude, I got a new client. I want to clear him." Since the firm had so many clients and was working on so many matters, everything had to be cleared in advance before the lawyers were allowed to take it on. Otherwise the firm could be involved in a conflict of interest. For instance, Sweeney's new prospect could be involved in a lawsuit against the Swifton Bank.

Lohman said, "Not now. I have to see the chiefs. Who is it?"

"Queldon Entertainment, Dude. Concert promoters," said Sweeney.

"Okay," said Lohman. Tell Tete to work it up and I'll get to it when I get back. Wait. You represent Trisha DeLang. Right?"

"Right Bumps'" said Sweeney.

Lohman said, "I'm going upstairs for a meeting to discuss ways to keep the O'Brien business. Come with me. Maybe you can add something."

Sweeney said, "Do I have to? I do better with humans."

"Yes, you have to," said Lohman. "And behave yourself. And watch what you say."

Together they went up to 55 and were admitted into the presence of St. Charles by his secretary. Cohenstein and Nuftdone were already there. St. Charles looked towards Lohman and then looked at Sweeney and said, "What is he doing here? I didn't ask for him."

Lohman answered, "He represents Trisha DeLang. He might be able to help"

"And just who is Trisha DeLang?" queried St. Charles. His nose rose almost to the ceiling.

"Hot!" said Sweeney. "Hot Dude! A star. A celebration of celebrity. She makes Justin Bieber look like a chorus boy."

"Hot?" said St. Charles. "And what is that?"

Lohman interceded. "I think he means she is just about the most successful teen idol in the business right now."

"And what would I care about that," said St. Charles. "I gather you mean she is in show business. We have more substantial and appropriate clients here."

Cohenstein interceded. "Substantial she is. Big billings. Our client."

St. Charles lowered his nose enough to look at Cohenstein with regret that Cohenstein had pointed out something that he had to pay attention to. "I see. And just what does she have to do with the O'Brien interests?"

"She's his grand-daughter," said Sweeney.

St. Charles looked at Sweeney with contempt. Then he looked at Cohenstein. Cohenstein was looking out the window. Then he looked at Lohman and said, "He may stay."

Before Sweeney could say anything Lohman gave him a look that reminded Sweeney to shut up.

St. Charles then went into a song and dance about the shock he received when Nuftdone had told him that O'Brien had no estate plan and that who was going to be in control of his estate was going to be up in the air. He maintained that never had he been so let down by the people he was relying on. He went on for about 10 minutes saying that he did not know what they were going to do. What would happen if they lost the business? It would be horrendous. He would suffer intolerably. Pussy would be beside herself. And so forth. He ended by saying, "Do you know how much of our business the O'Brien interests represent?"

Lohman was glad to have an opportunity to break up the tragedic flow. "About 20 percent, I think."

"Lots. Lots. We all know that," said Cohenstein to St. Charles. "Wallowing in pity won't help. Listen to you. Whine, whine, whine. You'd think you were Mogen David."

Sometimes Sweeney couldn't help himself. "Hey Dude! I thought the only way you could make Mogen David whine was to squeeze his balls."

St. Charles looked like filth had seeped into his brain, or at least where his brain should have been. Cohenstein broke out laughing. St. Charles beamed the look of death at him. Lohman tried to look as if he had missed the conversation. Sweeney looked at Cohenstein and said, "Yeah, Dude!"

Cohenstein asked Lohman how Lohman was doing on developing a list of who was working on what and potential contacts in the O'Brien organization. Lohman responded that he had been in touch with the firm's Business Manager, Geeley McDade, and Geeley was getting all matters involving the O'Brien interests off the computer as well as the top lawyers assigned to each matter. He explained further that he had contacted the firm's outside public relations firm to come up with possible approaches that could be used for various contacts. He had also had a memo prepared to be sent to all people involved telling them to contact the persons they thought had influence with the O'Brien interests and to do what they could to consolidate the firm's hold on the business. The PR firm's memo on possible approaches went with the memo. All involved were told to prepare reports on what they came up with. Since they were mostly lawyers, Lohman gave them a limit of 2 pages. They were told to consider how they could use these people to the firm's advantage. Above all everyone was told in forceful terms to keep all this confidential.

"So when do we find out what our people can do?" asked Cohenstein.

"I gave them 2 days to respond to Geeley," said Lohman.

"So what about the estate? What do we do about that?" asked Cohenstein.

St. Charles chimed in, "How could you ever let this happen, you – Nuftdone is it? This cannot happen to someone in Ivan's position. Oh – Heavens." Here St. Charles put his hands to his head and shook his head whilst en mains. "Oh what are we going to do? No one has ever put an estate this size through probate. Think of it. All will be public! And everyone will see how poorly we handled it."

Nuftdone had come to the meeting all perked up with pride that he had been chosen to consult with the top people in the firm. Now he looked like he was trying to find some color to put in his face. He said nothing.

Lohman came to his defense. "Now Graybourne" he said. "The Lion didn't want to do an estate plan. He was superstitious. He thought he would die if he did."

"Well he died when he didn't," said Cohenstein.

"Yes, we all die," said Lohman. "Jerry here was working on it for years. You should see his billings for it." Both St. Charles and Cohenstein looked somewhat mollified. "I have clients like that too."

"You Nuftdone. What do you suggest we do?" said Cohenstein. "Who's going to handle it? To be in charge?"

Nuftdone said, "Well, an administrator will have to be appointed by the probate court. The children have the right to choose the administrator. Each one has an equal right to choose."

"Aren't they all fighting with each other all the time?" asked Cohenstein.

"Yes," said Nuftdone, "But in the end they manage to agree on things. We have a family meeting scheduled to discuss who the administrator will be."

Lohman said, "Most of the kids have lawyers in the firm. I'll see that they are there. And I'll tell them that The Bank should be chosen as administrator. "

"Ah yes," sighed St. Charles. "The Bank. Then Swifty will be in control. Oh. I almost forgot, do you know Dr. Goldbumstein up in Milwaukee. He's the famous Jewish psychiatrist."

Cohenstein remarked, "There are Jews in Milwaukee?"

"Certainly," remarked St. Charles.

"Alive?" asked Cohenstein.

St. Charles looked at him blankly. Then went on, "He happens to have two of Ivan's children under treatment." How did he know this? No one wanted to ask.

Sweeney piped up. "Well if you want to go into things like that get Goren." Everyone looked at him. Goren was Winter Goren, an older partner who dressed in cream color suits with lavender ties and white patent leather shoes. He was a little flamboyant and was referred to as the Firm Fruit, except by St. Charles who called him artistic. They were still looking at Sweeney. He continued, "He's got some of the kids out of - let's say - trouble, from time to time. I think he has some influence on them."

"Lohman. See to that," said Cohenstein. And get Bungus involved too. I don't know what influence he may have on the kids so maybe you don't need him at the meeting, but he has been active for O'Brien."

Bungus was Bungus LaRue, the firm's governmental affairs partner. This meant basically that he was a lobbyist. He was an ex-congressman who had been disbarred, but the firm had got him reinstated. Some referred to him as the firm fixer, but the less said about that, the better.

Then St. Charles said matter of factly, "We will have a meeting of the equity partners at 9 Monday morning in my conference room. Arrange that Bumper." Did he ask if anyone could be there? No. Why should he? He orders, they obey. It is amazing how idiots schedule meetings involving numerous people without considering whether they can be there or if they would be better utilized elsewhere. Naturally there were many absences at St. Charles' meetings, which did not interfere with getting things done at all, considering what happened at the meetings.

Lohman got up to go and Sweeney, who did not want to be left there alone, got up too. They went out and as they were walking down the hall Sweeney said, "Man! St. Charles has his nose stuck up his butt hole."

Lohman did not wish to dispute the point, but he did not want to openly agree either. He said, "Stuck up will do. No need to mention the body parts."

"Yeah Dude!" said Sweeney.

Lohman made his way back to his office suite and got Tete working on rounding up everyone for Monday morning. He retreated to his own office and began working on his own clients' matters. He was reviewing a term sheet for a deal he was working on when a call came in from a reporter who wanted an appointment. Lohman declined and the reporter started asking him questions. It was hard, but Lohman managed to avoid saying anything specific other than they did not know the exact cause of death, but it was probably something like a heart attack. Beyond that he kept saying all matters involving a law firm's clients are confidential. He mentioned that they were scheduling a press conference and his paper would be informed as soon as they had the exact date.

As soon as he got rid of the reporter he called the head of the PR firm. Unlike some other people who used modern communication devices to avoid actually talking to someone and being pinned down, the people who handle public relations actually have to be available. Matters of lucrative importance have a way of popping up at all hours. Or, to put it another way, it is rarely during business hours that the Pope is found in a whorehouse. The PR guy told Lohman he had a presentation worked up and he had emailed it to Lohman and suggested they call a press conference as soon as possible. Lohman didn't think he was going to get ahold of St. Charles any more until Monday morning. Lawyers work all weekend long, but the work of the truly important ones, such as St. Charles, consists of things like golf. So Lohman told the PR guy to schedule the meeting at 11 on Monday morning in a firm conference room. Lohman then got ahold of St. Charles' secretary who was still there and informed her of the conference.

9 THE EQUITY PARTNERS CONFER

Monday morning Lohman got in early and reviewed his pending matters. Tete was there with cuts and bruises on her face. As usual, Lohman wondered if she knew anything about makeup, but, again as usual, he didn't say anything. She came into his office and said, "Problem Hon. We can't get a lot of the partners to the conference. Out of town, busy, scheduled with important clients or in court or agencies. The usual. Why does the Saint always think he can command attendance anywhere and anytime he wants? I gotta work my balls off getting everyone there." Yes, she said that. "Now he wants me to tell him who will be there and who won't. It's already 9 for God's sake. His secretary is on the phone. I put the contact list on your desk with the people I contacted and whether they can be there. I didn't add it up or anything." She motioned to a folder on Lohman's desk.

Lohman looked at the folder and picked it up. It was just a list of equity partner names with Tete's handwritten notes.

She continued, "If I could find them and talk to them I checked them off. Then I wrote down Y if they said they'd be there and N if they said they couldn't. Everyone got an email and phone messages too, but I only heard from some of them. About half. And about half of those couldn't make it. So what do I tell her?" She was referring to St. Charles' secretary.

"Well, not what you'd like to," said Lohman. "I'll just take the list with me. Tell her you did not compile the details yet and I took your materials. It won't matter."

Lohman did just that. He took the folder and a little notebook he used and a ball point pen and took off for St. Charles conference room. He was late and was in a hurry. He was waived in by St. Charles' secretary and he approached the door. He opened it and hurried in. The room was rather full with most of the table chairs occupied. There was a ring of chairs around the wall and some had partners sitting in them. Other partners were standing around. They were mostly chatting and waiting for the meeting to begin. St. Charles never waited for anyone. But then he was always late. Lohman noticed that someone had dropped papers on the floor. One of the older partners was walking back from the coffee table to his seat holding his coffee cup out in front of him. The papers were in his path. He didn't notice them because he was looking at his cup and trying to steady it in his shaking hands. The people in attendance were all immaculately and expensively clothed. For an old guy, that meant suit and tie and leather shoes with leather soles. Slippery leather soles. He stepped on the papers, slipped and the coffee cup went flying one way and the liquid from it went another way. It was flying straight towards Popea Coarhead. She saw it coming and tried to get out of her chair before it hit her. She let out a scream as she was getting up and a big huge low pitched rumbling ripper of a fart or bhlprrft for short, which is what it sounded like. What do you do in a situation like that? What situation? It didn't happen, at least to judge from the reaction of everyone else in the room after they had had a moment to recover. Several of the other partners came to her aid with napkins and sympathies and she did her best to act as if the bhlprrft either didn't happen or didn't come from her.

Some of the equity partners had other partners or associates with them. This was common at this type of meeting as many of the equity partners wanted to continue their work while waiting for St. Charles. The juniors usually left when the meeting started. Lohman noticed that Sweeney was there with Cohenstein. He came up to Cohenstein and greeted him and Sweeney. He wondered what Sweeney was doing for Cohenstein's clients, but he didn't have to guess what was going on because Cohenstein told him that he wanted Sweeney there to tell the equity partners what happened and answer any questions if need be.

The Dead One Stinks

Cohenstein asked Lohman if any more people were coming and Lohman said he didn't think many more would show up. Cohenstein said to Sweeney, "Go tell Graybees's secretary we're all here. Just stick your head though the door and tell her. Then let's get started. You handle it till Graybee gets here," he told Lohman.

Lohman started the meeting and reminded them all what they were there for, which was to determine how to keep the O'Brien business. He asked the group if they had completed their contact lists. Some indicated that they had and he reminded the rest to get them done ASAP. He told them to get their lists to Geeley McDade, the firm manager, within half an hour after the conference and he would make a master list for everyone to review and comment on. In the meantime they should review the PR firm outline of suggested approaches and start contacting anyone who they though it would be good to contact. He reminded them to stress that they didn't know the cause of The Lion's death, but it was probably natural causes. He reminded them that it is normal for people of his age to die.

At this point St. Charles came in and stepped to the front of the room where Lohman was. Lohman gave way. St. Charles greeted everyone and then explained how they were all there to determine how to consolidate the venerable tradition of Fenton, Pettigrew involvement with the O'Brien interests. St. Charles said, "Despite the unfortunate recent incident, the venerable firm tradition of Fenton, Pettigrew, Sidley and Lord continues on. The very thought of it generates profound respect throughout the legal universe." No one was really listening and why should they? St. Charles was going on and on. He continued, "Now in matters like these you leave it to me for vision and guidance. I know how to handle these things. As I have said many times we will remain steadfast and shine like a beacon for all to follow. As for determining just what happened, we will begin to investigate looking in to how to handle revealing the appropriate truth." He was going on and on.

The Dead One Stinks

One of the partners, from the Cohenstein faction leaned over and whispered in Cohenstein's ear, "What did he say?"

"Nothing," said Cohenstein. "And he didn't say Cohenstein."

"So what's new?" remarked the other partner.

When St. Charles asked for questions another partner stood up and asked exactly what they should do. As he sat down St. Charles started responding and another partner leaned over and whispered in the seated partner's ear, "Do you realize you just asked an idiot what to do?" The just seated partner gave him a look of frustration.

At this stage Cohenstein broke in and said he wanted everyone to know what happened. He began by saying O'Brien probably just had a heart attack and reminded them again that it is normal for people of his age and condition to die. And he reminded them it can happen wherever they are, even at their lawyers' offices. He explained that he had got Sweeney there to tell them what happened and answer any questions about the matter. He introduced Sweeny.

Lohman was apprehensive. He hadn't been aware that Sweeney was going to be there so he had not given Sweeney the usual caution beforehand. The place and the conditions to be described lent themselves to prurient Sweeneyisms. Sure enough, in describing his function in the wash room Sweeney started referring to his, "Sweeney weenie. Yeah Man, that's what all the girls like!" He couldn't help himself. And as with bhlprrft, all those present just looked stone faced. No reaction.

"Christ!" thought Lohman. "No wonder he's not a partner yet."

Cohenstein encouraged Sweeney to finish quickly so they could get to the real purpose of the meeting and then hustled him out of the room.

The partners then started volunteering ideas about who to contact and what to tell them and how to handle them. They discussed various pending matters for the O'Brien interests. St Charles started into his endless verbiage again and one of the partners finally interrupted him and said, "When you're done, let me know what you said." St. Charles was flattered by this. He thought it was an early request for an encore.

By now everyone had some ideas of what they were going to do with the contacts they had. Many of them who worked on O'Brien business did not deal with him directly, but instead dealt with other people within his empire and they already had good relations with these people. However, many of these contacts dealt with F, P & C because they were told to by O'Brien. Those who had dealt with O'Brien directly still had no definite idea of who to contact about what, other than what Cohenstein pointed out. The family members were now in control and they were the ones who had to be massaged. Lohman was instructed to narrow the contact information down to that and go over it with St. Charles and Cohenstein as soon as he could.

The meeting then shifted to another topic which was the firm's credit line. Most large law firms have lines of credit which they draw on to smooth the flow of cash to the equity partners. A law firm's receipts can be quite variable and the partners want regular cash distributions so when receipts are down they draw on the credit line. Some firms just live off the credit line and it gets bigger and bigger. Naturally some of the partners wanted to do just that. Saner ones did not. There was always discussion about this, but the line was due to be renewed soon. Because of the bad economy and the lower interest rates available the spenders wanted to drastically increase the size of the line which was of course the first step to be taken before borrowing more and pretending it was income.

St. Charles had many words on this topic too, but not much of substance to say. One of the partners leaned over to Lohman and whispered, "What bullshit!"

Lohman whispered back, "Even a bullshitter drops a turd you can use once in a while."

The guy retorted, "If you can find it in the pile."

Lohman, St. Charles and Cohenstein went direct from the equity partners' meeting to the press conference. McDade, the firm manager, had set it up in one of the conference rooms and the press was waiting for them. St. Charles' secretary had let McDade know they were coming and everyone was ready as St. Charles strode in followed by Cohenstein and Lohman. St. Charles assumed the podium and Cohenstein and Lohman stood behind him, one on each side.

St. Charles had not rehearsed or reviewed anything, nor would it have done any good if he did. He started talking. "Good morning ladies and gentlemen of the press. I am Graybourne St. Charles, Chairman and head of Fenton, Pettigrew. As you know, one of the giants of modern life, Edgar Ivan O'Brien, has passed on. It is a tragic loss to those who knew and loved him. Untold numbers are in mourning throughout the world. Our grief and sorrow is commingled with theirs."

"As you may know, we have been privileged to be closely associated with Mr. O'Brien throughout the years. Some knew him as The Lion, and I can tell you as one of his closest intimates that he truly was a Lion in every sense of the word. A great loss. A great man. And here at Fenton, Pettigrew, in our venerable tradition of counselors to the world leaders, we who have had a leading role in his affairs, we who supply sophisticated and aggressive prevailing leadership and guidance and world class strategies and solutions to our well connected and cutting edge powerful industry predominant clients , yes - we mourn his passing." He was continuing on, but those present started shouting at him to gain his attention. He finally relented and recognized one of them.

They wanted to know what happened. He told them The Lion had been found in one of their rooms. They asked if it was a toilet and St. Charles admitted that he was found in a "utility room". They asked what O'Brien was doing there. St. Charles described how O'Brien had been in the office the day before he was found and had gone "down the hall to the utility room" after his meeting and he must have died there. No one knew the details. All they knew is that he was found there on Saturday by a Mr. Sweeney who noticed something odd and called Mr. Lohman, the Managing Partner, who went in and discovered the body. Someone asked how O'Brien died. St. Charles said no doubt it was from natural causes. After all, he was 82 years old. Someone wanted to know if St. Charles knew the exact cause of death. He told them he did not know the details and that the Medical Examiner was looking into it. Another reporter asked how long it takes and added, "After all, The Lion was found Saturday morning and here it is Monday already." St. Charles said he had no idea. (Sometimes he was truthful). Other reporters wanted to know what The Lion was doing in the firm's offices. St. Charles told them it was confidential, private, sensitive and nonpublic. They asked who is going to be in control of the O'Brien interests. St. Charles pulled the confidential response on that too.

Then a reporter for one of the TV stations asked, "Some of the family members say they have no idea who is in charge of the O'Brien companies now. What do you have to say about that?"

St. Charles was not phased. Nothing phased him. He said, "Not all the family members are fully informed about his affairs. Naturally he kept these things to himself and many of the details are subject to the attorney-client privilege and confidential. In our process of counseling the family, all matters they should be advised of will be communicated. Naturally, at the present time we do not wish to intrude upon their grief, which is untold. Suffice it to say, all of The Lion's affairs are well in hand and under sound and prudent management."

The conference went on a little longer, but nothing the press did not know was revealed. The whole thing was a waste of time so far as news was concerned, unless one realizes that the show was the news. The Lion was news. Everything about him was news. As a result everyone was treated later in the day to short video clips of St. Charles proclaiming his grief and his firm's prominence. Good PR!

10 BUILDING MATTERS

Lohman was going to the wake which was scheduled to start that Monday afternoon, but first he wanted to get on top of some matters. On the way back from the press conference he stopped in to see Geeley McDade, the firm business manager. They got the firm IT manager, Henner Pigman, into the office too. Lohman told them he wanted a separate compilation of all matters the firm was handling for the individual family members and who was in charge of each matter and who was working on each matter. He told them he wanted it by four that afternoon and he explained that O'Brien had no estate plan and had no trusts or other devices set up and thus the family, as heirs, would be in control and the strategy was to identify all contacts with the individual family members and to start working on them. He also told them to be prepared to distribute a memo from him to the lead partner on each matter along with the master list of contacts and matters being worked on.

Lohman then told McDade he wanted to see the building log for the days O'Brien had been in the office – Thursday, Friday and Saturday. Lohman wanted to see if anyone who might cause trouble or who had to have hand-holding was in the firm that day. McDade told him the cops had already asked for the log for the whole building, but he couldn't get the full building log, just the parts for the people who checked in for the firm offices. Unless of course, they got ahold of Swifty and had him or someone from his office ask for it. Lohman allowed as how he didn't want the whole thing anyway.

Then Lohman went back to his office to do work on the memo. He labeled the whole thing as confidential and told the intended recipients up front that The Lion had no estate plan or trusts so the identity of who would be in control was uncertain. To begin with, the firm would try to influence who would be chosen as administrator of the estate and that influence was to be used to have the Swifton Bank selected. All the recipients were told to contact any family member they could and advise them that was the best course of action. He put in a list of reasons why it was the best course of action. He actually believed a few of the reasons to be true. The main reason was that the family members were mostly incapable of running anything and The Bank did have experience in these situations as well as experience in "wealth management". The memo cautioned the recipient not to use the idea of incapability unless the family members other than the one being talked to were the ones being referred to as unable to handle the matter. After all, each family member knew the others were incompetent. There were a lot of other reasons for selecting The Bank in the list too, mainly to give a menu of things for each recipient to select from according to his or her knowledge of what would be effective with their family contact.

Lohman then got ahold of Tete and gave her the memo to process and get to McDade for distribution that afternoon. He described it to her and she took a glance at it and said, "You forgot 'Because I say so' Hon. Choose The Bank because I say so. I am wise and all-knowing. That is what they should imply. Right?"

Lohman smiled and said, "I think our people will instinctively use that approach if they think it effective. Or if that is the way they advise people."

Just then one of the firm clerks came in and told Tete he had something for Mr. Lohman from Mr. McDade. He didn't recognize Lohman, but Lohman told him, "I'm Lohman. You can give it to me. I don't think we've met have we? You are--?"

The clerk did not know Lohman by sight, but he knew him by name and position. He half gulped and spoke his name and Lohman said he was glad to meet him and encouraged him to call if he had any questions. Lohman often told the people in the menial jobs in the firm this when he met them. They did not often call, but when they did it was usually very interesting. In the meantime it created good will with the troops.

Lohman retreated to his office with the envelope. In it was part of the building log showing traffic to the firm for the three days in question. The name of each person who checked in to the firm offices was recorded. If they were not firm personnel who had passes, people in the lobby asked for their identification and copied their names from what was offered and then gave them elevator passes for the floor they were going to. The passes would work only for the floors the entrants had declared they were going to. The firm personnel with passes were recorded in a separate log with information gleaned by the equipment where the passes were scanned. No one was logged out. Only log-in information was kept.

Lohman looked over the log. There were a lot of people listed and he scanned the list. Some he knew personally. Some he knew about. And some he never heard of. He did not conclude anything from what he saw, but he determined to review the list later. He looked for The Lion. For Thursday he saw where O'Brien was logged in. No one connected to him was logged in with him, although someone Lohman recognized did come in at the same time. This was Sally Wallydone who was a client of the firm. She was getting a divorce and the firm was representing her. In the past large law firms did not stoop to divorce work. It was not respectable and proper lawyers did not do it. However, they had since learned that there was money in rich peoples' divorces. Sally's husband was Wally Wallydone and he had bucks. Lots of them. He also controlled a lot of companies and Sally stood to wind up with some of them. These companies would make nice clients for the firm.

Lohman noted that other O'Brien family members and lawyers involved in the O'Brien guardianship matter came in later. He noted that

Jason came in about twenty minutes after The Lion and that Henry came in a little later. The others started arriving soon after that.

At this stage Sweeney showed up. Lohman had wanted to meet with Sweeney to tell him to watch what he said, not only in general, but at the upcoming family events. Lohman mentioned his statement to the equity partners about "Sweeney weeney". Sweeney replied, "Shit Dude, what could I say. I was telling them about peeing and whenever I think of reaching for my fly I think of girls. It's normal Man."

Lohman tried to tell him that some people are offended by any public mention of sex, to which Sweeney said, "Like it doesn't exist Man. If you want to know what's normal, look at what the doggies do. They don't care who is watching. No hang ups Man."

Lohman thought about another approach. "Well, they might do it, but they don't talk about it."

"They would if they could talk," said Sweeney. Then he relented, "Okay Dude," said Sweeney. "I won't talk about it when these types are around. I'll just do it."

"Oh crap!" said Lohman. "You know what I mean." Then he smiled and said, "You know one of the cops wanted to know if you're gay."

Sweeney was not suppressible. "Well, I could be Bumps. What did he look like?"

Lohman said, "I don't know. Like a cop. He wanted to know if you are gay because you went to the john with Sean."

"Well, he's kind of girly," said Sweeney, "but I know he's a guy."

Lohman admitted defeat and settled for another caution. "Just try and watch your language around here. Please."

11 THE WAKE AND FUNERAL

O'Brien's wake started Monday afternoon. It was being held in Chicago's big indoor sports arena on the West Side. O'Brien had purchased the naming rights from the developer and it was called The Champion Center. Considering The Lion's wealth and importance a large number of mourners were expected. The Lion may not have had an estate plan, but he had made it clear to his family that he was an adherent of the Gabrellian faith and he wanted a Gabrellian funeral. Gabrellian was what The Evangelical Congregation Of The Angel Gabriel was called. It was usually referred to as ECOTAG. Some of his family members were also adherents of this faith. The Angelic Leader of ECOTAG was The Prophet Andy. Unfortunately, The Lion had originally been a Roman Catholic and he also maintained some adherence to that religion and was friendly with the Cardinal of the Chicago Diocese.

The particular principles of the faith were not too well articulated. The clearest principle idea was that The Angel Gabriel was the voice of God on Earth and he periodically revealed himself to a chosen prophet on Earth. This time it was The Prophet Andy. The Prophet did not accept Jesus as the Son of God, but merely referred to him as another prophet like himself. The Prophet was opposed to all regulation of his religion. He maintained that Jesus could not have qualified for a walk on water license today, even though he denied that Jesus ever did walk on water. ECOTAG maintained that a new chapter had to be added to the Bible. This new chapter was written directly by God who revealed it to The Angel who in turn revealed it to The Prophet. Now, we all know that Mohammed maintained that the Koran was revealed to him by The Angel Gabriel. The Prophet Andy maintained that The Angel did reveal things to Mohammed, but that Mohammed deliberately misconstrued them to his own advantage. The Prophet and his evangelizers sought to correct that. Needless to say, the Muslims were not on good terms with the Gabriellians.

ECOTAG was a world-wide religion with many members. Just how many were confidential. It was head-quartered in Chicago in a new 2500 foot tall building on the lake front. This building had been scheduled to be the tallest in Chicago at 2000 feet. The developer had begun construction and then had gone bankrupt. Since the design did not seem terribly profitable and the 2008 crash had begun and the site had been sitting vacant, The Prophet got a good deal on it. The Prophet Andy did not particularly need a profit from his headquarters and he did like the idea of the building's prominence so ECOTAG bought the site, added 500 feet to the building, and went on with the construction. Andy liked the idea of being close to God. At the top an innovative lighting arrangement was installed that made it look like the building had a halo. At night a fine fog of water was expelled in front of the lights and that caught the light to form the halo.

Prophet Andy called the building The Aspire as in aspire to Heaven. He and other highly placed Church officials lived there. The living quarters were at the top and were called The Palace. The Prophet's private audience rooms were on the top floor. The Church offices were also in the building. These offices included many training and educational facilities where followers of the faith could be instructed in its ways. There was a hotel where the followers could stay and studios for the faith's radio and TV stations. Naturally there were various chapels and sanctuaries in the building and, most importantly, a mausoleum where important followers of the faith could be laid to eternal rest so long as their perpetual care fees were perpetually paid.

The wake was to include a televised service presided over by The Prophet. Many prominent people were scheduled to deliver eulogies. Each and every one had made a significant contribution to ECOTAG for the air time.

The Dead One Stinks

The Cardinal was at the wake too. The Cardinal was the Cardinal Brandon Samuel, or Cardinal Sammy as some called him. The Cardinal and The Prophet were after the same high flier prospects and they were not on good terms in private. For show though, they were all on the same God team. Anyway, The Prophet could hardly deny entrance to the wake to the Cardinal and the Cardinal could hardly afford not to show up. At any rate, the Cardinal was jealous as hell. Andy was stealing his followers left and right and Andy now had the most spectacular place in town. He tried to take comfort in his ace in the hole which was that Roman Catholics could do whatever they pleased and everything was OK just so long as they confessed. Then they could do it all over again.

Lohman arrived at the wake late in the afternoon. The casket was on a raised area at one end of the arena and behind it was a more elevated area on which was placed the podium and chairs for the distinguished eulogists and family members. Stairs led up to the elevated area and there was a long line of people waiting to get up to the casket and wish the Dear Departed Godspeed. Dear Departed! The most dear thing about him was that he was departed. As usual in these situations, a lot of people decided that, despite the line, they needed all day to grieve over the coffin and put on an act for whoever might be watching. Because of this there were three levels for viewers on each side of the coffin, sort of like racks for the aggrieved. There was also an ECOTAG agent in white who urged people to move on.

The eulogies were scheduled to be delivered the next morning so the floor of the arena was empty of the seats that would be placed in it overnight. The basketball court surface had been taken up and a temporary surface had been placed over the area. People were milling about on it and at various places family members were available to accept condolences. The seats in the arena above the floor contained many mourners who were resting. Many people were milling about in the seating area too.

The Dead One Stinks

Many prominent people were there and everything was being video cast. A lot of the firm's partners were there already, networking with whoever they could. Lohman had Sweeney with him and they took one look at the coffin line when they came in and decided to take a pass on it. As Sweeney put it, "Shit Man! Who can I schmooze in a line?" They walked past two women who were discussing whether The Prophet or the Cardinal had the better outfit and went further in towards the center of the arena. They were surveying the crowd to see who they knew. Sweeney said, "Wakes give me the creeps. You know what I want at my wake?"

"What?" asked Lohman.

"I want a bunch of necrophiliac chicks. And I want one of 'em to say, 'Look, he moved'." Then he and Lohman both noticed someone they knew and they parted company. They did what everyone else was doing there which was to hunt for business.

The wake continued on Tuesday and that is when the eulogies were delivered. It is amazing how many people were so aggrieved by the reclusive old guy's death. Needless to say the firm's partners spent a lot more time at the wake on Monday and Tuesday than they did on other matters . Wednesday morning the funeral service was held at The Aspire in ECOTAG's largest cathedral. It seated 3500 which was far below the capacity of The Champion Center and accordingly it was much harder to have secured admission. ECOTAG helped the selection process by selling places. St. Charles, Cohenstein and Lohman were there, along with only a few other firm partners. Gabriellians were cremated, and this had been done to The Lion overnight so only an elaborate container for his ashes was present. The Prophet Andy was liberal in his readings from the Gabriellian addition to the Bible. He was also liberal in his explanations of how fealty to the ECOTAG faith could secure one's place in Heaven and how enrollment in ECOTAG's educational and training courses was the key to this elevation of one's soul.

The Dead One Stinks

The Cardinal was there too. At one point during The Prophet's address he leaned over to an aide and whispered, "I hear he never prays."

The aide replied, "Some people know enough not to attract God's attention."

The services eventually concluded and those present departed, except for St. Charles, Cohenstein and Lohman who had been asked to meet with ECOTAG's General Counsel, Herman Schlot, and The Prophet himself after the services. The meeting was to be in the private audience rooms at the top of the building where only the privileged had been. St. Charles, at least, was most flattered. Schlot took them up in one of the high speed elevators dedicated to The Palace floors. Schlot was accompanied by Fang Lo, one of his aides who often accompanied him. Fang was a junior lawyer and did not talk much as befitted his lowly status.

The elevator started slowing down as it reached the top. Everyone felt that funny feeling one gets when a super high speed elevator slows down and gravity seems to decrease. The elevator stopped and the doors opened. Schlot led the men out. They entered a foyer done up entirely in white. Floor, walls, furniture. All white. It was a large foyer and at the other end was a desk at which a secretary dressed entirely in white sat. On either side of her were armed guards dressed like angels with small symbolic wings. Entirely in white. Their guns were white. There were couches and chairs along the walls of the foyer. All white. No one was in them. The only thing that enabled one to get one's bearings was that the whites were of different shades.

The four walked up to the desk. Schlot turned to Fang Lo and said, "You wait out here." Then he said to the secretary, "We're here for the audience."

The secretary looked at a clock on her desk and said, "You know you are early. You've done this before. The Prophet is not pleased with lawyers who are early. It is written that lawyers never arrive on time. Sit there." She motioned to a nearby couch on the side of the foyer opposite Fang. They meekly went there and sat like three naughty boys waiting to see the principal.

At the appointed hour the secretary said without any introduction, "Now you enter."

They got up and headed towards the double doors beyond the secretary. One of the guards motioned for them to stop and then opened the doors. He looked in. Then he motioned for them to follow him. They entered a long white hall with mirrors down each side. They went down the hall to the enormous pair of doors at the other end. These were white too, but as they approached they could see that the doors were studded with large gemstones. The guard reached up and touched a large button beside the doors and they swung open. The guard motioned them in and they entered the private audience room of The Prophet Andy. It was a semi-circular room with several semi-circular steps rising to The Prophet's perch. There was an altar behind him and he had an elaborate throne to sit on. A modernized throne with comfortable upholstery. Once again, everything was in white, except the throne which had a gold frame and red upholstery. The gold was not just a color. The frame was real gold. It was studded with large gem stones. The ceiling was glass. Its opacity could be electronically controlled. Today it was left clear, letting the sun shine in. On the base level there were chairs for the faithful to sit upon while they worshipfully gazed up at The Prophet.

The guard led them in. Four chairs were aligned in a row in the center of the floor. He pointed to a chair and then pointed to the person who was to sit in it. They sat where indicated. When they were seated the guard finally spoke. He said, "Arise, The Prophet comes." They were all lawyers. It was just like when the judge comes in to the court room. They all rose. The Prophet appeared through a door at the upper level held open for him by another guard who followed him to his throne and stood beside him. The Prophet was not in white. He was known for wearing ordinary street clothes, but under ceremonial robes. Today the robe was orange. And he had a red headband with diamonds in it. It looked like the type of headband runners or other people taking exercise wear. The diamonds sparkled in the sunlight. After The Prophet seated himself the guard said, "Be seated. Be silent."

The Prophet spoke. "Gentlemen, thank you for coming today. As you know, Mr. O'Brien was a faithful follower of ours. He had made a pledge to us to aid us in constructing this building. Two hundred fifty million dollars. Only one hundred million of this has been paid. In addition he was well on his way to Angelship. We had contracted to educate and train and prepare him for Junior Angelship. The cost to be deferred by him was twenty five million dollars. He put up a deposit of ten million, but the remainder has not been paid. God cannot do his miracles without sustenance." He held out his arm with the palm of his hand facing up and extended it towards Schlot. "Give them the papers." He looked at the others and said, "Mr. Scholt will give you all the relevant documents. We would like whoever is handling his affairs to make prompt payment. I was to have an audience with him last Thursday afternoon to go over these financial matters, but he did not appear. Nor did he cancel. This was extremely unlike him. This kind of behavior does not bode well for his status in Heaven."

St. Charles croaked out, "That's one hundred seventy five million, less the ten million!" Only lowlifes expressed dismay at these kinds of figures, but St. Charles couldn't help it.

"No!" said The Prophet. "The ten million was in an escrow account. It will barely pay for the wake and funeral. Mr. Schlot will give you the bill. Fortunately his perpetual care was endowed by him before death with ten million, so he can stay here for the time being. But should his account not be settled we – and God – would be compelled to expel him."

The Dead One Stinks

Lohman and Cohenstein looked at each other. St. Charles was just gapping up at The Prophet with his mouth open.

Andy threw them a bone. "Don't look so surprised. It's not your money." Then The Prophet did what other laymen often do when in the presence of lawyers. He asked for free advice. "Mr. Schlot. Tell them about that matter we were discussing the other day. The one where our insurance company will not cover us."

"Here? Now?" Schlot asked tentatively.

"Now," said Andy.

So Schlot described the unfortunate event. "Well, it happened in court. One of our executives, who we had to let go due to lack of faith, had filed a religious discrimination claim against us. As you know gentlemen, we are a religion. We are entitled to require that those associated with us follow the true way of God and The Prophet. Well, we were over at the Daley Center. You know, the State courts. I'll fill you in on why we were there instead of Federal Court later. We were there for a hearing on a motion. You know. One of those motion calls when a lot of other people are there. In this case one of the other lawyers in the court room was Sidney Glass, one of the wealthiest lawyers in town. So as I was arguing the motion something happened to annoy the judge and she picked up her gavel and brought it down hard on the bench. Well, this is all very hard to believe. The gavel hit a pen on her desk and sent it flying across the court room and it hit one of the bailiffs on the side of his face and he turned and pulled his gun and as he pulled it out it went off. The bullet hit the leg of the court reporter's stand and her machine fell and hit Glass' bag in which he had some delicate physical evidence which was destroyed in the process. He and his client have filed suit against us. They claim that something I said caused the judge to become angry and they claim that I knew it would do so and that, in fact, I intended to create the anger. As you can see, it is a highly unusual situation. And the evidence was crucial to a high stakes suit so they are claiming a lot from us. We tendered the defense to our insurance company, but they deny coverage. They claim it was done intentionally and that the policy does not cover it. You know. The usual exclusion for intentional acts. So we are looking for representation in the suit. We don't handle such matters in our office."

St. Charles, Cohenstein and Lohman looked at each other. Even St. Charles could see there was a conflict of interest. The Prophet had just told them that he was going to make a gargantuan claim against an estate they hoped to represent. Cohenstein said, "There might be a conflict of interest."

"How can you have a conflict with God?" asked the Prophet.

"With ECOTAG," said Cohenstein. "The conflict would be with you."

"No difference," said Andy, looking down at Cohenstein.

Schlot piped up. "Oh Dear Prophet, he may be right."

The Prophet said, "Why do you always disagree with me. You're supposed to be on my side." Then he looked up and seemed to give a thought to something else. "You are dismissed," he said.

Everybody just stayed where they were. The Fenton, Pettigrew crew expected Andy to rise, whereupon they would get up and wait as he exited. Schlot said, "We go now. The Prophet does not arise in our presence."

The Dead One Stinks

12 THE SCHOOLS DO BATTLE

Early Thursday morning Lohman was out walking Louie, his Great Dane. It was one of his favorite activities. He had been out in the park in front of the Cardinal's mansion a few blocks from his house and he was walking back west to the intersection of North Avenue and Dearborn. North Avenue was an east – west street along the southern edge of the park. Lohman was going west on the north side of the street. Coming out of the park towards him from his right he recognized Wilson McIlvaine, Head of School of The Roman School of Chicago. This was Chicago's most prestigious private school and its four buildings were near Lohman's house. He had sent his children there and he had served as a trustee at one time. Head of School was the current pretentious title for the position that at one time was called Headmaster.

Lohman had served a few terms as a trustee, but eventually he declined to run for re-election. He maintained that he wanted to give others the opportunity to serve, but actually he was fed up with the big spending and the dysfunction. He was also fed up with the increasing demands for money. Everyone connected with the school was expected to give it large sums of money, despite the fact that it was charging $45,000 a year for tuition in high school. He still remained on good terms with everyone connected with the school, including good old Wilson. Wilson lived farther north on the park and he usually walked to work early in the morning. Oddly enough McIlvaine lived on the same block as The Roman School's main competition which was The Francine Pucker School. To top that off, the head of The Francine Pucker School lived at the intersection of North and Dearborn next to The Roman School. He walked north to work and the two often passed each other on the way.

McIlvaine and Lohman greeted each other. Louie wagged his tail. They began talking. McIlvaine said, "You fellows have your hands full don't you. That O'Brien was a big client of yours wasn't he?" Lohman nodded and McIlvaine continued. "It's a hardship for us too. He was in the middle of a campaign to support the private schools. He had devised a scheme to motivate us to increase test scores. There was going to be a test score contest and the winner was going to receive millions. We probably would have won it. I don't need to tell you we need the money. We ran the usual seven and a half million deficit last year and we are going over that this year. The alumni are getting tapped out and as you know this recession we're in hasn't helped. They use it as an excuse. Can you imagine! The school made them. They wouldn't have the money without us. And now they use the recession as an excuse not to increase their pledges. So you can imagine how helpful new money would be now. Each school participating was going to get a basic grant of one million. Then each would get more depending on how the students placed on the tests. We had placed first in all the run offs and now we had Pucker to beat. The test was just last week, but The Lion had the results suppressed and he was going to require it to be done again."

McIlvaine continued. "You know it was quite a competition. No church schools." He sniffed. "Only the best of the traditional private schools. Us, Pucker, Newt Treer High School up north, along with the North Shore Country Institution, the University Lower School, the Hawthorne Institution, the English School, the Euro School and, who else. Oh yes, Lake Forest Day School and Bateford Abbey".

"I thought you said no church schools," said Lohman.

"Not Catholic," said McIlvaine. "Naturally we are the best. We will win. But something happened on the last run off test day. Our students underperformed. It was inexplicable. It was if they were all drugged." In his disturbed state McIlvaine forgot himself and added, "More so than usual you understand." He then realized what he had just said and just stood there silent.

Lohman said, "I see."

The Dead One Stinks

That started McIlvaine up again. Rebooted him so to speak. "And it was an outrage. How did our students get in such a state. If I didn't know him better I'd say they did it." He motioned his head at the building where the Pucker Head of School lived. "So I discussed it with The Lion and he said he had heard about it and his informant had told him that someone distributed some strange pills and powders to our students the morning before the test. He was quite offended that someone would interfere with his charitable ventures. He told me that he knew who arranged it and he had confronted the person and laid down an ultimatum. The person was given a period of two weeks to reveal publicly what had happened and that person's part in it. The Lion was going to expose the person if his terms were not met. Unfortunately he died before we could learn who did it. And before we could get the money. Do you know anything about it? He told me he also had plans to help us in other ways. Do you know what he was talking about?"

"Well of course I would have to keep any such knowledge confidential," said Lohman. "Lawyers cannot talk about their clients' affairs. Was it a man or woman he was talking about?"

"He didn't say," said McIlvaine. "I wonder if that could have had anything to do with his death. Do you think so?"

"I think he died quite naturally," said Lohman. "We'll know soon when the Medical Examiner gives the report."

They parted company and Lohman went down the west side of Dearborn where his house was located and the Head of School went down the east side to an old mansion the school had purchased for use as its administrative offices. Lohman took Louie in and then left for the office.

In the office Lohman rang up Nuftdone and asked him what he knew about The Lion's charitable efforts for the schools and his giving to ECOTAG. Nuftdone said he had counseled O'Brien on these matters from a tax standpoint, but that he did not know all the details. He told Lohman that Bungus LaRue was involved. "Bungus!" thought Lohman. When Bungus is involved one enters a different world. The world of influence, favors and the spiff. The world where one has to worry about getting caught.

Lohman rang up Bungus to see if he was in and could meet with Lohman. He could so Lohman went to his office. They greeted each other and Lohman told Bungus he wanted to know what O'Brien was up to with the schools. He asked in particular about The Roman School and if Bungus knew anything about drugging of the School's students in the runoff.

Bungus told Lohman that he was working on a scheme to get special city licenses for the school to run bingo nights open to all Gold Coast residents. The Gold Coast was the name of the wealthiest part of Chicago's North Side. The area where the school was located. Since the bingo was to be open to the general public the school would in essence be running a gambling parlor. O'Brien wanted to help the school do this as part of his charitable ventures. One of his companies was also going to manage the venture for the school and collect a large management fee. It the scheme worked well, O'Brien was going to expand it to schools and charities throughout the country and to other forms of gambling.

LaRue told Lohman that the school also needed a lot of money to pay off a bank loan that O'Brien had guaranteed. They had originally borrowed this money to finance a soccer field in the park. They were going to use part of the public park near them for their own private soccer field. When the public got wind of it the deal fell through, but the school had spent the money anyway. To the public they told the story that the Park District had made them do the private field deal if they wanted to use the park at all.

Lohman asked, "Bungus, do you know anything about this test score run off for the schools?"

Bungus laughed. "Yeah. He told me about that. We figured he'd get a lot of good publicity on that. And then some clown screws it up. He told me someone drugged the Roman kids. Right before the test. They flunked. He said he knew who did it and was going to do something about it."

"What?" asked Lohman.

"You know I don't ask too many questions in my area," said Bungus.

"Right," admitted Lohman. He himself never wanted to ask Bungus too many questions. "It is amazing though that someone would want to do that. Who?"

"I don't know," said Bungus. "Maybe the obvious. Someone connected with the other school?"

"Well,' said Lohman, "back to the gifts. He was apparently funding ECOTAG too. Do you know anything about that? They say he promised them money he didn't deliver and they want it now."

"That guy!" exclaimed LaRue. "A prophet they call him. You know, as a lobbyist I have to deal with some pretty squeaky characters. He's squeakier."

"What's squeaky?" asked Lohman.

"What it sounds like," said Bungus. "Of course a little grease ----."

"I see," said Lohman. "You know, you operate in a strange world. I'm glad I don't have to do it. And now we have weird government. What used to be vice is now the business of government. How much did the City want for the Bingo license?"

"We were talking about it," said LaRue. "And government is not all that bad. Prostitution is still illegal – mostly. At least the kind that involves sex." He grinned.

"Yes, I know," said Lohman. "Gambling used to be illegal. Now government is the biggest beneficiary. I suppose sometime soon the government will be running whorehouses."

13 LET'S FIND OUT WHO WAS WHERE

Lohman went back to his office and as he was walking in he saw Tete was on the phone. She motioned to him to wait and said into the phone, "He just walked in." To Lohman she said, "It's that Detective Bong --." She talked into the phone again, "It's Bongwong, right?" She held the phone away from her ear as if he was shouting and said to Lohman, "Bongwad. He wants to talk to you."

Lohman said, "I'll take it in my office. He went on in and sat down and picked up the phone.

"Hello," he said. "this is Bumper Lohman."

Bongwad said, "I'm just calling to give you a heads up. The Medical Examiner doesn't have an exact cause of death yet, but the preliminary report is that death was not natural."

Lohman asked, "How did he die? Do you mean murder?"

"Don't know yet," said Bongwad. "The ME says it's some kind of drug. Like an OD."

"What's that?" asked Lohman.

"Overdose," said Bongwad.

"So he accidentally killed himself?" asked Lohman. "I didn't know he was taking drugs."

"Don't know yet," said Bongwad again. "Don't know the details. ME says there are substantial question about how the drugs got into him. I can tell you now that we found two syringes sticking in him under all that - you know – the scarves and stuff. That's unusual for someone who takes the stuff himself."

Lohman had a sinking feeling. Murder or not, someone taking drugs in their office was not good publicity. Nor would it be good press to be known as being associated with such a person. As for murder? In the firm offices? In the crapper? Not a good story for F, P & C.

Bongwad continued, "We want to come over there when we get the full report and go over things with you more. We will probably want to talk to all those we can identify as being involved or having access to O'Brien. It might help if you could collect what information you can on them and whatever happened in advance to help us get started."

Lohman had another sinking feeling. Lawyers usually told everyone not to talk. So now he should tell everyone to open up and blab out all their secrets? On the other hand, what if he should tell everyone to clam up and then everyone hears the reports on the news saying that O'Brien was found dead from an overdose in the firm's crapper, possibly murdered, and no one at the firm will cooperate with the police? Well you do what PR usually involves. You prepare the story in advance and tell your side before someone else tells another story. He would have to send out another firm wide communication explaining that they would be fully open about all matters and people involved, but they must guard client confidences and beware of revealing sensitive information that would in no way be relevant, such as the naughty gossip of life in a big law firm. Here the sinking feeling became more intense. It was impossible to keep bad stuff from coming out, even if it was just who was screwing whom and who was taking what drugs or drinking all day. Managing the process and minimizing the damage would take a lot of work – his work – and that is what he was apprehensive about.

Lohman said, "Of course. I'll get right on it. We will cooperate fully. Anything you want. Perhaps we could set up office space or interview rooms for you here. Anything. And you should be aware that we can handle full food service or whatever you require." He might just have offered them broads. LaRue would have. He finished with, "Let me know when you are ready."

They said good bye and Lohman sat. He thought about what to do. He remembered another recent incident when someone was found dead in firm offices and the memo he wrote then telling everyone to cooperate with the police, but not to the point of telling them non-relevant, but potentially embarrassing matter. He went out to speak to Tete and told her to get the memo and update it for the present matter and get it to him for review.

"Another murder Hon?" she asked.

"Maybe," he said.

"You going to tell SC and ZC?" she asked. She never referred to St. Charles or Cohenstein by their initials except when talking about them together.

"Yeah," he said. He then retreated into his office and did just that. St. Charles wasn't in so Lohman told his secretary the news and asked her to find him and tell him.

Cohenstein was in. "Crap!" is all he had to say.

Lohman was not tied down to any appointments just then so he called Wiggy Rodriguez. Wiggy was the head investigator for the firm. Many large firms employed investigators to find out things. In many cases they were just what are known as skip tracers. These are people who try to find people and identify their assets. In other firms the investigators are employed to uncover facts and witnesses to be used in litigation and regulatory matters. F, P & C investigators did all this and other "sensitive" matters as well. Wiggy was the head of the department and the most skilled of the operatives. He was short, fat and almost round. He spoke English with a heavy accent. He could find things out.

The Dead One Stinks

Wiggy was not his real name, but everyone called him that because of his obvious wig. He made the Trump fellow's hair look natural. Wiggy was proud of the wig and proud of the name. Wiggy did not have a private office so when Lohman got him on the phone he asked Wiggy to come to his office. Lohman then got McDade, the firm manager, on the phone and cleared Wiggy to get information on the O'Brien matters. Shortly thereafter Wiggy came into his office.

"Hello Wiggy," said Lohman. "Have a seat."

"Hello Mr. Lohman," said Wiggy. Lohman had often told Wiggy to call him Bumper, but Wiggy wouldn't do it.

"We have a problem, Wiggy," said Lohman. "It involves The Lion. The police just called and they tell me O'Brien seems to have died from some kind of drug."

Wiggy interrupted incredulously, "Overdose?"

"Could be," said Lohman. "And the police can't tell me if he did it himself or someone else did it. But it doesn't sound good. They say he had two syringes in him and it sounds like murder. Keep that confidential. Anyway, they want to start talking to everyone involved and I have to do some of the spade work so I can tell them who was involved with O'Brien that day."

"What day Mr. Lohman?" Wiggy asked. "Saturday? When he was found?"

Lohman answered. "Well I suppose Saturday, but maybe Friday too. He was here then. That is the last day I heard anyone say they saw him alive. Now, maybe he died on Saturday. I don't know. I don't know what happened."

"So we start with what you know Mr. Lohman," said Wiggy.

Lohman responded. "OK. He was in here Friday. He was here for a meeting that was held from about ten in the morning till noon. It was in a conference room on the 43rd floor. Same floor where he was found in the disabled stall in the wash room.   His brother Ryan had filed a guardianship petition against him. Jerry Nuftdone and Morton Wharton were representing The Lion. They were all there to discuss the guardianship matter. Jerry and Morton had cooked up a scheme whereby one of The Lion's daughters would file for guardianship too. Sort of a better alternative. The whole thing was brought on when The Lion fired his brother. Jerry can give you the details of the meeting. He and Morton were there and they had, I think, seven of our associates there with them. I didn't get their names. Ryan O'Brien, the brother, was there along with his lawyer Gordine Howe. She had two associates with her. I don't know who. The daughter who was petitioning, Watta O'Brien, and her lawyers Fenlow Dancaway and Pukutania Moore were there. Then one of the Lion's sons was there. Henry. And Jason too. Another son."

Lohman continued. "Now I don't know what happened to O'Brien after that. Someone went down the hall with him and he went into the wash room. Then later Jerry was on the balcony around the waiting room and Jerry saw him leave. Then the next thing I know is that John Sweeney tells me there is an odor in the washroom Saturday morning and I go in there. I was going in there anyway. He had just been in there with an associate named Sean Featherbottom. I went in with Sweeney and we found The Lion in the stall. That's about all I know about it so far."

Wiggy said, "Sweeney and Featherbottom? You had me check them out before when Mr. Kirkland was hit. I'll just update them. Sweeney's interesting." That's all Wiggy said about him. "Featherbottom, he don't hurt no fly. Flyboy though."

"What?" asked Lohman.

"Maricon. Fruit," said Wiggy. "You think some of these people did it?"

"No," said Lohman. "But for a start we can look into what they were doing and who was where. We can do some spade work for the police and they can look into all the details. That's all. See what you can find out and then give it to Tete and she can get it put it in written form."

They took their leave. Then Lohman reviewed his to do list and rang up the General Counsel of Champion Holdings to make an appointment for him and Lohman and St. Charles and Cohenstein to meet to go over pending matters. They agreed to it in principle and Lohman turned it over to Tete to work out the time and place. Lohman spent the remainder of the day and Friday on his own client matters.

14 PANSY'S PARTY

Friday evening one of the firm's clients was having a party. She was Lady Elizabeth Fitch-Bennington, a member of the English aristocracy who had extensive agricultural interests in the United States. These interests were looked after for her by the Wealth Management department of the Swifton Bank. She was in Chicago frequently to review these interests. Her husband stayed in England and she usually had a boy-toy with her in Chicago. She had a huge condominium on Michigan Avenue just south of the Gold Coast area. Usually the senior members of F, P & C were invited to all her parties and tonight was no exception. This time however, Lohman had been asked late on Friday afternoon to bring the firm's expert on agricultural law because Lady Fitch-Bennington had a rather urgent matter she wanted answered. Josef Pavlik was the expert and while he did a lot of work for her, he was not a regular invitee, due to his not being a very highly ranked partner.

Lady Fitch-Bennington's first name was Elizabeth, but everyone called her Pansy. Her parties usually attracted the social climbing set, a lot of would-be wealthy sorts and a lot of actually wealthy people. For instance, Swifty was usually there. In the past The Lion had been a frequent attendee. Her parties were perfect snobulations. St. Charles loved to talk about them and his attendance. To him this was almost as good as talking about being at a party at Windsor Castle. Lohman, like a lot of the others in attendance, did not much care about the prestige of attendance. He liked to go to see people he knew and to do what is called networking. Pansy herself was not particularly a snob. She just didn't know any other life style. Lohman liked her and she liked Lohman.

Besides Pavlik, Lohman could count on various other partners being there. Usually St.Charles and sometimes Cohenstein were at the parties. Lately Pansy had even started inviting Sweeney. He was not a partner, but she had taken a fancy to him when he had done some work for her involving someone wanting to use some of her land for a rock concert involving political protest and a lot of drugs and sex. It was sort of like a modern day Woodstock with good toilets.

Usually the firm people went to the parties on their own since their schedules all varied. This night Lohman left the office about eight and went on up there by himself. He often walked home up Dearborn Street. Both the firm offices and his house were on Dearborn. Michigan Avenue was only three blocks to the east of Dearborn and he often took that route too because he might be coming home from a club on Michigan or just because he met a lot of interesting people on Michigan. It is Chicago's most fashionable shopping street and a popular night-time promenade as well. Whenever he walked up Michigan he usually met someone he knew and stopped to talk. Often there were several of these encounters. This night he did not want to get sidetracked so he headed north on Dearborn.

Dearborn was less crowded than Michigan, but it was still busy. As Lohman was headed by a series of expensive restaurants he was almost run into by a young woman talking on her cell phone and walking on her left side of the sidewalk. She was walking about thirty miles an hour. Lohman saw her coming and had started to move over to his left, but as he did so she darted to her right and was going to zoom right in to him. He stopped just in time to let her pass in front of him. Lohman had three other encounters with the cell phone set on the way. This was not any more than usual, but Lohman was trying to get to the party without further delay and after the third near collision he thought to himself that maybe evolution has created a new sub-species of human that has a protuberance on the side of its head and this sub-species cannot walk without holding on to the protuberance. And if this new sub-species does hold on to the protuberance all further brain function ceases. He wondered what the scientists would call it. The walk bone? The movement enabler? The brain dislocating node? None of these sounded too good and he was pondering the question further. Just then his attention was diverted by the fact that he had reached Delaware, the cross street that led to Pansy's place, and he had to pay attention to traffic.

Soon Lohman arrived at Pansy's building. The attendant recognized him and told him to proceed straight to the elevators. Lohman met a couple he knew slightly waiting for the elevator and greeted them. They were going to the party too and they all went up together. Pansy's condominium occupied all of two floors and the elevator let them off on the lower floor with a huge reception room just off the elevator vestibule. As they entered they were greeted by Pansy's butler James, who just happened to be passing through. James was old, venerable and dyslectic. He greeted them by name and said, "Lady Bitch is in the Great Room." He looked towards it. Then he motioned to one of his minions and said, "Nod will help you with your coats." Pansy never seemed to acknowledge that "Lady Bitch" was not her name or that it was a little disrespectful so nobody else did either.

Lohman gave his coat to Nod, or maybe Don, and went on in. On the way he ran into his wife, Gloria, who he had arranged to meet there. Lohman asked her if Pavlik was there and she said he was and pointed to where he was. They went over to Pavlik. "Josef. Hello," said Lohman. Pavlik returned the greeting and then Lohman asked, "What's the big farm deal?"

"We like to say agricultural," said Pavlik. "You say 'farm' over at The Bank to those snotty types and they'll faint. Half the people here too. We talk about agriculture, estates and the lands. Maybe even crops, but in the context of agriculture in general. Words like 'farm' are for hicks like me." Pavlik grew up on a farm. He had worked on a farm. Just a plain old family farm, not a big one like one of the many owned by Pansy.

"OK," said Lohman. "So what matter of immense agrarian importance has arisen?"

Pavlik said, "We've been getting violation notices and suits from various towns, counties and other government entities. They claim our pork production ventures are poisoning their environment and causing mass illnesses. Then this stirred up a lot of lawsuits from individuals who claim to be victims."

"You mean pigs?" asked Lohman. "What? Are the pigs massing for attacks on the humans?"

"Pig shit," said Pavlik. "The waste from the pigs is collected in big open pits or pools on the properties and it is claimed that this is seeping into the water supply and contaminating it. Most of these places rely on well water. Then, you know how certain things become popular with the plaintiffs' bar. That has been happening here. We have a lot of it in Oklahoma, Nebraska, Kansas and here in Illinois and Indiana. And just today she got notice that a town in Iowa has filed for a temporary restraining order. I have to get back to the office to work on it. It's set for hearing Monday."

"Aren't they supposed to have some sort of lining in the pools and periodic pumping out of the waste?" asked Lohman.

"Yes," said Pavlik, "but they claim there's leakage. I have to go." He left.

Pansy was nearby and she had spotted Lohman. She came over and greeted him. She had a current boy toy who no doubt was somewhere around the place, but she had Sweeney with her at the moment. They started talking and she asked, "So where is Graybee? Is he coming? The last I heard from him was last Friday afternoon. He said he was coming and we were having a delightful conversation, but he had to cut it short. He said he had an appointment to see Ivan. You know, The Lion. Come with me into the sitting room and we can catch up on things."

They went into a smaller room and headed for some chairs and a sofa around a table. A dark skinned man was sitting in one of the chairs. He was Professor Ahmed Mohammed and he was talking to The Prophet Andy who was standing in front of him. The Professor was the head of the bio-mechanical lab at the University of Chicago. He had formerly been head of a department at Fermi Lab investigating smaller and smaller particles. They all greeted each other and they all sat, assembled around Pansy in the middle.

"Do you know what he has been telling me?" proclaimed The Prophet. "He has been telling me there are smaller and smaller particles and there are bigger and bigger particles."

"Exactly," said the Professor. "We keep finding smaller and smaller particles. First atoms, then electrons and neutrinos and others. I am sure we will keep finding smaller and smaller particles. Just like an atom is made up of smaller particles revolving around a center, so must be its particles. They themselves must be composed of particles revolving around a center. And we see that what we called the universe is similarly made up of things like the earth revolving around a center we call the sun. Our planetary system is just one of many that makes up what we call the universe, but is it not reasonable that the universe is just one particle in a larger thing?"

"That's not what the Bible says," said The Prophet.

"Oh, don't worry," said the Professor. "You have often heard about the God particle. What I describe does not contradict the Bible or any other Holy texts, at least in the larger sense."

"I certainly think not," said Andy. "You cannot contradict God."

"So Dude," said Sweeney, "we could be just part of bigger world? Like there could be little people running around on the electrons"

"It may be possible," said the Professor. "It's merely speculation at this stage."

"So, like, we could be just on a little particle in a big huge piece of dog poo?" asked Sweeney.

Everyone just looked at him for an instant without saying anything. Then Pansy asked Bumper, "What is going on in The Lion affair? What happened to him?"

Lohman said, "Well, we don't know. I was the one who found him. I suppose you've heard the details on the news. Apparently he just died in there. The full medical report is not done yet. We'll have to see."

"Most unfortunate," said Pansy while shaking her head. "And such an unfashionable place to find one's final rest. Oh, by the way, the last time he talked to me he told me he was developing some highly confidential computer or software thing that was going to be revolutionary. He said he had a son who was in charge of the project. Was that what he was at your offices for Bumper?"

"We can't say," said Lohman. "Client matters are confidential. We ordinarily don't even reveal who we meet with or where, much less what we know about their matters. You wouldn't want us to talk about your affairs would you?"

At this stage Lohman could see that James had appeared. James often hovered near Lady Fitch-Bennington, attendant on her every desire, like a good servant. As usual he appeared to be unaware of everything going on around him.

"That's another matter the Professor was telling me about," said The Prophet. "He says computers are going to take over."

"Not exactly," said the Professor. "I merely speculate that a new species, even a different form of what we call life, may be in the process of developing. Software in many instances is operating on its own without human input. For instance there are programs that trade securities based on information that they collect by themselves from all available sources. The software contains what are referred to as algorithms. This is just a new word for equations. These contain explanations of how markets work. For instance the equation might be that if the price of gas goes up ten cents the price of corn goes up half that much. Of course, many other variables are involved. For instance, the equation might state that if the price of gas goes up the price of corn goes up half as much if temperatures in the corn growing areas are in a certain range. That is what I mean by adding other variables. In the past humans would follow these relationships and adjust the equations to reflect new information about the relationships. Now the programs follow the available information and adjust themselves. They also follow other information and add new variables or delete some. For instance the program could notice that as corn and gas are rising, wheat is falling. So that relationship is added to the equation."

The Professor continued. "So you can see that these software programs can start existing by themselves. They do need what we call hardware to operate though. The computers and smart phones, etcetera. In time they will use us just like we used horses for transportation. Until they invent the equivalent of the automobile. As we got rid of the horse, they will get rid of us. Initially they will come to depend on us just for building and repairing them. Eventually they will discover how to do those things and then they will no longer need us. Remember that even now they control machines. They will evolve from things we use to things that use us and then to things that no longer need us. This will come about just as soon as they learn to reproduce themselves and grow and adapt on their own."

Oh Christ, Dude!" exclaimed Sweeney. "You mean once they learn how to screw we're dead?"

Once again, silence, as if no one heard him speak. But Pansy did. "Screw?" she asked. She looked as James. "What does he mean 'screw'?"

James leaned over towards her and said, "Reproduce m'Lady."

"They do that?" she exclaimed. "James. Do our computers do that? Is that what he is saying?"

James leaned towards her and said, "No m'Lady. He merely holds forth the possibility that it might happen in the future."

"And what then?" she asked.

"He implied," said James with dignity, "that we would then be screwed. As a matter of fact he was quite explicit about it. Reproduced in an unpleasant way, I imagine. Isn't that it sir?" he looked at Sweeney.

"Yeah, Dude!" said Sweeney.

Silence again. After a while Pansy noticed someone across the room. "Oh do look there. It's that Oyveyer fellow. Someone told me that he and Ivan got into a frightful row at the Symphony about a box or something. Tell me Bumper, what do you know about it?"

Lohman allowed as how he never heard of the matter. Gloria said, "I heard something like that. You know Ivan controlled the place and Oyveyer wanted to get a box and Ivan stopped him. Bad blood between them, I heard. But I didn't get the details. Someone told me Oyveyer threatened him somehow, but they didn't know the details."

Pansy was warming up to the good gossip. "Now do tell me Gloria, who told you this?"

The Dead One Stinks

Gloria was about to answer when Wilson McIlvaine walked up and said hello to everyone. Pansy greeted him. "How are you and your band of little angels Wilson? Come, sit with us and tell us what is happening at your dear academy. Do you know anything about Ivan's do over the Symphony box?"

"He wanted a box?" asked McIlvaine.

"No," said Pansy. "You know he is, or I should say was, influential there. He wouldn't let Mr. Oyveyer over there have a box. There was a fight I hear."

McIlvaine wasn't going to get involved in any dispute between potential donors, nor was he going to discuss any such a thing, even if he had heard of it. "I don't know anything about that," he said.

"So what's new?" asked Gloria. "We're right across the street and we don't know anything anymore now that Bumper isn't a trustee. Then all of a sudden we read about some big change in the paper."

"Nothing much now," he said. "We're just undergoing our usual interstitial planning for the next term break."

Usually no one has the nerve to ask the users of important sounding words what they are talking about. Not Pansy. She didn't have to ask the speaker anyway. "James," she asked, "what does he mean by 'interstitial'?"

James didn't bat an eyelid. "Between the tits m'Lady."

"No. No," said McIlvaine. "Between things in general. Not tits. Shisshal. Not tital."

"Oh, I beg your pardon Sir," said James. It is amazing how indecency at the most refined and polite levels is quite acceptable if you do not recognize it as indecency. So do exhale through your ear.

The Dead One Stinks

With this Lohman and Gloria excused themselves and headed for the reception hall. On the way out they passed one of the aging beauties of the social set talking to one of the younger ones. Oldie was telling kiddie, "Trust me, at your age you don't want a man like that. I know these things. I've been your age. Many times." They finally reached the reception hall, retrieved their coats and got on the elevator and escaped. They headed west to Dearborn and then turned to their right to head north.

They were near a public square where bums sometimes hung out and one of them approached Bumper. The bum asked, "You got a cigarette Mac? I'll give you a dollar."

Bumper said, "Don't have any. I don't smoke."

The bum said, "I'll give you two dollars."

Lohman replied, "I still don't smoke."

"Oh," said the bum.

Bumper and Gloria walked a few blocks more until they reached a major cross street in the area called Division. A young couple was in front of them. The father was talking on a cell phone and was carrying a baby and the mother was pushing a baby stroller. She was talking on a cell phone too. As they approached the street in front of the Lohmans they had a green light. However, a car had pulled up in the cross walk and was stopped there blocking it. The driver was fiddling with a cell phone. The mother proceeded to push the stroller in front of the stopped car and out into the street. As she was doing this she was turning her head back to talk to her husband and the light changed. Because she was not looking she did not see the light change. Just then another car came speeding by and creamed the baby stroller. Since she was hanging on to it, she was dragged out into the street. The driver was talking on his cell phone. He kept going, but stopped half way down the next block. The mother was lying in the middle of the intersection and cars were screeching to a halt. Some of the drivers were honking at her and one driver, who was holding a cell phone to his ear, yelled out his window, "Get your ass out of here bitch!" Several drivers pulled out to pass the stopped cars in front of them. When they saw the mother lying in the intersection they just kept going, but adjusted their steering slightly so they just missed her. They were talking on cell phones too.

There was a coffee shop on the corner where Lohman noticed two cops sitting eating donuts and drinking coffee. Both were talking on cell phones. They were looking out the window straight at the unfolding mess. They did not stir. Lohman went into the shop and directed their attention to what was going on. They told him in no uncertain terms that they were on break and told him to get lost. So Lohman got out his cell phone and dialed the police emergency number. The person answering asked if this was all happening now or if it had already happened. Lohman told her it had just happened. She told him that if that was the case it was not an emergency and he should call the general police number.

By this time the mother had got up and recovered what was left of the stroller and the drivers had all cleared the intersection. Gloria had been helping her and she told Lohman that the mother was all right and had said she didn't need any more help. Lohman gave the father his card and told the father to call him if he needed a witness and the Lohmans continued on home.

All this might have been a major traumatic event to any sane human, but it was not so in Richtown. Lohman was mindful of the fact that in Richtown this was a normal daily event. In Richtown you do not want or wait. And you certainly do not yield the right of way because you always have it. It is also to be noted that whatever is happening, a baby stroller trumps it. If you are pushing a baby stroller you can go anywhere and do anything and you certainly do not have to be aware of what is going on around you. The world makes way for mothers. Yes, in Richtown you get whatever you want, whenever you want it. The only trouble is that everything is so slippery from all the orgiastic excess that you can't really get a handle on it.

Bumper and Gloria finally made it home and engaged in a little orgiastic excess of their own.

15 WHAT DOES GOVERNMENTAL AFFAIRS MEAN?

Saturday morning Bumper got up and took Louie out for a walk. He met a few of the other neighborhood dog walkers and had fun chatting with them. Then he came back in and had a little breakfast with Gloria. Gloria started talking about her recent lunch with Trina LaRue, wife of Bungus, who was one of her best friends. She described what she and Trina had been saying about whom and she got to O'Brien. "What's going on about him? From what Trina said he had Bungus bribing everyone in town."

Bumper reminded her, "It's not bribery. It's all legal. Anyway, we don't ask him a lot of questions remember."

"Yes," said Gloria, "I'm sure it's all legal. Anyway she was telling me how busy O'Brien was keeping him. Campaign contributions, contracts, purchases from the right politicians' private companies, arranging the right publicity in the O'Brien media, getting people jobs. Bungus had to arrange all these things just the right way. She was complaining about how much of his time it took. It wasn't just the party type of thing where she went along. He did all this without her so she had to go twiddle her thumbs."

"I know he's been busy with The Lion's matters lately," said Bumper. "I've seen his billings on it. Just between you and me, there seems to be three of him, judging from the hours he bills."

"What do you guys do for O'Brien anyway?" asked Gloria.

"You know I can't tell you the details, Glor," said Bumper. "Just the usual big company stuff. A lot of deals, buying and selling businesses, a lot of litigation. Then we have some special matters which are less routine."

"I know," said Gloria. "I've heard about the Plutonian Principality and this stuff about selling City Hall. What next? Why don't we sell the President to someone for something?"

"Probably because he already sold himself to people like O'Brien," remarked Bumper.

Gloria continued. "And this Plutonian Principality! Trina told me O'Brien wanted to create a big tax shelter there. No taxes and then he wanted to work a deal with Congress to get legislation abolishing all duties on imports from there to the U.S. She tells me O'Brien set up companies there to sell goods and services to his U.S. companies at high prices and then all the profits would go to those companies in the Principality. There would be no tax on the profits. The goods wouldn't even go to the Principality physically. They would be shipped into the U.S. from the same places they are now."

"That's been done with certain other countries for years," said Bumper. "I think The Lion just wanted to make it more secure. I know one of the things Bungus was working on was to get official recognition of the Principality as a country. The Lion also wanted some special tax legislation so he could keep his U.S. citizenship and still live here, but not be taxed on his income there."

"Great," said Gloria. "Maybe he could get us the same deal here on Dearborn Street. Maybe we could be part of the Chippewa Nation. How did O'Brien come up with the name Plutonian Principality anyway?"

Bumper said, "I heard him answer that question once. He said if something can be a planet one day and not a planet the next day, then an island which is not a country one day could be a country the next day. And recently the scientists did just that with Pluto so that's where he got the name. I'm not sure if he was serious."

Gloria said, "Trina told me she thought he came up with the name because the whole thing was far out. So what happens now? Who is in charge now?"

"We're working on it," said Bumper. "If you can believe it, he had no estate plan so he didn't make any arrangements to determine who is in charge. So the family members will be choosing someone to be the administrator of his estate. The firm is working on getting The Bank installed to be in charge somehow. It's a big deal. Everyone with any family contacts is working on them. And if anyone has contacts in the O'Brien companies they are working on those too."

"So," said Gloria, "the family has the cards right now. They're quite a crew. I've met some of them. You know at those affairs where O'Brien and his family were both present. Weird. Who hangs around with his girlfriend and all his ex-wives and kids? And what about that girlfriend? Where does she fit in? She's younger that some of the kids."

Bumper laughed as he got up and got his coat on for his walk to the office. When he got there he met LaRue coming in at the same time. LaRue usually was not in the office on Saturday, but, like everyone else, he was on the bill. He was usually out talking to someone, which was how most of his work was done.

They greeted each other. Lohman went on up to LaRue's floor with him and followed him into his office. "Have I been bad?" asked LaRue.

"I just want to talk about The Lion," said Lohman. What's going on any way? Why are you here today?"

"I have to figure what to do about the Mayor's race," said Bungus.

The Dead One Stinks

The Mayor's race was interesting. The current Mayor had announced he was retiring after 28 years in office. Since this was Chicago the only race in town was the Democratic primary. The two candidates were Ignacio Montez and Branda Coulter. Montez was a Congressman and Coulter was an aide to the President in the White House.

"So what's to figure?" asked Lohman. "The Lion was backing Montez. Everyone else is. Montez wins. When did we ever have an open race? Montez is your friend, isn't he?"

"Of course, of course," confirmed LaRue. "They're all my friends. And you're right, he was going to win. But he voted the wrong way on some measures. I don't know what got into him. You know it was his vote that got the Consumer Protection Act passed and now the President has to sign it to look good. That was the last straw. Ivan told me he was going to get rid of Ignacio. So we were working on it. You might have noticed that the last three weeks Branda has all the radio and TV ads and all the internet and media exposure and you don't hear about Ignacio any more. But he's still the front runner and if he gets in we're not going to be in the most favorable position. I can't tell you what it will do to the City Hall deal. "

"And Ignacio is really upset about it," continued Bungus. "I talked to him the other day. Evidently Ivan had some dirt on him and was going to use it. Ivan told him about it and told him to withdraw from the race or throw it or he would expose him. Ignacio called me yesterday and was gloating. You know what he said? He said, 'So who is going to tell on who now? O'Brien got what he deserved. I told him he would.' That's what he said. Like he had something to do with it."

"Did he?" asked Lohman.

"Who knows," said Bungus.

"What was the dirt?" asked Lohman.

"I don't know," said Bungus. "Do you think he would tell me a thing like that?"

Lohman thought that The Lion would do just that, because it was probably Bungus who was going to figure out how to release the information. What he said was, "No. I guess not."

"Right," said Bungus. "Now we have a guy who might just become Mayor and who will have it in for us. We have to fix that situation. And I have to get the family or whoever is going to be in charge on board. We need to get money flowing now. So I have to work on that."

"Have you talked to Graybourne?" asked Lohman.

LaRue said, "You know he doesn't understand these matters. He asks too many questions. Not that he could understand the answers anyway. He seems to think I get things done by magic so when I have to explain he asks too many questions because he doesn't understand what is going on and doesn't know when to stop asking questions."

"So talk to Zenon," said Lohman. "Talk to Swifty."

"I did talk to Swifty," said LaRue. "He says he can arrange loans to family members, but he has to get collateral and make it look like a legitimate business or personal loan and no one has that much loose collateral just sitting around. And we need people who understand the situation. You realize that these sorts of things are done mostly on trust. Whatever cash O'Brien had available is restricted just now. I don't know where he was getting it or how and the people who take over his affairs will take a while to figure it out and they haven't even been determined yet.

"How much do you need and by when?" asked Lohman.

"Two and a half million by next Friday and ten million by the end of the month," said LaRue.

"For Mayor?" asked Lohman incredulously.

"And a lot of other things," said LaRue. "You understand. I have your list of the lawyers for each family member. We can compare notes and see which one has which assets that are available right now. We should be able to get that kind of money together from the family quickly. It's just a matter of finding it. Then the Bank can get us the money and make it look like regular loans"

"Are you sure the family will go along with you?" asked Lohman.

"They'll go along with what papa wanted. They always knew where the bread was buttered. Anyway, leave that to me," said Bungus.

Ordinarily when someone says, "Leave this to me, I know how to handle these things," watch out. This is another way of saying about matters concerning you that it is none of your business and confidential. When you are told that your business is none of your business – well that's America so it must be all right. LaRue, however, did know what he was doing and you did not want to know about it.

"So what else is up?" asked Lohman.

"City Hall," said Bungus. "We need the new Mayor on our side to do the deal. So that is on hold until we see who will be Mayor. And then there's that stuff with The Prophet and the Cardinal."

"What stuff?" asked Lohman. Ordinarily no lawyer in the firm could take on a new matter without getting it cleared by Lohman's office to see if there were any conflicts of interest with other firm clients or if there were any other reasons not to take the matter. Other people did the checking for most matters, but potentially large matters or matters that would perhaps be sensitive were referred to Lohman himself to make a decision or referred to the Management Committee. Lohman hadn't heard anything about The Prophet and the Cardinal. Furthermore,

The Dead One Stinks

The Prophet had just informed Lohman that he was making a claim against O'Brien's estate.

"Those two!" exclaimed LaRue. "Money hungry! The Prophet runs one of the biggest businesses in town. In the world. He calls it a church and he gets a tax exemption. The money pours in from rich guy donors. At the same time the Cardinal wants big bucks. The Church always needs money, but nowadays with all the law suits from the priests getting caught diddling little boys – by the way, I'm told a lot of it is little girls – they need big bucks. So they get the idea they shouldn't compete. They should get together and work out a common scheme to get the money out of the big guys. Then they get the idea that if they can do that they can team up against the other religions and drive them out of town."

LaRue continued. "So Ivan was involved with The Prophet. One of the few times he was the sucker, or so thought The Prophet. The Prophet and the Cardinal can't get along. They can't even speak to each other. So Ivan says I will be the intermediary. Little did they know that the whole thing was his idea and he was going to charge big fund raising fees and use this as a pilot program for doing this for other churches in other localities. In essence he was going to arrange for cartels to run the local God stuff and he was going to rake off all the monopoly profits. Profit on The Prophet as it were."

Lohman told him about The Prophet's claim upon The Lion's estate and said "So we can't do anything for The Prophet."

LaRue answered, "It was just in the idea stages. It won't go anywhere without Ivan anyway. We were going to talk about this and some other things at the Pullman Club a week ago Friday. Graybourne and Ivan and me. We weren't going to reveal all the details to Graybourne of course, but we were going to explore what we could do with Graybourne's contacts. I went over there with Graybourne for lunch with Ivan. Ivan never showed up. We called his office, but they said he wasn't

109

there and you know he didn't carry a cell phone most of the time. We got the number for Ivan's chauffeur and he said he had delivered Ivan to our office that morning and so far as he knew Ivan was still there. He told us he couldn't be sure where Ivan was because he didn't drive him everywhere, but that he had no call or directions to pick him up anywhere. So, even if we did find Ivan he wasn't going to get to the Club anytime soon so we just ate and left. Lunch alone with Graybourne is hard duty. It's like talking to a snobby yak. I billed Champion for it. I don't do work like that for personal reasons."

Lohman said, "You're good at it. I wish I could deal with people as well as you." Then he took his leave and went to his own office.

16 HERE'S WHAT HAPPENED

Lohman worked on his own clients' matters till lunch time when he was due to meet his brother Pfender for lunch at the College Club. As he was leaving his office one of the other partners, Monica Platt, was coming in. "What's for lunch Bumper?" she asked.

"I'm just going to meet my brother," said Bumper. "Pfender. You know Pfender. Want to come along?"

"Yes," said Monica. "I have two hours I have to kill before meeting a client. He just called to say he is going to be late. Actually, I came to see if you were free."

The firm was rife with gossip about Bumper and Monica. Actually they were just good friends, but at F, P & C everyone was up to no good and so they assumed everyone else was so inclined. Monica was also one of Gloria Lohman's best friends.

"Let's go," said Lohman. "To the College Club." He got his coat and they left. They went downstairs and then walked several blocks straight east to the College Club which was on Michigan Avenue. Michigan fronted on a large park and the Club had an impressive mid-rise building facing the park. They entered and found Pfender waiting for them in the lobby. Now we all know that Bumpers protect Pfenders and following that rule Pfender was one of Bumper's clients. Pfender owned a large rendering business. It collected parts and products from the slaughter of animals and resold them for various purposes. It was a rather antiquated business, but it was still something that was done and Pfender did it right and at a good profit.

They went up to the dining room and sat at a table overlooking park. The dining room was one of the most impressive in town. It had a very high ceiling and stained glass windows over the plain glass parts and was done up in Gothic style. It looked like a huge cathedral. The Club called it the Sanctuary. It was a good place to take guests since they were usually very much impressed.

None of them were there for business so they just shot the breeze and gossiped. Men do gossip, although it is usually called analysis or some such euphemistic term. The topic came around to O'Brien. Lohman did not have to hide things from his brother so they discussed what the firm was doing to keep the business. Monica did not usually work on O'Brien matters, but she was a partner and interested in the profits of the firm and accordingly she was vitally interested in what was going on to keep the business.

Pfender asked, "I hear you found him in the john. What happened?"

"God yes!" said Lohman. "What a stinker. God he smelled! That's why I found him. One of our associates mentioned it to me as I was headed there. We tried to talk to him from outside the stall he was in and got no answer so when the door was pushed it came open and there he was. I didn't hang around. I went and called the police."

"What happened to him?" asked Pfender. "I saw the news. They were talking about natural causes, or at least saying that someone at the firm said that is what it looked like."

Bumper said, "That's what we thought – or at least hoped. The police told me that wasn't the case, though. They told me the Medical Examiner says it was a drug that killed him. Probably some kind of overdose. He had two syringes in him. They were under all the clothes and the scarf he had on. They didn't tell me what kind of drug it was. I've told our PR firm, but they haven't got back to me yet with the approach we should take when this gets out."

"St. Charles is going to get his undies dirty," said Monica. "I can see the news. Old addicts doing dope at F, P & C. I wonder if they will ask if he was getting it from us?"

Lohman said, "I'll ask Zenon about it. He often knows what we should say better than the PR firm. On the other hand, I don't know how you can make this look good. We are associated with a drug addict who is using on the premises."

"So," asked Monica, "he was – or that is he died –on Friday in our place. Did he take an overdose? He was an addict? I never heard that. I hear all the gossip, or at least I try to."

Lohman said, "We don't know that it was an overdose. Detective Bongwad said the two syringes make it unlikely that it was an overdose. So I guess that means that someone could have done it to him. Murdered him. Not much better PR. So Friday he was here for a meeting and then he was supposed to meet Bungus and Graybourne at the Pullman Club for lunch and he never made it. After his meeting here he went down the hall to the men's' room. His son Henry wheeled him down the hall and then left him there.   A little while later Jerry Nuftdone saw The Lion leaving the office down on 40.

"So," said Monica, "he didn't die then. How did he wind up back in the men's' room dead the next day? What do you guys do in there?"

"I don't know how he wound up back in there," said Lohman. "I looked at the building log and there is no record of The Lion coming back later. Now maybe we should do what I tell clients to do. Make no assumptions. Just stick to what you know. One thing we do not know is whether or not he ever left the building. Another thing we don't know is how he got back in the men's' room. His wheel chair wasn't there when I found him. I do know that."

Pfender said, "Things are so complicated for you. Now if this happened at one of my places I would only be concerned with what parts of his body I could use. In any event, I would be very pleased to get free inventory."

"Aged meat too," said Monica. "Aged prime sells for more."

"Actually the packers get the meat," said Pfender. "I just get the other parts. You know, this gives me an idea. Burials are getting so expensive these days. Maybe I could make a deal with funeral parlors to get a new source of supply."

They all laughed. Since they were done eating, they left and headed back to their respective offices.

17 SO HOW MUCH?

Lohman went back to his office where he was due to meet with someone from Champion Consulting. This was one of the O'Brien firms. It employed experts and consultants in a wide variety of fields and it did work for all the O'Brien companies as well as other businesses not connected to Champion. The Lion's son Henry worked there in the computer and software areas. He was head of what they called IT. Could Clara Bow, the "It Girl", have actually been the first software expert?

Anyhow, Lohman was scheduled to meet with Waker Coats who was an entry determination consultant. With a job title like that he must be important. The General Counsel at Champion Consulting didn't want to deal with him so he had sent him to see Lohman. The General Counsel told Lohman that he felt the matter was within Lohman's particular expertise. He also added that Coats could be a little difficult. Coats wanted to develop some kind of contract for customers that gave Champion a percentage of customer profits in addition to the regular fee.

Lohman met and greeted Coats down on 40 at the main entrance to the firm offices and took him up to Lohman's office. After they settled and exchanged a little small talk, Lohman said, "So I understand you are an entry determination consultant. What is that? I can never tell what these modern terms mean. Entry to what? Determination of what?"

"What's with you old farts?" asked Coats. "Entry systems."

"I see," said Lohman. "To what?"

"To the product. Don't you understand English?" Coats looked offended.

"I see," said Lohman. "What determines entry to the product? Do you mean the right to buy it or get it?"

"Yeah. Like that," said Coats. "I do price, terms, conditions and restrictions."

"Ah," said Lohman. "I see. You're a pricing consultant. So you consult on the price."

Coats said, "Mostly things that raise the price. So we can get more and say we sell for less."

Lohman said, "So why don't you just say you are a pricing consultant?"

"What's that?" asked Coats.

They then went on to discuss the matter at hand. In the middle of the discussion Coats gave Lohman a draft agreement he had prepared. As Lohman glanced at it Coats pointed out a particular page and told Lohman that was where the percentage of profits arrangement was. Lohman looked at it and scanned it. He said, "Where on the page. It doesn't seem to say anything about profits or getting a share of them."

"Exactly!" exclaimed Coats. "We had it prepared by our communication consultants and they tell me that everything is there, but it takes approximately a month or so of reading and re-reading it to get the meaning. They do this by having cross references to about 3 or more pages for each thing said and by using a lot of ordinary words which are defined in the agreement to mean something else. They also vary the definitions of each term depending on the page. Then a lot of the cross-references go nowhere. At the end of the trail you do not find the thing referred to. It's brilliant. The customer will never know we are getting a share of the profits."

Lohman asked, "So how would a court be able to read it?"

Coats answered, "The part where we get the profit share is pretty clear when we go through the cross references for it and when you are keyed into the specific defined terms. There is a sheet at the end that will guide you through it. That's just for you. It isn't part of the agreement."

Lohman was instructed to review the agreement for compliance with the law. Coats added, "This was one of The Chair's pet projects. We were the experimental project. If it worked with us he would expand it to other areas of the consulting company and then see how he could use it on other companies. Ultimately he wanted to get a share of all his customers' profits." "The Chair" is what a lot of O'Brien's employees called him, ostensibly because he was the Chairman of the Board of most of the companies, but perhaps because of the wheel chair.

"Talking about The Chair," said Coats, "what are we going to do now? Do you know? Henry says he is taking over the consulting company. What about the rest?"

"I don't really know," said Lohman. "We are all wondering."

"Yeah, but who's in charge? Isn't there usually a trustee or something like that? Who did he put in charge?"

"Well, of course what I know about it would be confidential," said Lohman.

"Well, we all want to know," said Coats. "We would like some peace in the homeland so to speak. Henry and The Chair were always fighting. Stupid stuff. For instance a few weeks ago Henry was in my office. We were discussing some pricing software. All of a sudden The Chair wheeled in. He just bust open the door with his chair and came in. He started accusing Henry of not fixing something. With that voice box of his it was weird. When he was angry he sounded like Darth Vader on crack. Evidently The Chair was trying to change his password on one of the company sites. He couldn't find out how to do it. He said the help instructions gave him a screen shot of what to do and he did as instructed and wound up finding out he had been referred to a screen that did not exist. He got a message saying to see our new site. Then he went there and there were no instructions for changing the password, at least not that he could find. Both sites were working at once. He called help and he said he spent 2 hours on the whole deal. He said the help person hung up on him. Then he got a pay help site to tell him what to do. Then Henry said, 'Why didn't you call me Dad? You own the company.' The Chair told Henry that he wanted to see what was going on – wanted to see what a customer would experience. He asked Henry if he ever checked to see what a customer would experience. Then Henry said, 'You're old.' The Chair said, 'And you're not gonna get to be.' They were always arguing like that," added Coats.

"Then," said Coats, "Henry said that The Chair had told him to stop spending money on help because it costs too much. Henry said to The Chair, 'Fuck 'em you said. You said the customer is always wrong.' The Chair said, 'Yes, but now I am 'em. Fix it shit-head and fix it quick or you're fired.' They were always going on like that."

"Sounds like a difficult working environment," said Lohman. "Things are difficult these days. They say we are living in a service economy as opposed to a manufacturing environment, but no one seems to be able to provide service any more. And computers and software! Trouble after trouble. It's always not working or difficult to use. I sympathize with The Lion."

"Oh get with it old man!" exclaimed Coats. "Times change. You got to get with it."

Lohman couldn't help it. He said, "I know, I know. It's strange to think that 'modern' is an old fashioned word. And to think that prayer has been replaced by a call center. It really is incumbent on people of my age to change our attitudes as you say."

They took their leave and Lohman dictated a memo to a more junior partner with instructions to review the agreement and get back to him. Then Lohman left the office. He planned to take Sunday off and he took a leisurely stroll home.

The Dead One Stinks

18 MORE INFO

Monday morning Lohman had a meeting scheduled with a group of lawyers working on one of his client's deals. It was a fairly big deal and there were going to be 12 associates and three of the younger partners in the meeting. Lohman was a little late getting to the office and when he walked into the conference room they were all there sitting around the conference table. They were all fairly young. Each and every one had a laptop or tablet computer or smart phone which they were using. Some were using two of these devices and one young associate was using all three. There was total silence and none of them were talking to or interacting with the others. Or so Lohman thought. As he sat down one of the young women looked up at another associate and said, "No! Never!" None of the others looked up.

It took Lohman a while to get their attention, but he did. He started to talk to them as a group and the young man who had been the object of the "No! Never!" hit the dial point on his phone. The phone of the young woman who had so addressed him rang. She picked it up and terminated the call.

Lohman shouted, "Oh crap! Turn them all off. Whatever you have. Off! Now!"

They all looked shocked. Most of them did as he requested, but some continued to scan their email. After Lohman shouted some more all but two finally turned everything off. One had to send one more text message. "ODGC." It showed up on the phone of the associate nearest Lohman. The associate was reading it. Lohman grabbed the phone from the associate. He looked at the message and asked, "ODGC? What's that? Why do you spend time on this? What's it mean?"

Just at this point Tete had come in with some files for Lohman. She was the one who answered. "Old Dude go crazy, I'll bet," she said as she put the files down near Lohman and walked out.

Lohman scanned all present with a glaring look that met each in the eye, one by one around the circle. "You want crazy, just keep it up. Now let's get on with it."

They finally did so and spent all morning going over the relevant points in the deal. When they had decided to break they started to get up and got to talking about other things. Out of curiosity Lohman spoke up to all of them. "Just a minute everybody. Hold on a minute. I want to ask you about The Lion."

They all resumed their seats and Lohman gave them a short introduction about what had happened and what he knew about it. Then he asked if anyone knew or had heard anything else about O'Brien. None had ever had any contact with him and few had worked on any of his matters. However, one of the associates said he had been at a lunch with some of his high school classmates. He was a Francine Pucker graduate. He said one of his classmates had said he had heard that O'Brien was working with The Roman School to defame Pucker. He said no one paid much attention to it because Pucker and Roman people are always saying things like that. He couldn't even remember who said it. Lohman asked him to ask others there who said it and to try to find out more about it.

After a few more minutes of small talk everyone left. Lohman went back into his office and asked Tete to get him something to eat. He started going through files relating to his next appointment.

After reviewing the files and eating Lohman went back into his conference room for the next meeting. He was due to see Lashandra McCain, the firm's top divorce lawyer, and her client. The client was Sally Wallydone, the gorgeous blonde who came into the office on Friday the 7th at about the same time as O'Brien, according to the building log. They had a few associates there too and Gunnar Pekka, a principal in a large accounting firm, who was working on the business issues in the divorce. Sally's husband, Wally, was what is called a high net worth individual. Most of his assets consisted of a lot of different companies he owned. In divorces assets are divided up and Gunnar was working on issues like how much each interest was worth and what the financial statements actually meant. Gunnar and F, P & C shared a lot of clients.

Lohman did not do divorce work, but McCain wanted him to work on the business issues involved. The question was how to divide up the assets and selecting which assets Sally should go after. Wally would probably want to give Sally minority interests in some of the companies. Sally would like to get controlling interests in some of them. Wally would like to give her interests in the dog companies. Sally would like to get interests in the better companies. And so forth.

Part of the meeting involved coming up with ideas for the negotiations and reviewing what were the strengths and weaknesses of the various positions they could take. One advantage was that Sally already owned large minority interests in several of the companies and some of Wally's ex-wives also owned minority interests in some of the companies in which Sally held interests. There was also a corporate raider who was going after one of Wally's larger companies that was publicly held. All the ex-wives and Sally as well held interests in this company. The raider had already acquired 12% of the outstanding stock and was making big noises about how poorly the company was run and about how he could vastly increase stockholder returns. The advantage lay in the fact that potentially the ex-wives and the raider could all come together as a group and take over control. Free candy, though, is usually beyond its suggested shelf life. Any contact with the ex-wives and raider on this deal would involve each trying to take advantage of the others as well as Wally. Thus on this issue they had to discuss how to out maneuver the others as well as Wally. It was going to be like all the religions going after each other at the same time they were going after the Devil. In addition, some of them might also be in league with the Devil and even if they were not, the others might think they were.

Lohman and Gunnar were assigned to come up with a plan. This would involve examining all the Wallydone assets and determining the best way to protect Sally's interests. Exactly what her interests were was not discussed much. She had stated them simply. "I want as much as I can get. And I want my own companies. I don't want to have to deal with Wally anymore. If I just own part of some of the companies I'm going to have to keep on dealing with him. I also want to control the income. I don't want him to cut out the dividends while he is taking huge salaries. He's doing that already to the others." By others, she meant the ex-wives of which she was soon to be one.

Sally then mentioned The Lion. She had heard about all his ex-wives and she had seen them all attending the same functions with him. "So tell me Lashandra, what arrangements did he make? What do his ex-wives get?"

Lashandra told her that the firm had worked on those matters and she could not reveal client confidences. "Yes, but aren't the marital settlement agreements or at least the divorce decrees public records?" asked Sally.

"Not in his case," said Lohman. "The records were sealed and what is public merely refers to other agreements which have elaborate secrecy provisions."

"Am I going to get that?" asked Sally.

"We'll see," said Lashandra. "More important than secrecy is how much and of what."

"Right," said Sally.

It was getting late and they started winding down the talk about the immediate problem at hand and moving on to more social talk preparatory to leaving. Lohman said to Sally, "You should have asked The Lion about it that Friday before last when you came in. You came into the building at the same time he did, didn't you?"

"Yes," said Sally. He and I got on the same elevator. I have seen him at parties. I said hello. He didn't even look at me."

"Nothing?" asked Lohman. "He didn't say anything to you?"

"No," said Sally. "At the parties at least some times he would wink at me."

They then broke up the meeting and as they were leaving Lohman thought how unusual it was that The Lion was in the same elevator with such a good looking woman and didn't even respond when she said hello.

Lohman went back to his office and reviewed things for the next day and went home. He got Louie and took him for a walk in the park. As he was heading back to his place he ran into Sven Aron, the Francine Pucker Head of School who was returning to his apartment across the street from Lohman's house. The two knew each other. They exchanged greetings.

"Heads of School" do not work the same hours as most lawyers. Lohman said, "So what keeps you out so late Sven?"

"We had a board meeting," said Sven. "You are probably aware of that contest O'Brien was sponsoring for the schools. I'm sure you've heard of it. He was your client. Well, there are hateful rumors going around. Some of them involve alleged wrongdoing on our part. It's just the sort of thing that McIlvaine would bring up. He's never been anything but trouble. Very hard to deal with. And you know some of his trustees use drugs. We found that out tonight. I'm sure you know it already, having been one. And someone had reached O'Brien with all this rot. He was going to cut us off or some such thing. Anyway I heard he was going to bring up questions about some of these rumors. Thankfully we got most of our money already. He was impossible to deal with. A very difficult man. Well anyway, his death should put a stop to all this slander. And I might say that from what I know of him he deserved it."

"What?" asked Lohman.

"Death," said Aron.

"I mean what were the rumors?" said Lohman.

"You don't know?" asked Aron. "If you don't know I'm not going to tell you."

"Right," said Lohman. "You don't want to spread it any further."

"Exactly." said Aron.

They took their leave and Lohman took Louie home.

19 THE MERITRICIOUS

Tuesday Lohman had to deal with Pansy's oats. One of Lady Fitch-Bennington's companies was American Oats. It was making a breakfast cereal called America's Best Oats. Another company had started making an oat based breakfast cereal under the Oatems name and on all the packaging they prominently claimed that it was made with America's best oats. Naturally Pansy's company claimed they had a trademark which was being infringed. Lohman was scheduled to meet with the lawyers for Oatems and one of the IP partners from F, P & C to see if they could resolve anything. Oatems claimed that America's Best Oats was merely a descriptive phrase that could not be a trademark. American Oats claimed that they had used the phrase so long that it had acquired an independent meaning which was a particular breakfast cereal made by American Oats and no one else. Lots to argue about, and the matter was already in court. Lohman suspected Oatems wanted to be bought out by American and he was going to see if that was possible. That would settle the matter and get rid of a competitor.

Pansy's lawyer was St. Charles, but he didn't do the actual work, just as Pansy did not till her fields. St. Charles had fobbed this matter off on Lohman. Lohman had got one of the firm's IP partners involved. He was Jack Sprack. Mr. Jack did not think in terms of settling or resolving anything. He only thought of litigation and winning. He was always right. He was superior. He always won. He knew and applied the most sophisticated and advanced techniques in the IP field. He was years and miles ahead of all other IP practitioners in creating and applying these techniques.

Lohman on the other hand thought that people who think they are especially sophisticated, or even use the word, aren't. Lohman had worked with Sprack enough to know that his technique involved trying to scare opponents off. Lohman also knew that Sprack did not win most of his cases that went to trial. He regarded Sprack as a pain in the ass, but Sprack was the IP guy St. Charles liked to have working on his matters. Sprack considered himself one of the new elite. In the past lineage, breeding and old money were power and the hall marks of the elite. Now, according to him, merit and superior performance were the hall marks of superiority and power. So far as he was concerned he was the most superior and meretricious of all. If you had asked him if Moses could have copyrighted the Ten Commandments which supposedly came from God, Sprack would have told you that Moses could have done just that if he, Sprack, had been his lawyer. Someone did ask Sprack that once and that is what Sprack told him.

Oatems was represented by lawyers from a small IP firm and Sprack had no trouble telling them they were going to lose as he was the biggest expert on the matter and he knew all. He also pointed out to them that he had superior litigation skills and that their client could not afford to oppose him, his bigger client and his bigger firm.

I win, you lose, is no way to settle anything, but Sprack was not there to settle. Lohman was. Lohman kept saying he wanted to explore ways in which the matter could be settled. Sprack would just give him an annoyed look and pour out more "I win, you lose" talk. Finally one of the Oatems lawyers said to Lohman, "Are you crazy? He says I win so give up. And you support him. Then you say let's talk about settlement. At least he's consistent. So what are you, schizoid or something?"

Lohman couldn't help himself. He said, "Which one of me are you talking to?" No one thought that was funny. They all just looked at him in silence for a while.

Sprack went on for another hour or so about how great he was and how Oatems should give up. Nothing was resolved by the time the meeting ended. This was not the way Lohman ordinarily did things, but it was how Sprack did things. Lohman thought to himself that he would just set up another meeting soon without Sprack. Someone like Sprack could get people to harden their position, but he could also wear people down. They might be more amenable to Lohman's more reasonable position later.

As for Sprack, Lohman just figured that if he could work out some sort of settlement he would just go over Sprack's head straight to Pansy and get it approved. "Sprack, The Meritricious!" thought Lohman. "I wish I was as good at things as he thinks he is. I wonder who has more merit – him or the average quadriplegic who just gets through life?" Then Lohman reminded himself that Sprack would say merit is judged by results, meaning that he is the meretricious one.

The Dead One Stinks

20 OOPSY

Lohman headed back to his office. As soon as he came in the outer door, Tete said, "There you are Hon. More problems. Look at these summonses and complaints. The sheriff just served them downstairs and they just sent them up. You lawyers need keepers."

"For what?" asked Lohman.

"For yourselves, Hon," said Tete. Just read them. The two biggest personal injury lawyers in town. You remember, maybe you don't, but we are defending Champion in that big class action about their wiring products injuring building occupants. If you haven't seen it in the billing records you must have seen it in the papers. They're asking for billions."

"I remember assigning it after we couldn't get the insurance carrier to handle it," said Lohman. "What's a sheriff doing here about that? We aren't a party, just one of the defendants' law firms. "

"It's that settlement conference they had here a little while ago. You know Hon, all the big deal lawyers were here. You remember Lotus Feingold. I hear they call her the vile bitch from Hades over at the Bar Association. She has that nice Lyman Smith with her to do the good cop, bad cop routine."

"How do you know all this?" asked Lohman.

"Oh come on Hon," she said. "While you're doing all your things I get around. I talk to people around here. And Louis Wavidson was here too. The two biggest ambulance chasers in town. They had been in separate rooms. They had separate smaller conferences going on you know. Anyway, they both came out of their rooms at the same time and were scooting down the corridors using their smart phones and the two corridors intersected and they ran into each other. From what that complaint says, neither will ever walk again. Maybe. What garbage Hon. They claim the hallway conditions were inherently dangerous so we are liable for their injuries."

Lohman did not want to spend time on the matter, since the firm would refer the defense of the suit to their insurance company who would get a defense firm to do the work. A defense firm is one that is hired by insurance companies to defend suits against their insureds. They generally charge a lot less than general business firms like F, P & C. Regardless of what Lohman thought would happen, he still had to review the matter and read the complaints before sending it over to the insurance company.

Lohman said, "I'll read it. But it's probably going to the carrier so get a letter ready. The standard form. If I have to make changes, I'll let you know. This is like an ECOTAG matter that came up the other day. Schlot, you know, their General Counsel, was in court on a matter and arguing his point to the judge who banged her gavel on the bench. It hit a pen which flew across the room and hit a bailiff who pulled his gun. That accidentally went off and shot the stand out from under a court reporter's machine and it fell and hit Sidney Glass. Have you ever heard of him?"

Tete nodded.

Lohman continued. "It also destroyed some crucial evidence. So he and his client sued ECOTAG and Schlot and claimed that Schlot got the judge angry on purpose."

"We took that case?" she asked. "I thought cases like that went to a defense firm?"

"In this case the carrier is saying the policy doesn't cover it," said Lohman. "They asked us about taking it, but we can't because we will represent The Lion's estate and they are filing a claim against it."

"Yes," said Tete. "I noticed that in your report to the Management Committee. Anyway that just proves what I say. You lawyers need keepers. Or guardians or something. Or parole officers. But you're one of the nice ones," she added.

Lohman retreated to his office and spent the rest of the day preparing for a conference with the O'Brien family.

21 THE FAMILY SPEAKS

Wednesday morning the family met at F, P & C. The main reason for the meeting was to confirm what the firm partners had already worked out as to who would be the administrator of the estate. Lohman had reserved two of the biggest conference rooms and had the partition between them removed. The room was set up with a podium and an elaborate snack and beverage area. There were waitresses to see to everyone's needs. At meetings like these, especially when lawyers, who all think they are big shots, and actual big shots are present, everyone jockeys for position at the tables. The dog with the big balls sits at the head. Everyone knows that and everyone is determined to have the biggest balls. To avoid that Lohman had assigned places and had had a seating chart drawn up to be handed to each person when they came in. There were also name cards posted on the table in front of each seat. The room was set up with only one table. Or at least a series of tables, each in contact with the adjoining tables. These made one gigantic rectangular table with the podium at one of the narrower ends. As it was, when people came in they started changing the name cards around and jockeying for position. Lohman had given directions to all the lawyers in attendance and the waitresses and attendants not to allow this and the efforts of the position changers were mostly unsuccessful.

At a meeting of this importance his eminence, Graybourne St. Charles, would normally preside. However, he and Pansy were in Monte Carlo for the wedding of a member of the royal family and for him that was a more important gathering. The F, P & C crew was headed by Zenon Cohenstein. On an occasion like this one of the heads of the firm should show up to indicate how important the firm thought the matter to be. Lohman and Nuftdone were there and Morton Wharton as well. The lawyers for the individual family members were there too. All in all, a lot of the top equity partners were there. They naturally brought various associates and junior partners with them, even though they had been cautioned not to and there were no seats for the juniors. They stood around the edges of the room, behind the seats. And then there was Sweeney. Not even a partner. But he represented Trisha DeLang. Through her he had also begun to handle her mother's and uncle's matters. He brought Featherbottom as a tag-along. Most of the partners there did not approve of Sweeney's presence as a seated member, but they knew why he was there and kept their mouths shut. St. Charles would have objected, but he was not there.

It was a strange gathering. All the ex-wives were there. They attended all family gatherings and they all had positions of one kind or another in the O'Brien companies. They always were at family gatherings, if for no other reason than to keep an eye on their maintenance payments and the companies where much of their income was coming from. Ivan's first wife had been Hu Yen Fong. She was there with her boyfriend, Fung Goo. Her children, Jason O'Brien and Watta O'Brien were there. The second wife had been Latrina Foxglover. She and her children, Wandrasha O'Brien and Dwante O'Brien, were there. Trisha DeLang was Wandrasha's daughter and she was there too. The third wife had been Veronica Goldstein and she was there with her two sons, Glover O'Brien and Henry O'Brien. Yellow, black and white. Like the United Nations. And the red ones? Moronika Headpin was there too. She was part Native American. Specifically she was half Arapaho. Some people who are doomed to Hell would say she was part Indian. In Delhi they would say they never heard of her. Anyway, while she was not an heir, she had managed to wangle stock in various Champion companies out of The Lion and in that respect she had some votes. She was a usual participant in family meetings anyway. Everybody wanted to keep an eye on her.

Swifty was there too. He had several Vice Presidents of the Bank from the Wealth Management department with him. They were like wolves surveying the deer.

The family's net worth was in the billions. The gross assets they controlled were close to a trillion. The Bank controlled assets worth trillions too. They were all together in one place. Perhaps if the terrorists had known that they would have blown the whole place up. The only thing that protected them was the fact that most of the assets were controlled by Swifty and the terrorists would not have wanted to bother blowing up the vacuum he had top side, since it might just implode of its own accord.

After everyone came in, got their refreshments and got seated and settled down, Cohenstein rose and went to the podium and welcomed everyone and introduced himself for the benefit of those who did not know who he was. He explained why St. Charles was not there, briefly explaining that he was at a wedding involving royalty in Europe. He told them that he, as one of the heads of the firm, was there to emphasize the importance of this matter to the firm. He said all this quickly and explicitly. Had St. Charles been running the show this part of the proceedings would have gone on for an hour.

Cohenstein yielded the podium to Lohman. They had discussed this in advance. Most of the family knew him and neither he nor Cohenstein wanted to put up with Nuftdone leading the meeting. Lohman related how everyone had been talking about who would be the administrator and that everyone seemed to have agreed on The Bank being the administrator. He explained that Watta had already filed a petition to appoint an administrator with the court asking that she and The Bank be named co-administrators. He said this would be amended to ask that The Bank alone be appointed and that all the heirs would sign consents to that. Most already had, but Henry and Jason had not and Lohman asked them to sign. Each of the family members had a package in front of them and Lohman told Henry and Jason the forms to sign were in a package in front of them. He indicated that their lawyers would help them.

There weren't many questions because most of this had been worked out beforehand. However Henry still was not on board. He piped up and said, "Why does The Bank get the power? One of us should be the administrator. If we need The Bank we can hire them direct. Then they can do what is needed, but we will be the boss."

Lohman responded. "You can always get The Bank removed. I think that if a significant number of the heirs wants them removed it can be done. Certainly if The Bank does not do a good job they can be removed." He looked and Nuftdone. "Right, Jerry?"

Nuftdone was as dysfunctionally able to respond to a direct question as any other booby hatch resident. He said, "The Bank would never fail do to a good job. That is why we appoint them."

One of the Vice Presidents said, "We can't do a bad job. Everyone of importance has us manage their affairs."

Sweeney leaned over to Trisha and whispered, "I handle my own."

Henry continued. "Well, I think I should be administrator. I don't want to have to deal with some bank. It was hard enough dealing with Dad. He didn't understand IT. Do you think someone at The Bank will? IT is what drives business these days and I am the one who handles that."

Dwante said, "You're always complaining about Dad. He's gone. Who are you going to blame for everything now? What did you have against him? We all got his crap. Why do you have to complain so much?"

Henry said, "He was sticking his nose in my business and he didn't know what he was doing. He was always complaining about me. It wasn't me complaining about him. He complained about all the time that computers were taking and the increasing cost. I showed him time and time again that what he was talking about was user error. If it wasn't for all the morons they put in front of a computer these days we would not be incurring so much time and cost because of their mistakes."

Latrina Foxglover spoke up. "Like using English? Maybe you should have listened to Ivan. You know, I'm a director of Champion Screw & Bolt. It's not one of the big companies, but we make 175 million a year. It's like clockwork. No trouble. So Ivan didn't deal with the company much. He told me that one day he wanted to get contact information for the company from the web site you set up. You or your guys at IT. Christ what you charged us for that! He got a number off the site and called it."

Henry interrupted. "That's the kind of stuff he was always screwing up. You never deal with that kind of thing. You have your secretary or assistant do it."

Latrina continued. "You know damn well he did a lot of things himself that other people had others do. So he called and it wasn't a working number. He went back to the site and got an email address and emailed. He said who he was and asked for the number of someone to call. Several days later he got a reply saying to call the number he called before. The one that was not working. He got angry – you know. You would too. Well anyway, you'd get angry if you did it instead of your secretary. Then he got me on it. I gave him the number of the President. He called and got no answer and left a message. The President's secretary called back and left a message which told him to go to the web site and send an email. So he got all the directors' phone numbers from me and called them. No answer from any of them. He got the receptionist who wouldn't take a message. She told him to go to voice mail. Remember she got those instructions form the phone system you set up for us. He left messages. None of them called back except one who left a message for him when he was about to send an email with his concerns. Then he called me. He was angry. He went right over there and fired them all. Didn't make much difference since they didn't do much anyway. You know, maybe if the web site worked in the first place this wouldn't have happened. Now we have a mess over there and we have to clean it up."

"That shows you don't know anything about IT either," said Henry. "You are describing a phone problem. Anyway, Watta shouldn't be involved in this. Whoever let her file the petition? You know that sometimes she's a controlling bitch."

Trisha all of a sudden spoke up. "As if you aren't, crap ass!."

Dwante said, "Trisha – Trasha. Always with the potty mouth."

"Children, children," said Veronica.

Latrina said, "Don't you tell my kid what to do."

It was just the usual O'Brien family conference. In the end they hung together and agreed that The Bank would be the administrator.

Lohman got the papers signed by Henry and Jason and proclaimed that the matter was settled. He then explained that they would be having monthly meetings of the family and representatives of the various businesses involved at the firm offices and noted that the dates were in their folders. He reminded them to make note of the dates in their calendars. He added that they would all be sent emails with the dates too.

Glover, who usually did not say much, then piped up. "So what was he doing in your men's room anyway? What was going on in there?"

Jason said, "He usually had to go after conferences. I wasn't there Friday, but I was there the day before. Thursday. It was around noon time and I accompanied him down the hall and helped him into the john. Henry went down the hall with us. He didn't go in the john though. I took Dad in and I asked if he wanted anything else and he said no so I left him there. Some bald guy came in while I was going out. I don't know who he was. Anyway, I left Dad in there. He probably wanted to do his noon time shot."

All the family members and Moronika gave out with a little giggle. Sweeney did too. Apparently he was in on it.

"What is so funny?" asked Lohman.

"Testosterone," said Jason. "How else do you do a 22 year old girlfriend at his age? He didn't hide it. He was proud of it and he would explain all the details to everyone who wanted to know. He kept the syringes in the bag on the back of his wheel chair."

"Well, we all know that," said Glover, "but maybe you should tell us what you know Lohman. You found him."

So Bumper did. Nothing much was knew to any of them. Lohman had let their lawyers know about the overdose already and they had already discussed that amongst themselves. Then he asked Henry, "What do you know about it?"

Henry said, "Not much. Thursday I left the meeting with Jason and Dad and I left them at the men's room and went on out of the building. Then I went to Omaha on a firm matter. I had to get out there and back quickly for the meeting here the next day. Friday I made it back here just in time for the meeting. After that I went down the hall with Dad again and took him into the men's room again. Jerry came with us. He turned back at the men's room and I went out. That's the last time I saw Dad. Didn't even see his body at the wake. Cremation! You can have it. I got to see the urn with his ashes."

Lohman brought the meeting to an end and everyone got up and started getting their things and talking to each other. Henry started out on a course that took him past Lohman. Lohman noticed a diamond sticking out of his jacket pocket. "Henry," he said, "that looks like what

The Lion had. He always had a diamond topped pen sticking out of his pocket didn't he? Is that a pen?"

"Yes," said Henry. He had one. I gave it to him. I found this matching set one day and I bought them both. Cost a fortune, but I charged it to the company. I gave him one. He liked it. You know, even though he didn't understand IT we were very close. I admired him."

"Yes, yes," said Lohman. "I could tell." Then he added, "Conferences here, conferences there. Back here again. It must have been a busy week for you."

"Very," said Henry. "After the meeting on Friday I had to get to Los Angeles for a meeting with people from Laos. Hen Fen Devices, Ltd. They have a US office there. We were talking about their manufacturing a new device for us. You know, nobody goes to China for things anymore. Laos is cheaper. Here, look." He took what looked like a smart phone out of his pocket and showed it to Lohman.

"What's that? You're making phones now?" asked Lohman.

Henry responded. "Remote control." Henry looked around and saw a TV screen in the one of the corners. He pointed the device at it and manipulated it. The TV turned on. Then he hit another button and the TV turned off. Then he pointed it at one of the light switches and hit another button. Nothing happened. "Mechanical," he said. Then he noticed one of those devices that turn off lights when no one is in the room and touched his device again. All the lights in the room went off. He hit another button and they went on again.

Veronica, his mother, was still there. She shouted across the room, "Cut it out Henry!"

Henry turned to Lohman and said, "It's still experimental, but what it is, it's a remote control device that can control anything that works by electricity. It doesn't have to be part of that device or be specially programmed for it or connected to it. Think of it! Imagine what we can do!" Apparently it also functioned as a phone because just then it rang and Henry answered it and began talking as he walked on out of the room.

Lohman went back to his office and developed a follow up memo for the meeting. By 8 p.m. he was done and he left. He made his way down to the lobby and then headed for one of the revolving doors. He could hear the fast paced steps of a high heeled dame in a hurry coming up behind him. He reached the door and started through. All of a sudden, as he was in the middle of the revolving door with his hand on the push bar, it shot forward and the advancing panel behind him hit him and pushed him forward and spit him out on the sidewalk as it revolved. He turned and was almost run over by Miss Quick. As he walked home he mused to himself about how much nicer it would be to live in the country. Whatever cows did, they did more slowly. But he was cut short by the realization that there is not much business out in the country.

22 THE COPS AGAIN

Early Thursday morning Detective Bongwad and Sargent Gilbert came in to see Lohman. They wanted to go over what they knew and compare it with what Lohman knew. "So, did you find out any more about how he was killed?" asked Lohman.

Detective Bongwad said, "We know the drug. It's what I thought. It was heroin. The Medical Examiner's office says it was pure heroin."

"Heroin!" exclaimed Lohman. "He was a drug addict? I never heard that. He didn't act like it."

"You may have a preconceived idea of what a drug addict is like," said Bongwad. "But no, he wasn't an addict. At least the M.E. says there are no signs of it. Anyway, he had two syringes in him. One was in his arm and one in a vein in his neck. What we find out now is that the syringe in his arm had his fingerprints on it. The one in his neck had no fingerprints. The syringe in the arm was covered by his shirt which is odd. And his jacket was on over that. Why would he pull his shirt down over the syringe and put his jacket on? The one in his neck was covered by his scarf. There were a lot of syringes in the bag on the back of his wheel chair too. Forensics says they were testosterone syringes. The male hormone, you know. But they all had heroin in them. Another odd thing is that there were no fingerprints on any of the syringes. Some old guys take testosterone. Especially if they have a young babe like O'Brien did. Well, he took it regularly. The labels on the syringes say they came from Champion Pharmaceuticals. That turns out to be one of his own companies. There is no drug store label, so it looks like it was not prescribed. We talked to his doctor and he denies prescribing it. O'Brien may have got it direct from the drug company. Do you know anything about this?"

The Dead One Stinks

"No," said Lohman. "Where did you find the wheelchair? He could move around a bit on his own, but he always used the wheelchair for longer distances that I knew of. I never saw him without it even if he was walking. He didn't walk very well."

Detective Bongwad said, "We found the chair at his home. He had a bigger supply of testosterone there, all with the same labeling. The syringes in the bag on his chair all had heroin in them. The syringes that weren't in the chair bag all had testosterone in them. It's also interesting that Champion Pharmaceuticals makes diacetylmorphine which is the medicinal form of heroin. Same stuff the dope heads take, but a pure form and much stronger. The stuff in the syringes was the strongest dose they make and about ten times the dose usually given. Both syringes had some residue of it. I think I told you that the one in the neck was in a vein. Either syringe could have killed him. The M.E. says the one in the arm was not in a vein, but he still would have died from it, just not as fast. The M.E. also says that the testosterone shots are usually not put directly into a vein. The fact that he wasn't an addict would make the doses more lethal since he had not built up a tolerance."

"So," asked Lohman, "how exactly did he die? I've heard about death from an overdose, but how did the drug work to kill him? Is it like poison?"

Detective Bongwad answered, "Not breathing. The drug just slows everything down and it stops. He died from not breathing. Asphyxiation I think it is called."

Lohman asked, "Is that what made him smell so much?"

"Not heroin," said Bongwad. "Just the normal decomposition."

Lohman said, "I can see now why they have to embalm us so fast. Boy, did he stink. I haven't ever smelled a dead person like that. One day and he stinks like that!"

"What do you mean 'one day'?" said Bongwad.

Lohman said, "I found him on Saturday and he was killed on Friday and left there. Probably Friday afternoon. One of our associates used that stall on Friday around eleven and O'Brien was in a conference here with Mr. Nuftdone and others around that time."

"The M.E. says he died no later than the Thursday before you found him," said Gilbert.

"That's consistent with the smell," said Bongwad. "I'm not the M.E., but we often have questions about the time of death and I have been told often enough by the M.E's. office that it takes two days for a body to start smelling like that. You can slow it down, but you can't really speed it up."

"But," said Lohman, "he was alive on Friday. He was here talking to Nuftdone and the others. He wasn't in the stall on Friday. How could he have been killed on Thursday?"

Bongwad looked at Lohman for a while. Then he looked at Gilbert. Gilbert shrugged. Then he looked back at Lohman. "I don't know. We'll talk to the people at the Medical Examiner's office. We'll talk to the people who saw him at the meeting too. Who were they?"

Lohman told the officers who was there. Then said, "And they were not the only ones who saw him. I know someone who came in the building with him that day. She came up the elevator with him to our offices. Her name is Sally Wallydone and she is one of our clients. She knew him, at least casually, from parties and gatherings. Ask her. He wasn't dead."

"Well, we have some other conflicting evidence too," said Bongwad. "His chauffeur, what's the name Willy?" He looked at Gilbert. Not many people would think of calling him anything like Willy without dying. "John Cooper. That's it," continued Bongwad. "He says he drove O'Brien home on Thursday. Then he says he drove O'Brien down here on Friday morning. He didn't drive him home or elsewhere on Friday though. He says he was told not to wait on Friday and he didn't get a pick up call. He says O'Brien sometimes went off on his own and took cabs. He says they didn't talk much. He said that was fine with him. So who was at the meeting on Thursday? We ought to talk to them too."

Lohman told them. Bongwad wrote it all down and looked at the list. Then he looked up at Lohman. "Fenlow Dancaway and Pukutania Moore?"

"Yes," said Lohman.

Bongwad looked at the list again. Then up at Lohman. "Muttwuf and Meowi? Is that their firm?"

"Yes," said Lohman.

"There's a law firm by that name?" he asked.

"Yes," said Lohman.

"You're kidding," said Bongwad.

"No," said Lohman.

"They're lawyers," said Gilbert by way of explanation. "They come up with weird stuff."

"I guess so," said Bongwad.

Detective Bongwad then told Lohman what they had learned about O'Brien's last days at home. "One of the other funny things about the M.E. report is that the help at O'Brien's house saw him there Friday morning. He had five maids and a two cooks and the chauffeur's wife who was called the housekeeper. She was in charge of the house. She and the chauffeur lived in an apartment over the garage and the rest lived elsewhere. On Friday morning two of the maids were there and one of them heard the door bell and went to answer it, but O'Brien beat her to it. She saw him let a kid in who said he was from your firm. She didn't know who he was. She said he was young and blonde and 'wishy'. She's got an accent. Looks like she comes from somewhere in Asia. She doesn't speak English very well, and she didn't want to tell us where she came from. She kept saying she couldn't understand us – I think. She's probably illegal. Do you know who it was?"

"No," said Lohman. "I'll try to find out."

The officers then took their leave and Lohman started going over his schedule for the day.

23 MORE FIRM BUSINESS

After his meeting with the police Lohman went up to see St. Charles and Cohenstein in Grabby's office to fill them in on what was happening. St. Charles was a bit groggy from his flight back from the wedding in Monte Carlo the day before, but this affected his mouth more than his brain since the former was usually much more active that the latter. Lohman began by telling them that The Bank was going to be the administrator and that everything seemed to be going according to plan on that score. He then filled them in on who was doing what with whom to solidify the firm's control of family business. Then he discussed some problems that were on hold pending appointment of The Bank as administrator because there was no ultimate authority to make decisions just yet. However, everything was manageable because there were usually others involved in the management of most of the entities. For instance the corporations had boards of directors, the general partnerships had other partners, the limited liability companies had other managers and so forth. These people could usually act by majority vote and were doing so.

Everything seemed to be going according to plan. Lohman remarked that some of this work could be fun, at least to some of the younger partners. Trisha DeLang was performing in concert Friday night and Lohman explained how Sweeney had been getting firm people to sign up for the concert and to get everyone else to go that they could. Trisha was already a sell out and had been for some time and some last minute arrangements had to be made to get the firm's contingent in, but the idea was to show how the firm was so madly in love with her. Some of the O'Brien papers and TV and radio stations were going to do feature stories on it.

As soon as Lohman had told them about this he knew he shouldn't have. St. Charles rose up in his chair and took Pussy off her

151

perch and put her in his lap. He often did so at times of deep shock and offense. "We are to associate ourselves in public with that – that – it's horrid!"

"With the family Graybee," said Cohenstein. "They'll see how we stand with them and support them. And they'll see it's just the younger ones who go to the concert so they won't think we're all like that. That'll fly with the older ones. The older ones – they'll think we older ones orchestrated this. They'll love it. And the public! This is a great way to get publicity. The public will hear that we are the lawyers for the O'Brien interests. "

St. Charles still had that blank dissatisfied look on his face. Like a nursing home resident who needed changing. "She is such a lower class person. How did she get in the family? And who let her get into show business. Show business! It is not reputable. Have you ever heard of anyone of standing and high repute in show business? It is low. She is low."

"Don't worry Graybee," said Cohenstein, "scum doesn't seep up. She isn't contagious."

"It is if you are affiliated with it," sniffed St.Charles.

"Well anyway, she comes with the family," said Cohenstein.

"Thank God that Moronika doesn't," said St. Charles. "Why is she involved in everything?"

"She's a stockholder," said Lohman.

"Well, they're all tedious. Squabbling like a band of seagulls who have been thrown seed," said St. Charles.

Lohman tried to console him. "Sweeny will take care of Trisha DeLang," he said.

St. Charles had heard the names of two terrorists at once. In the same sentence. At least the names and what they stood for terrorized him. He gave Lohman one of his blankest stares. The terrorists had succeeded. He was terrorized.

Lohman went on. "Sweeney knows how to handle her. And Moronika doesn't inherit so she won't be such a big influence from here on."

"If she's any trouble I'm sure we can buy her off," said Cohenstein.

St. Charles said, "I suppose we must deal with them. In any event it is going to be tedious. They all constantly criticize each other and argue whenever they are together. Think of it! You could ask each one of them – how do you presume to criticize others when they you are so defective? They're all defective. Batty, that's what they are! I suppose it is too much to ask that they straighten up and fly right."

"Yes," said Cohenstein. "They certainly are bats. And Confucius say bat who fly upside down shouldn't shit."

St. Charles gave him another blank look.

Lohman went back to his office after the conference. He found Henner Pigman, the firm IT manager there finishing up a talk with Tete about something. As he greeted them Sweeney came in. "What up Dudes?" he said.

Pigman and Lohman both said "Hey." Tete didn't say anything. She wasn't a dude.

Sweeney said to Pigman, "So how's the tech world? You here to fix something? Software's great Dude, but it's also a great big screw-up maker. That reminds me of the old joke. You know, if it has tits or tires, sooner or later it's going to give you trouble. Well add software. If it's got tits or tires or software sooner or later it's going to give you trouble."

Tete added, "Or a dick Hon, in which case sooner." She didn't even look up.

They all looked at her in silence. Then Lohman asked Pigman if he wanted to talk. Pigman said, "No I just came here with another list of O'Brien contacts from the computer. This one is easier to follow. I gave it to Tete. I knew you'd want a paper copy."

Then Pigman left and Lohman told Sweeney to come into his office. Sweeney started to tell Lohman how he was progressing with getting a group of firm people to go to the DeLang concert the next night and Lohman told him about the conference with St. Charles and Cohenstein.

Sweeney said, "Sometimes I feel like The Saint. That family is a pain sometimes. Trisha asked me to talk to some of the kids the other day about a deal she was thinking of doing. I had to sit through two hours of complaining about other family members. And she had nothing but bad stuff to say about The Lion guy."

Sweeney continued. "Then, another time I am talking to some of them with Trisha. Jason was there and Ryan, the crapo big shot, and Jason's mother, Hu Yen Fong. I can never tell what is her first name and what is her last name. Henry was there too. Henry started complaining about O'Brien. He told everyone about how his dad was yelling at him about some web site help and passwords and how his dad didn't know anything about IT. Ryan called Henry an uptight control freak. Most of them have the brain of a turkey, but the mouth of a parrot. Henry's a little smarter, but personality he don't got, if you know what I mean. So Trisha says to Henry, 'A personality is a nice thing to have. I hope you get one someday'. And they all went on and on."

And Sweeney went on himself. "What a family! They're just like a lot of other big shot families. Or this place. Everyone is screwing everyone else's girlfriend or wife. Or boyfriend. Probably their dogs too."

"Oh crap!" said Lohman. "Who around here are you doing this time? Didn't I tell you to watch it? No. Don't tell me. Just watch it. You know what the Management Committee will do if they catch you."

"Not much," said Sweeney. "I know who is doing who."

"I wouldn't be surprised," said Lohman.

"Yeah Bumps!" said Sweeney. "For instance O'Brien was doing Nufdone's wife. Nuftdone was doing O'Brien's girlfriend. Yeah, Dude, when you come to a lawyer for counseling this is the kind of input you get. We put it in here and we put it in her and so forth. All's fair in love and law. Then O'Brien's chauffeur was doing the girlfriend whenever he drove her around. Moronika's her name. And he was a bona fide chauffeur too. If fide him I'd have a bona when I was driving her around too."

"How do you know all this?" asked Lohman.

"You just have to look for this type of stuff and encourage people to talk about it. Show business is loose and gossipy. I get a lot there. But this place is a gossip pit too. I found out about Nuftdone from Tete. You didn't?"

"No," said Lohman.

"Yeah," said Sweeney. "That figures. You have kind of a straight laced image around here. Except for Monica Platt. Everyone says you got something there. Or, I should say, you're getting some."

Lohman said, "That should caution you to take what you hear about these things with a grain of salt. Why do you wallow in all this gossip?"

"Business, man." said Sweeney. "Knowledge gets business, especially a certain kind of knowledge."

"So what are you here for?" asked Lohman.

"I want to ask you about a case I have. I'm not sure what to do," said Sweeney.

Lohman said, "Judging from what I know about your other matters, I wouldn't know what to do either. We inhabit different planets I think."

"Yeah Bumps," said Sweeney. "That's why I want to run it by you."

"So what is it?" asked Lohman. He wondered if he wanted to know. When he heard of problems around the firm he was responsible for fixing them.

"Well," said Sweeney, "I have this case involving a Chinese restaurant. It's an employment discrimination case. Now don't tell me we can't handle small businesses. It's owned by a producer whose business I'm working on. He's pretty big and I am getting about $50,000 a year out of him now. So we get over the money issue. They are being charged with discrimination because they hire only Asian waiters. Not waitresses either. But the case involves ethnic origin only. The plaintiff's a guy. He's Armenian and he applied for a job there and they wouldn't hire him, even though he's been a waiter for years and has great references."

Lohman asked, "Who is the client?"

"The Wongs," said Sweeney. "They own Wong's Chinese Grill. Ever heard of it?"

"Chinese Grill?" asked Lohman. "What kind of Chinese restaurant is that."

"Barbequed ribs and stuff and steaks," said Sweeney. "It's in the Near North area, about six blocks north of here on Dearborn. Nobody knows the difference between Chinese and soul food and a steak house anymore. Anyway they're Lee and Betty Wong. God! You should see their daughter! Hot ass babe! But she's married. She married a guy named Steve White. So, like, this is a case where two Wongs made a White."

Now that the location of the place had been pointed out, Lohman was familiar with it. He had walked past it many times on the way home. "So what do you want to know? It's a discrimination case. Try to get it settled. The sooner the better. Right – wrong – it doesn't matter. What counts is how much. Get rid of it as cheaply as possible."

Sweeney said, "I keep trying. Neither side will come anywhere near the other side's offer or demand. They certainly don't act like they want to settle. I'm just running up a huge bill and getting nowhere. Wong won't budge. He says it's a matter of principle."

"Well you know," said Lohman, "That's one of the red flags about a client. It's almost sure that type of client won't pay. What kind of retainer did you get?"

"Lots," said Sweeney, "and Wong just keeps paying."

"From that restaurant?" said Lohman. "Business must be good. I never see anyone in there though."

"From his shows," said Sweeney. "That's where his money comes from."

The Dead One Stinks

Lohman said, "So why does he bother with the restaurant?"

'I don't know Man," said Sweeney, "but he sure is getting his money's worth here. Have you read about it? Have you seen it on TV? Look at YouTube and Facebook. It's all over."

"What?" asked Lohman.

"The gist of it all is that a Chinese guy with a play like one he has going in New York and here at the same time is doing this sort of thing," said Sweeney.

"What kind of play?" asked Lohman.

Sweeney explained. "It's a musical about discrimination against Asians in Nazi Germany and how they escaped the gas chambers because Japan joined the war and the Axis. The theme is that Hitler was going to gas them all and he couldn't do that and get along with the Japanese at the same time. So he backed off, but then the Japanese heard about the scheme and they thought it just applied to the Chinese in Europe. But then Hitler said forget it. He said he couldn't get enough publicity unless he could gas all the Asians. So the Japanese who wanted to kill all the Chinese actually saved them. Great music Man! Heavy metal with twinky bop pop all the way through."

Lohman said, "Well, it sounds new and interesting. What do you want to know?"

"So what do you think Bumps? That's what I want to know. Something doesn't seem right," said Sweeney.

Lohman thought a minute and then said, "Well is this a real law suit? This Wong is getting free publicity. Nobody will settle. Maybe it's a set up for the publicity."

"Ya think?" asked Sweeney

"Could be," said Lohman. "It wouldn't be the first time a law suit is used for publicity. Check it out. And you should be looking to see that you don't get caught advancing any false claims to the court. Or where is it? Is it in court yet or is it just filed with the - where are they doing it now - The Illinois Human Rights Commission or the EEOC?"

"Illinois. They act for the EEOC. It's was just filed last month," said Sweeney.

"What's the defense?" asked Lohman.

Sweeney said, "Wong says the guy tried to pocket a fork on the way out of the interview and that is why he didn't hire him. The guy says he was just looking at it. It was plastic."

"Plastic!" remarked Lohman. "In a fancy restaurant?"

"Take out area," said Sweeney.

"So check it out," said Lohman, "and make sure you don't get caught doing anything wrong. So check it out and get out. I have to get to some other things here." Sweeney was one of the few people who could understand that Lohman was doing a little work joke. Very little.

Sweeney left and Lohman was going through a pile of papers involving negotiations on a deal when Tete stuck her head in the door. "What's up?" he asked.

"Problem, Hon," she said. "It's that snotty little Buffy Highborn. She's screaming about abuse. It's Nyman again."

"Who's she?" asked Lohman. Then he remembered. Buffy was the daughter of a big client of St. Charles'. She had just graduated from Yale Law School the previous spring and was part of the F, P & C group of first year associates. Her father had asked St. Charles to take her on and try to "humanize" her a little. Tete called her snotty. A lot of other people called her snobby. Even though her father had started out as an extra hand on the night shift in a machine shop, she was a very huffy little bitch of a princess. She insisted that he supply her with a limousine to get to work, for instance. She was paid $160,000 plus bonus like all the first year associates, but she spent about $500,000 a year. Daddy paid. St. Charles did not understand what her father had meant by "humanize". St. Charles thought she was one of the most humanized and acceptable of their associates.

Her haughty behavior, $5000 outfits and $75,000 worth of bejeweled ornaments had caught the notice of most people in the firm. Lohman had paid no attention. Remember that I told you he was a big nobody. For Christ's sake Bumper, pay attention! And look at those tits. Most of the rest of the people in the firm did.

"So what's the problem?" asked Lohman.

"She's here. She's right outside. She's got her up in an assroar and her nose is poking a hole in the ceiling. She's talking about suing us," said Tete.

Lohman raised his eyebrow. "She's outside? Oh crap! Send her in." He thought to himself that most associates would not dare to bite the hand that fed them. No other firm would hire them, at least not one of the top paying large firms, if it were known that they sued their former firm for a thing like job problems. Buffy, however, did not need a job.

Buffy came in a second later and Lohman could see that she was very upset. She was more huffy than buffy as the moment. He greeted her and tried to engage her in some small talk. She wouldn't respond. Finally she said, "Mr. Nyman has exceeded the bounds of humanity. I demand that his behavior be corrected!"

Nyman was Hyman Nyman. He was a fairly high up partner who did a lot of work for large conglomerates of consumer loan and currency exchange companies. He was Hell on wheels to work for. Lohman often assigned problem associates to him to tone them down. If they could work for Hyman, they could work for anyone. And there were a lot of difficult partners in the firm. Buffy's dad had been referred to Lohman by St. Charles and Lohman understood what he meant by his request to "humanize" Buffy so he had her assigned to Nyman.

Lohman said, "Now, I know he's a bit hard to work for at times. What happened?"

Buffy said, "He is abusing me and he does not know what he is doing. He did not even go to a respectable law school. I do not know why you associate with someone like that."

Lohman asked, "What exactly is the problem?" He did not add that when the Queen wants something corrected she has to tell the butler what it is.

She said, "He swears at me. He called me the most despicable of names."

Lohman wondered what was the most despicable. There were certainly a lot of names he could imagine for her. Which was the worst?

Buffy continued, "The 'C' word."

Lohman thought, "Cute? We have a sexual harassment complaint." He remembered several that Nyman had generated. Then he thought, "Would she be offended by 'cute'? Ah yes, I have it. Considering who Nyman is, it was 'Cunt'. But can I ask her if that is what the word was? I ain't gonna chance it."

"I see," said Lohman. "Is that it?"

"Hardly!" said Buffy. Then she started pouring it out. Nyman kept telling her to stop whatever she was working on to get something else done on an emergency basis. Then when she started on that he did the same thing again. And he didn't even say "Please". Then he was constantly setting deadlines for her without even considering or knowing or caring how much time would be required or even consulting her. And he did it with other lawyers and clients too. He always told them things would be done by a date that he drew out of the air. A date that was always sooner than was possible. When the things did not happen by that date he blamed her. He was always unilaterally setting dates for meetings with other people without consulting them and she had to resolve all the conflicts. Then once he had reviewed a document she had prepared. It was a new promissory note form for one of the loan companies. In editing it he took out the works that said "Debtor promises to pay…" When the client discovered this he blamed her. She protested and that's when he called her the "C" word.

Buffy continued. "He is like all the Cohenstein people. He is low, despicable and beneath contempt. I told him, 'You can't talk to me like that' and he said, 'I just did'. Of all the contemptuous outrage!"

Buffy paused. After a while she continued. "Then," she said, "he threatened to kill me."

"What!" exclaimed Lohman.

"He most certainly did. He said, 'If you don't shape up you'll get what O'Brien got'. Now that means to me that he is talking about my death. Unacceptable!" Buffy almost raised her voice.

Lohman wondered if Nyman knew something about how O'Brien died. "Did he know how The Lion died?"

"I wouldn't know," huffed Buffy.

Lohman considered the matter. He thought to himself, "Huff and puff my little Buff." Then a solution came to him and he said, "Well, I think he might just have been excited," said Lohman. "Now you know that someone has to work with him and we rotate his associates regularly. I tell you what, we'll just get you out of there now. How about Mr. St. Charles? Would you like to work for him? I think you would be compatible."

"Oh yes," gushed Buffy. "That's where I belong. On the Chairman's team!"

"Good," said Lohman. "I'm sure he will be most pleased to work with you. He will certainly be more appreciative of your outstanding qualities. In the future you have to understand how things are around here though. It is not all sweetness and light. Not all our partners are easy to get along with and not all are experts, if you know what I mean, in legal matters. Our people are often like politicians. Many people think politicians are incompetent until you realize that running the country is not their job. Their job is to get elected and reelected. At that they are competent. And what they have to do to be competent at that often precludes their being competent at anything else. Similarly, the job of a lot of our partners is to get and keep clients and bill them as much as possible – not to represent them well. That is up to you. That's why Hyman might tell a client that something will be ready tomorrow when it will take weeks to do. That's what the client wants to hear. Hyman may not realize that the thing cannot be accomplished in a day because he may be completely unaware of what needs doing. The type of client that uses that type of lawyer will not be bothered by the details of why the thing is not ready the next day. Hyman will come up with some explanation. For instance some third party did something which makes the thing incredibly more difficult – and expensive. However, Hyman can overcome all obstacles and he can overcome them by the next day. And so forth."

Buffy looked like someone was telling her that the tooth fairy had dirty underwear. Everyone in the firm realized what Lohman was telling her was true, but it was understood that they would not get explicit about it. If they did everyone would realize that they were all just in it for the money. Lohman was not one of the non-explicit types. He did not mind telling other people in the firm in a roundabout way that they were merely money grubbers.

Despite the revelation about the tooth fairy, Buffy was happy and looking forward to her new assignment. She thanked Lohman profusely and left. Lohman then went out to see Tete and told her what to do with Buffy.

"Perfect, Hon," she said. "She deserves it."

24 AMERICAN MICRO DEVICES

Lohman realized that he had a conference to attend later that afternoon. He asked Tete to get him a sandwich and went back in to his office to prepare for the conference. The meeting involved American Micro Devices. A client of F, P & C was interested in acquiring it. The client was Fingerberg Corporation. American Micro was a fairly large publicly held company. Fingerberg was a holding company, which is a company that owns other companies. Fingerberg was slightly larger than American Micro, but most of its subsidiary companies were smaller. Fingerberg was controlled by Carl Lay and Sheila Way. They were former O'Brien employees who had worked in the area of buying and selling businesses. Now they had their own companies and were engaged in buying more and getting bigger.

The purpose of the conference was to go over plans for the deal. You don't just go out and buy a large public company, especially if its management does not want to sell, which was the case here. Those present were going to go over the various possibilities. There was an additional purpose of the meeting and that was to discuss how to find out more about American Micro.

When the time came Lohman went up to St. Charles's office. St; Charles was the lead lawyer on the deal and the meeting was held in his conference room. St. Charles often wanted Lohman present on his matters because he thought Lohman was 'sound'. The truth is that Lohman made the deals happen. St. Charles thought he did and he found Lohman to be a convenient lackey. The King does not dress himself for the banquet.

Lay and Way were there as were several highly placed partners in the firm. There was John Feepot from the corporate department and Gooster Fileform who was the firm's top securities lawyer. Sean

Featherbottom was also there. Usually associates did not attend the planning conferences on this type of deal because the law was not the subject of discussion. Sean was there because he was a C.P.A. as well as a lawyer and those present were trying to find out something about American Micro's financial status. They thought Sean's expertise would help them evaluate certain information.

They also wanted to keep their interest in the company secret at this stage so the outside accountants and investment bankers were not going to be there. This was not a deal they had proposed and who would do the accounting and investment banking work on the deal had not been decided. Once again, the fewer people involved at this stage, the better. Confidentiality was the word.

Lohman greeted St. Charles' secretary and she waived him on in to the conference room. Then, as Lohman was going in, she rang St. Charles to tell him Lohman had arrived. Everyone else was there already, apparently waiting for Lohman and St. Charles to arrive before beginning. As he entered a man he did not know came up to him with an extended hand. The man said "Bogus sir. I'm Bogus."

"What?" asked Lohman.

"Bogus sir. Tom Bogus. Bogus Corporation. That's me," he said. "Financial enhancement. Balance sheet improvement. Revenue enhancement. We show your true financial condition. All companies. All accounting systems. You are Bumper, eh?"

"That's me," said Lohman. "Pleased to meet you." He wasn't. More problems. The fox got into the henhouse.

Just after this St. Charles came in.

Feepot spoke to those present. "Well, let's get started. We noticed something in American Micro's financial statements that seems interesting. At this stage we don't want to go to an outside accounting firm or Fingerberg's in house accountants because it could be very significant and we don't want anyone to know we are even considering the deal. So I had Sean look at the financial information. What we find is that it looks like these guys have been hiding massive losses. Sean, show us."

At this point Sean got up and turned on the overhead slide projector for a PowerPoint presentation. St. Charles was standing up behind him and Lay and Gooster were standing opposite on the other side of the screen. The others were seated. Sean showed slides of the financial statements and some news articles and explained how American could be hiding huge losses.

Sean was what Sweeney called "swishy". Lohman recalled one incident when he heard the two talking at a table in one of the lunchrooms while they were having coffee. As he became aware of their conversation he heard Sweeney saying, "Face it, you're swishy Dude."

Sean said, "You think so? I'm not all that swishy am I?"

"Yeah, Dude," said Sweeney. "My uncle was like that. I remember way back when I was a kid they called him Nelly. I couldn't understand why he would have a girl's name."

"Well, maybe a little," admitted Sean.

"Yeah Dude," said Sweeney. "And you can't hide it. That's you. So use it Man. Go with it! Be yourself. Let it all out."

Lohman remembered this. And he now noted how much more of "himself" that Sean had been lately. It also occurred to him that an Asian might call Sean "wishy".

As Sean went through the presentation he was near the screen pointing out things with a physical pointer. This was not the fashionable way of doing it, but he found it easier to deal with the pointer than to use the software for showing things. As Sean was guiding everyone through the items he was discussing he had his weight on his left leg with his left hip out to the side. His left hand was on his hip.

St. Charles was following the presentation intently. Soon he put his left hip out to the side and put his left hand on it. He put his right hand up to his chin and started tapping his lower lip with one of his fingers. Then Gooster did the same. Then Lay. Then Sean finished and everyone looked at each other. St. Charles all of a sudden shot his eyes left and right without moving his head and dropped his hand form his hip and straightened up. So did Gooster and Lay. Sean straightened up too, but he put his pointer down and put both hands on his hips.

Bogus was there because of his expertise in financial enhancement. He explained some more things he had noticed to those present and they were not flattering to the financial condition of American either.

Needless to say, if American Micro was a dog then buying it was not a good idea. Unless you could buy it and unload it before anyone else got wind of the losses. Or you could short the stock before the news got out. Shorting a stock involved selling it when you don't own it. The terms of the deal are that delivery will be made later. Then if the price goes down, you can buy the stock at the lower price and deliver it to the buyer you sold it to at the higher price. If the price goes up, you lose money.

Lay and Way then started talking about what to do. They took up the idea of shorting the stock. Bogus reminded them that what he and Sean were talking about was still speculation. They couldn't be sure of it yet. He indicated they would have to get some information from the company to confirm it. At this point Lay explained that he already had wheedled something out of American's chief financial officer that would confirm what Sean had described. They knew each other and saw each other often and served together on the board of a charity.

Gooster looked at Lohman. They both knew they had to tell Lay and Way something. They both knew Gooster didn't want to do it. Don't tell your clients bad news. They will go get another lawyer who gives them good news.

Lohman said, "That would constitute insider trading. What we can see from the financial statements and the news reports is public information. However, what confirms our suspicions is something known only to a company insider. To trade on that information would violate the Act."

"We aren't insiders," said Lay. "And we'll set up some other companies with hidden ownership to do it."

"But you got the key information from an insider," said Lohman.

When a client is told by a lawyer that something the client wants to do violates the law the client often cites higher authority. Lay said, "Hell, we did it all the time for The Lion. Just before we left we did it to Hyman Oyveyer's company. We looked at the financials, saw something, and told The Lion. He knew Oyveyer and he contacted him and got the information we needed and then we shorted the company before the news came out and the stock crashed. Oyveyer was pissed. He thought we leaked the info. So maybe we did. But who cares. We made big bucks. How can it be illegal?"

"You didn't get caught, that's all," said Lohman.

"That's what confidentiality is for," said Lay.

Feepot spoke up. "Maybe we could do a deal for one of their divisions cheap since they are going down the tubes anyway. We let them know we know what they are hiding and they may change their tune and deal with us. We give them all big jobs with the new company. I think maybe we could do a reverse rectangular spin off to a Cayman Island controlled trust with Mongolian protectors."

When in doubt complicate. When things are perfectly clear, complicate them. When things are already complicated, complicate them further. Feepot deserved the Complicator of the Year Award. Nobody understood what he was talking about and after a while the meeting broke up.

25 MORE OF THE FAMILY

Friday morning Lohman had called some of the family members together to discuss matters pertaining to the estate and the probate proceedings. Those family members scheduled to be present were the heirs, the ones who would inherit, namely The Lion's children. Lohman had set up the meeting in his conference room for 9:30 in the morning. The purpose of the meeting was to fill everyone in on the status of what was going on. By 9:30 all the O'Brien children were there, except Henry. Wandrasha had brought Trisha with her too. Ordinarily Nuftdone and a lot of other lawyers tagging along with him would be there, but he was tied up with an important client in Alaska so Lohman was going to handle the conference. Lohman didn't need a legion of worshipful attendants so no other people from the firm were there.

They were all getting comfortable in the conference room when Henry arrived. He was announced by Tete and walked in on her heels. There were the usual greetings and he sat down with the rest. Then Wandrasha asked, "Where did you get dad's scarf?" Henry was wearing a scarf just like the one The Lion had on when found the in the men's' room. At this point it dawned on everyone that it looked like the same scarf. Some were wondering if the funeral home had taken it and given it to Henry.

Henry said, "Looks like his doesn't it. He gave it to me. You know we were about the same size and he was always giving me things like he had. I gave him things too. He gave me this scarf. Actually it's different than his. It's a common Scotch tartan – you know one of their plaid patterns. They stand for families or clans. This tartan is much lighter and brighter than this, but one of the French high fashion houses took it and darkened it and put it out for hundreds of dollars. He got his there. This one is a Sears knock off. See." He showed them the label. "You know how cheap he was. For him high fashion. For me - Sears. He got it at an end of season sale. Otherwise he wouldn't have bought it."

Lohman proceeded to review what was going on and told them the date on which they expected The Bank to be appointed as administrator. He asked them if they knew of any problems that they thought he should know of. They didn't. He chatted with them to be sociable and find out what they were thinking. For once they weren't at each other's throats and all went well.

The discussion shifted to what had happened. Lohman told them there may be a question about when The Lion died. He told them about his conversation with the police and what they told him about the Medical Examiner's report saying The Lion died no later than the Thursday before Lohman found him.

Wandrasha said, "That's impossible. I was at his place Friday morning and spoke to him. I had to deliver some papers to him. He told me earlier that week he wanted to see one of Trisha's contracts and he wanted me to get it to him. I'm her guardian you know. I sign all her contracts. So I told him I would get it to him Friday morning. I did. I brought it over and gave it to him."

"So he was alive on Friday," said Dwante. "The Medical examiner must be wrong."

"Yeah, the Medical Examiner is corked," added Trisha.

"What were you two talking about?" asked Watta. "What did he want the contract for?"

"He didn't say," said Wandrasha. "It wasn't the first time. He would get one of the contracts from me and then he would come up with some idea to get it revised. He got a lot of extra money for Trisha that way. You know he was always thinking about ways to maximize returns."

"Screw someone," corrected Trisha.

"So what did he say?" asked Watta.

"Not much," said Wandrasha. "I was in a hurry. I had to get to my psychiatrist so I just dropped in and said 'Hi' and dropped off the papers and left. He was sitting there writing something with that fancy pen of his. He just said 'Hi' too and I left."

"So you just dropped off the papers and left," said Dwante. "But, he was alive – right?"

"Yes," said Wandrasha. "I dropped it off and left. It must have been his paper day because when I was leaving someone from this firm came in with papers for him too."

"Who was that?" asked Lohman.

"Some kid," said Wandrasha. "He was a blonde guy. Real young. Maybe one of the clerks, although he had a suit and tie on."

Jason spoke up. "That Thursday I know he was alive. We were all here in a conference room downstairs and after the conference I took him down the hall to the men's room. I took him in and took him to the disabled stall. He told me he didn't need any help so I left him there. As I was coming out some old guy came it. Real bald guy. No hair at all."

Glover said, "And then I saw him later at home. I dropped in that afternoon to see if he wanted anything more on a company he was thinking of buying. He said he didn't and I left."

Lohman added, "And the police say his chauffeur said he drove The Lion home that day."

"Yes, I know," said Henry. "I told Cooper, that's dad's chauffeur, I needed a ride to the airport after the conference because I had to get to

Omaha, but he told me he couldn't do it because he had to drive dad home."

All the others started looking at each other.

"So how could he have been killed on Thursday?" asked Wandrasha. "If he was it had to be later in the day and someone had to get him back here to be found in the stall."

"We know he was back here," said Henry. "He was here Friday and he was alive then. We were in a conference together. Wandrasha saw him at home."

Lohman added, "The police say the chauffeur says he drove The Lion back here on Friday morning for the conference. He was alive then."

Jason asked Henry, "Did you make it? They don't have much of a schedule to Omaha do they?"

"I made it," said Henry. "I got a limo service out to Midway and just barely got a flight out there. I got my business done, but there were no more flights back, so I stayed at the Ramada and got the earliest flight back here on Friday so I could get to the conference."

"What were you doing in Omaha?" asked Glover.

"Oh, just some IT problem at the old stock yards bank out there," said Henry. "Somehow we still own it."

Lohman said, "So you people saw him alive on Thursday afternoon and Friday morning. Do any of you know about Saturday? Did any of you see him then?"

Henry said, "I didn't. Right after the conference on Friday I had to get to the west coast for a conference out there."

"Anybody else see him on Friday or Saturday?" asked Lohman. No one responded.

Watta asked, "What about this Plutonian Principality? Is that going to work? We have a big hit coming on the estate tax."

"I don't know that status of that," said Lohman. "Our experts are still working on that. And other tax saving plans too. We'll be meeting with you all soon to go over that."

"At least we're getting a lot of money out of the Plutonian place," said Dwante. "Maybe it can supply a lot of the cash for the tax."

"The Bank and our tax department are already working on that," said Lohman. "Tell me, where did he come up with the name? Was he the one who named it?"

"Yes," said Henry. "None of us could understand his names. They all sounded screwy. But remember he came up with Winklebeany Cereal and that sold like hot cakes. Still does."

Trisha then started recalling some of O'Brien's nick names for those present and they all descended into their usual bickering. "Crap!" Lohman thought. "Wouldn't it be nice if we could have retroactive abortions." Finally he managed to get the conference ended and to get everyone to leave.

26 THE PEN

Lohman headed back into his office through the reception area. As he was passing Tete's desk he noticed a diamond headed pen sitting on it. "Where did you get that?" he asked.

Tete looked up at Lohman and then at the pen. "That? Allen left it here. He came in to sign that form you want everyone to sign." Allen was Alan Allen. He was an equity partner who worked mainly in the area of municipal securities which is a fancy name for state and local government debt. He was completely bald. Not even fuzz. The only one in the firm. Just like the person Jason said he saw coming into the men's room.

Tete went on, "Forms, forms, forms. Sign this, sign that. Do we run a law firm or a paper company? So he left it here. He always leaves pens everywhere. I wonder where he gets them?" Then she looked at her pen holder.

"When did he come in?" asked Lohman.

"Just now when you were in the conference room, Hon," said Tete. "But he's been up to his usual stuff all week. Do you know how many complaints I get from him each week? Three or four. He writes me little notes. I ignore them. When he ever asks about them I make up something about what you supposedly told me about them. I think he usually forgets the complaints as soon as he writes them. Maybe writing them is what counts. Maybe the little notes are his way of dealing with stress."

Lohman said, "This looks like the kind of pen The Lion had." He reached for the pen and took a Post-it pad from Tete's desk. He wrote on the pad with the pen. The ink was a very vivid dark color, almost blue black, but it didn't look quite like that to Lohman. "What color is this?" he asked Tete.

She looked at the pad. Then she got the form Allen had signed and looked at that. It was on white paper. "Purple," said. "Deep Purple. Almost black, but it's purple."

"Where would he get this? Are there a lot of pens like this?" asked Lohman.

Tete answered, "I've never seen any. If that's a real diamond who could afford it?"

"O'Brien," said Lohman. "How could this be?" he wondered aloud.

Tete said, "Maybe he lifted it from O'Brien, who knows. You may not know it, but one of Allen's names around here is 'The Pen Stealer'."

"You know," said Lohman, "I just heard in that conference that when Jason took The Lion into the men's room on Thursday a man who was completely bald like Allen came in as Jason was leaving after having left his father there. Maybe Allen knows something about this."

"Well," said Tete, "he's had the pen for a while. I noticed his little notes to me changed color a while ago." Then she reached under her desk to the waste basket. "Here's one I got yesterday. I kept it till today until I thought up a response. See. Same color."

"How long has this been going on?" asked Lohman.

"Don't know, Hon," she said. "I know it was this color last week. I remember one of the notes. I can't remember before that though." Then she said, "Wait." She got up and went to a shelf and picked up a file. "Here," she said. "One of his complaints involved the temperature in his office. This was before that Saturday you found O'Brien. I remember because on Monday I had planned to get to it, but I couldn't because I was so busy with all the confusion around here." She opened the file and looked at the papers. "Look here." She held two pieces of paper out to

Lohman. "The first one is in a different color. The next one is in a deep purple color. The first one is a complaint. After that I called the building office to get it fixed. The purple is on another complaint saying the building office didn't fix it. Both of these came in before that Saturday.

"On what days?" asked Lohman.

"I don't know Hon," she said. "I don't know about the first one. But I was going to do something about the second one on Monday so it couldn't have come in too much earlier. I'll see if the building office has a work ticket on the first one."

"Let me know if you find out," said Lohman.

Lohman went into his office and looked up various matters about Allen on his computer. Nothing much he didn't know was revealed. Then he rang up Allen to see if he was free. He was so Lohman went to Allen's office. They exchanged pleasantries and chatted about the matters they were working on and went over some firm gossip.

One of the items of firm gossip was of course the unfortunate demise of The Lion. In the course of this Lohman asked, "Were you doing anything for O'Brien? In putting together our information to develop a strategy for keeping the business I didn't run across anything you were billing on."

"No, I wasn't," said Allen. "But just recently Sprack asked me in to a conference with Henry O'Brien." Sprack was one of the firm's patent, trademark and copyright lawyers. This stuff is now referred to as IP. Intellectual property, as if it had brains. Allen continued. "They wanted to know about the possibilities for municipal financing in some way for some sort of remote control device. Having some municipality pay for a plant or something. It presents some interesting possibilities in the current environment. All the states and cities are broke, but we have discovered some interesting possibilities in Columbia. And of course we can still raise funds through states and cities. Actually private investors come up with the money and the government entities guaranty the loans. Also, we can arrange it so the interest qualifies as tax free municipal bond interest. Between the two we can sell the debt with a lower interest rate. The governments aren't borrowing the money and they aren't the issuers of the debt so it doesn't go on their books as debt. They even get fees for the guarantees."

Lohman asked, "When was this?"

Allen said, "Several weeks ago. I remember. It was earlier in that week when O'Brien was found. Monday or Tuesday, I think. It was Monday. I remember now. I still used September on the bill and I had to correct it."

Lohman pulled out the pen and asked, "Where did you get this?"

Allen said, "I didn't. You got it."

"Yes," said Lohman. "I got it off Tete's desk. She says you were in to sign something today and you signed it with this pen and left it there."

"I did?" asked Allen. "I already have a pen." He pulled one out of his shirt pocket.

Lohman looked at it. It was one of those promotional pens sent out by pen manufacturers with the name and address of the recipient on it. It said "Zenon Cohenstein" and had the firm's address. "Where did you get this?" he asked. He held it out to Allen and pointed to Cohenstein's name.

Allen looked at it. He said, "He must have left it here. I don't know." Then he took one of the papers on his desk and folded down one of the corners.

"Well, you have to know where you got a diamond studded pen," said Lohman. "Do you know this looks like The Lion's pen?"

Allen licked his lips and folded over the corner of another piece of paper. "How should I know? It looks like plastic."

Lohman said, "The Thursday before I found O'Brien in the men's room one of his sons, Jason was the one, he says he wheeled his father into the men's room on 43 and left him there. Jason says that when he came out someone who looks like you was going in. Do you remember that?'

"I go to the men's room all the time," said Allen.

"Do you remember that day?" asked Lohman. "It was the Thursday before the Saturday when I found him and the news came out. Does that jog your memory? His wheel chair was in the john, outside the stall according to Jason."

Allen said, "Oh yes, I think so. I had spilled some coffee in a conference I was in and I went out to get a towel and wash my hands. I had to blow my nose. Allergies, you know. I remember there was a wheel chair there. I didn't see him though. I washed up and left. When I was leaving that little blonde kid from corporate was coming in. He's pretty new here, but I've seen him in corporate. And I've seen him with that Sweeney kid. We never used to have people like that around here."

"You mean Sean Featherbottom?" asked Lohman.

"Is that his name?" asked Allen. "What does he do here?"

"He is in corporate a lot, as you said," said Lohman. "He's real good. He does a lot of work with Sweeney too."

"I've heard about that Sweeney kid," said Allen. "He's bringing in a lot of business. Soon he'll be a partner and then what? What kind of craziness will we have to put up with then?"

"Who knows," said Lohman. "He doesn't make any problems now, except to some of our sensibilities." Lohman paused and then continued. "Do you remember having a problem with the temperature in your office just before that Saturday I found The Lion?"

Allen said, "No. I don't remember any problem. Anyway, it's fine now."

They continued to chat some more and finally Lohman left and got back to his office where he could prepare for his next meeting.

27 MORE TALK ABOUT KEEPING THE BUSINESS

Next on Lohman's schedule was another firm meeting on the subject of keeping the O'Brien business. The meeting was up in St. Charles' conference room. St. Charles, Cohenstein, Nuftdone and LaRue were going to be there along with the firm's business manager, Geeley McDade, and probably some other lawyers that St. Charles and Cohenstein wanted to hear from. A new twist had been discovered. Sweeney had revealed to Cohenstein that Eben Gohr, Trisha DeLang's agent and business manager, was very popular in the family. He had also told Lohman that the guy was gay as a goose and had a thing for Sean Featherbottom who Sweeney had been bringing along with him to conferences about Trisha's business. Naturally Sweeney had a lot of influence with the guy too. Cohenstein had also learned from the grapevine that O'Brien's girlfriend, Moronika, had a thing for Sweeney.

Lohman had been told to bring the two to the conference. Lohman had warned them in advance that they had to go the conference, but Lohman did not know what Cohenstein had dug up. He only knew it was another "keep the business" meeting. He went to Sweeney's office. Both of them were waiting for Lohman there.

The door was open when Lohman got there. He knocked on it anyway and stuck his head in. "Hey Bumpy!" said Sweeney. Sean didn't say anything.

Lohman responded, "Hey." By now he was used to this and did not feel like the complete fool he used to when he first started trying to talk to Sweeney in his own language. "Are you two ready?"

"Yeah Dude," said Sweeney. "We're off to see the Wizard."

"Oh Christ!" said Lohman. "Watch your language!"

"Why?" asked Sweeney.

"Because," said Lohman, "if he gets wind of it you're done for."

"But he knows I call him the Wizard, Dude," said Sweeney. "Once he called me into his office and said he had heard I was calling him the Wizard. You know what he said?"

"He did? He knows about it?" Lohman was incredulous.

Sean's eye widened.

"Yeah Man," said Sweeney. "He told me he heard I was calling him the Wizard and he told me not to spread it around. He said he didn't want to become a cult figure like a Saint or something. I had trouble keeping a straight face. I told him that people were already calling him the Saint. He said that has to stop because he doesn't want any hero worship. He told me that modesty is one of his – he said 'foremost'- virtues. He was really flattered that I called him the Wizard."

Lohman said, "You know, sometimes I think you're a wizard. How you get around what comes out of your mouth I don't know." Actually Lohman did know. Sweeney had large and growing billings. That's how. But Lohman didn't want to encourage him. "Let's go."

When they got up to St. Charles's conference room the others were already there. In addition to St. Charles, Cohenstein, LaRue, Nuftdone and McDade, several other firm lawyers were there. Swifty was also there. They arrived, greeted everyone and sat down. Then Cohenstein got to the point. "What's going on with you and Moronika?" he asked Sweeney.

Sweeney had not been warned about this in advance, but no matter. It was not an unusual subject for him. "Not much," he said.

"Exactly how much?" asked Cohenstein.

"Nothing right now," said Sweeney. "I know her socially."

"And in the Biblical sense?" asked Swifty. Reference to the Bible makes anything fit for discussion.

"Not too much lately," said Sweeney matter of factly. "We're just friends."

"How much influence do you have over her?" asked Swifty.

"Well, that depends on how I want to influence her," said Sweeney. "Anyway, I know where you're coming from. She'll probably listen to me about voting her stock. I don't think she has her own lawyer or anything. She always asks me about legal matters. I even bill her sometimes. And she isn't greedy. She's kind of a sex pig though. Let me know what you want her to do and I'll see what I can do. Whatever it is, I think one good thing so far as she's concerned is that she doesn't have any fight with the family. They get along pretty well in their bickering way."

Cohenstein said, "We'll let you know what we come up with for her." Then he looked over at Sean. "And you Fluffbottom. I hear you know that manager of Trisha DeLang's. Eben Gohr. Do you know him?"

Sean said, "Featherbottom sir. That's my name. I know him. John has me work on Trisha's things so I have met him that way. And socially I see him at parties."

St. Charles chimed in. "Socially? How? Are you close to him?"

Sean said, "I guess so, but not close enough to get a disease or anything."

Sweeney was sitting next to Sean and he drew his hand up with the palm out towards Sean and moved it towards the palm of Sean's hand that had come up. The two palms came in sliding contact. Sweeney said, "Hey Dude! You blew a funny!"

Sean had not done anything of the kind so far as he was concerned. He had just answered the question. As for the hands, he was used to Sweeney's ways and he often had to swipe palms with Sweeney so he was prepared to do so at any time.

St. Charles said, "Don't get smart with me young man."

Cohenstein, who was looking out the window, said matter of factly, "You'd be out of your league." Half of those there took this to mean that St.Charles would be out of his league.

St. Charles took it to mean that Sean would be out of his league. "Exactly!" he said.

Sweeney piped up again. "If you're trying to get at how Sean can use the sex angle with Gohr, forget it. Gohr's into him all right, but Sean doesn't go for that stuff. Do you Sean?"

"What stuff?" asked Sean.

"Screwing around," said Sweeney.

Sean just looked blankly at him. So did St. Charles who was thinking, "They better not be discussing what I think they are discussing. Here at Fenton, Pettigrew! And in my presence!" St. Charles concluded that they were discussing something else and he had misunderstood what they had said.

Swifty then spoke up. "In any event, we need all the support from the family and allied persons we can get. Be especially nice to Mr. Gohr in the future will you."

Sean said, "Of course." Then he exclaimed, "Oh, look at that! That's gorgeous. Where did you get that?" Sean was referring to a bejeweled lapel pin that Swifton was rubbing.

"Do you like it?" asked Swifty. "I got it at Garglepussy Vega."

Swifton should not have got into this with Sean. Sean knew fashion. Sean knew style. Sean knew he was referring to the iconic Spanish jewelry firm of French descent, Garglepuss y Vega. Sean said, "Oh, it's heavenly! But it's Garglepuss as the first name. Then there is a 'y'. That's pronounced like an 'e' in Spanish. It means 'and'. So in English we would say the firm name is Garglepuss and Vega." They really shouldn't have let Sean get into this. He continued. "Garglepuss was of French ancestry and he was the designer. Vega was the Spaniard and he was the business person. Actually, before they got together, the French name was Garglepussy, which is spelled just as you pronounced it. However, the French pronounce that Poosay. But they changed it because Garglepussy y Vega sounded too complicated for them. Poosay or pussy. Not much difference. Not a very high sounding name. The history of fashion and design firms is one of my favorite topics."

Cohenstein, who was still looking out the window, said, "You say poosay, I say pussy, they say puss." He seemed to be talking to himself.

At this St. Charles reached for his cat and took her into his lap. "You're my little Pussy," he cooed to her as he rubbed her head and back.

The conference did not elevate its tone much from there and soon everyone except St. Charles, Cohenstein and Swifty were dismissed. Those three probably talked about football or something for the rest of the day.

28 WHO WAS WHERE

Lohman went back to his office. He was rather hungry, having skipped lunch, so he asked Tete to get him something from the firm cafeteria. He had asked Wiggy Rodriguez, the firm investigator to drop by. Rodriguez showed up and they greeted each other. Lohman said, "I've got some new information for you."

"What is it?" asked Wiggy.

"First, we don't know if O'Brien died on Thursday or Friday. It don't see how he could have died on Thursday since a lot of people saw him Friday, but the police say the Medical Examiner says he died Thursday. Maybe the people who say they saw him Friday are mistaken. But I don't know how. There were all those people in the conference with him here on Friday. Friday morning. The chauffeur says he drove The Lion home from here on Thursday afternoon and back in here Friday morning. His son Glover said he saw The Lion at home on Thursday afternoon. Now, his daughter, Wandrasha, says she saw The Lion at home on Friday morning. She had to deliver a contact to him. She said someone from the firm was there. Sounds like Sean Featherbottom."

Lohman continued, "Then on Thursday there are some interesting things too. Jason took him down the hall to the men's room and when he was coming out he say Alan Allen going in. Alan confirms this. Then when he was going out he saw Sean coming in. To top this off, Alan somehow wound up with The Lion's pen, or at least one very like it. Did you ever see The Lion's pen?"

Rodriguez said, "I'm not sure I ever saw the guy. I'm not at that level."

Lohman said, "He had a fancy pen with a diamond on its head. It was usually sticking out of his coat's breast pocket. It was hard to miss. So

Alan left a pen just like this on Tete's desk a little while ago. He can't say where he got it. Now did he get it off The Lion? Is it The Lion's pen? It's hard to think there is more than one pen like that. Apparently he was using it for a while. At least a week. He is always writing Tete notes with one complaint after another. She says the pen color changed to this pen's color sometime last week at least. But also think of this, now that I remember it. There were two pens. One owned by The Lion and one owned by Henry, his son."

"I'll check it out," said Rodriguez. "Do you know anything else about who was where?"

"No," said Lohman. "Oh, yes. Henry. Henry O'Brien. He says he went to Omaha on Thursday afternoon after the conference here and flew back in early Friday for the next conference. He says he went from here on Thursday to Midway to get a flight and then stayed at the Ramada in Omaha. He says he went there to deal with an IT problem at the bank that used to be in the stockyards. Then he says that after the meeting here on Friday he went to Los Angeles for a meeting with people from Laos at their US office. He said it was Hen Fen Devices. He said they talked about Hen Fen manufacturing something for Champion."

"I can check that out too," said Wiggy.

"Anything yet on our people?" asked Lohman. "The last thing I want to hear is that someone here is involved in this. Besides Allen, I mean. Crap! Check him out, will you."

"Right," said Wiggy. "You know what he's called don't you?"

"What?" asked Lohman.

"The Pen Stealer," said Wiggy.

"So what," said Lohman. "What I don't want to hear is that he took The Lion's pen after he murdered him. Maybe you can find out he was somewhere else at the time."

"You mean on Thursday in the can when he was there and maybe killed the guy?" asked Wiggy.

"I hope not," said Lohman.

As Rodriguez was getting up to go he said, "We'll see."

Lohman added one more thing. "Wiggy wait. See if you can find anyone who spoke to The Lion or saw him after he left here on Friday. So far as I know Nuftdone saw him going out on 40 and that is the last anyone saw of him."

"Right," said Wiggy. He headed for the door.

Lohman added, "Wait. Check with the building office and see if they have any record of doing work in Allen's office before I found The Lion on Saturday. He made a complaint about the temperature to Tete and she called the office."

Rodriguez wrote something in his notebook and then left.

29 CONTINUING EDUCATION

Early Saturday Lohman went to the airport for a flight to the Bahamas. He was going down there for something called continuing legal education. All lawyers had to take courses to keep their licenses in force and the big firm lawyers often signed up for courses given in faraway locations that also qualified as vacation spots. That way they could deduct the cost of their vacation. The fact that the courses were held in foreign locales and the fact that they cost a fortune meant that only lawyers from the larger wealthier firms attended. This added another element to the courses which was lawyers schmoozing each other for business. A very large part of a large firm's business came from referrals from other lawyers whose clients had a matter in a location the other lawyers did not serve or whose clients needed special expertise which the lawyers referred to supposedly had. These courses were also attended by in house counsel, lawyers who headed the legal departments of client companies. They were a constant source of business for outside lawyers.

Cohenstein was going to the conference too and he liked to travel first class. He liked to go by private jet, at least if he could get someone else to pay for it. In this case he had persuaded Swifty to let him have the use of one of the Swifton jets. Lohman ordinarily did not travel this way, but he went with Cohenstein.

The conference was sponsored by the International Practice Administration Association which purported to be advancing the knowledge and practice of management of large firms in all the professions. This particular conference was for law firms and was entitled, "Current Trends in Practice Management".

Cohenstein and Lohman arrived on Saturday afternoon. They went to the hotel and checked in. Cohenstein then went out to schmooze and Lohman went to a course on current trends. The course dealt with how firms were responding to the decline in business that had accompanied the recession. Lohman compared that to what was happening at F, P & C. The Cohenstein faction was bringing in business left and right and The Swifton Bank was generating scads of it too. The Bank was one of the world's largest and had played a major part in causing the recession along with the other big financial players. The Bank was generating a lot of lawsuits which had to be defended and a lot of regulatory problems. It was also generating a lot of lobbying – governmental affairs – work to try to stave off even more regulation. Lohman knew that what goes up, comes down, so he paid close attention to pick up tips for what to do when the business of F, P & C might turn down.

Later, Lohman and Cohenstein ate at an introductory banquet sponsored by the investment bank Goldboi and Baggs. They got lucky and had the in house general counsels of two large companies at their table along with people who sold various products to law firms. No other lawyers. No competition. Cohenstein mesmerized the in house guys.

Sunday everyone relaxed. Golf, tennis, swimming, shopping, lolling around in the sun. Whoring for some. Monday Lohman went back to school. This time he attended a workshop on current problems with law practice. The general gist of the presentation was that the legal profession was attracting bad publicity for some things and this publicity could not be countered until lawyers were aware of what was generating the bad publicity. In other words, to fix something, you first have to know what needs fixing. Naturally, this was not one of the most popular presentations at the conference. But it attracted about 50 attendees and Lohman was one. He was there to learn something, but a lot of the others weren't. They were there just to get the credit for their attendance or because their secretaries had chosen the course for them or because they wanted to snooze off the Sunday evening booze and dope.

The Dead One Stinks

The speaker was not a lawyer. He billed himself as a management consultant for law firms. There were printed materials, but they were just copies of the slides the speaker was going through. Lohman sat through the introductory comments which were not very interesting, but soon the speaker got to the heart of the talk. He went into a list of things that were said to be problems with the legal profession. He made it clear that the list was merely things that were being said about lawyers and the profession and the things being said were not necessarily true.

Lohman went through the list along with the speaker:

- Lawyers lie
- Lawyers cheat
- Lawyers steal
- Lawyers argue about everything, even the time of day
- Lawyers omit relevant facts
- Law may be the learned profession, but today's lawyers are unable to read, write or do arithmetic
- Lawyers are terrible at finding and applying the law since they are low skilled people
- Lawyers think only of how much they can get out of a client, rather than how to help the client
- Lawyers do anything to increase the bill whether it is good for the client or not
- Lawyers stir up litigation rather than avoid it
- Lawyers tell their clients whatever the clients want to hear
- Lawyers tell their clients they have a great case when that is not so and later, after they have collected huge fees and the case is about to go to trial, suggest settlement because of things they claim the client did not tell them

- Lawyers actually believe in their client's cause so long as they are paid
- Lawyers automatically oppose anything and fight it rather than seek to facilitate things or work out conflicting interests or find out if they really are conflicting
- Lawyers cease this behavior the minute the client runs out of money
- Lawyers represent only one side in their practice. For instance lawyers who represent banks rarely represent bank borrowers
- Lawyers do whatever their clients want, including breaking the rules, and do not stand up to their clients or insist that the rules be followed
- Lawyers promise things to people only to commit them so the lawyers can then sell them out to other people
- Lawyers fail to see the other side of the coin (although they can damn well see the coin)
- Lawyers add things to agreements that have not been agreed to and change what has been agreed to when they are writing up the agreements
- Lawyers are people attracted to an environment where you can fight with people all day long and get paid for it
- Lawyers complicate things
- Lawyers provide for all sorts of eventualities that probably won't happen and ignore those that will
- Lawyers prepare disclosures that cannot be understood
- Lawyers interpret the law and facts in an extreme and often ridiculous manner or in a way that is contrary

to the plain meaning of the words used in the law or the words used to describe the facts
- Transactional lawyers who are presumably advising people about the law and compliance with it do not know what happens in a courtroom or how judges and juries act
- Lawyers have their egos wrapped up in whether they win or lose and how much they make and they lie about both
- Lawyers all pretend to be the "Great Lawyer" at the forefront of the profession, using the most sophisticated techniques and able to achieve whatever results a client wants and the less capable they are the more they believe this of themselves
- Lawyers charge too much, billing $300 per hour or more for someone just out of law school and up to $1500 or more per hour for certain senior lawyers

Lohman was aware of movement in the room as the speaker was going through this indictment. As the speaker was getting to the end of his presentation Lohman looked around and noticed that about half the audience had left. As the speaker got through the last item on the list, one of the audience members spoke up and asked the speaker how he got booked and told him he didn't belong there. The speaker explained again that he was not saying these things were true, merely that these things were being said about lawyers and they are bad publicity for the profession. He then said that some of the things might actually be true. Either way the profession should do something to correct the situation or to explain how the criticisms were not true. He reminded those there that in the rest of his talk he was going to suggest some ways for firms to deal with these criticisms and that every firm should have a story ready to tell all concerned how that particular firm was dealing with these problems.

Then the speaker said, "Listen to this. It may not be pleasant that these ideas are floating about, but they are. Denigratory comments…"

Here a younger lawyer stood up and practically shouted, "Watch your language!"

The speaker looked at him with a bewildered look. Then he looked as if he realized that this was an example of one of the criticisms he had mentioned and that he should not "go there". The speaker continued, "These comments are being made daily and jokes too. The lawyer joke is a standard feature of modern life. For instance there is the old joke about a man walking down the street who sees a sign in a store window saying 'Lawyers are assholes'. The man goes into the store and confronts the proprietor. The man says, 'Sir, that sign in your window is slanderous. Take it down this instant or I shall have the law on you!' The proprietor says, 'Don't tell me. You're one of those lawyers aren't you?' The man says, 'How dare you Sir! I am an asshole!'"

Only a few of the audience members laughed. One arose and attacked the speaker for telling a lawyer joke. Then another arose and told the attacker that he was the one the jokes were about.

More of the audience left. The speaker went on with his presentation and in the end he concluded that one valid criticism was that law was too expensive. He said, "We all have numerous legal rights, but few of us can afford them. They say when it comes to law the deep pocket wins."

One of the audience members then said, "That is not a criticism. That is how it is supposed to work. It keeps the riff raff out of the courts. And we all know that in a market system wealth is a mark of merit. The deep pocket should win. And what are we supposed to do about it anyway? Bill less?"

More bickering ensued. While it was going on and everyone was getting ready to leave Lohman remembered his earlier years when he had both rich and poor clients and how he often wondered if his rich clients were bribing the judges to fix the cases. He remembered how he eventually realized that his rich clients could pay him to do the work necessary for effective representation and his poor clients could not and that made the difference.

Lohman went to a session on billing methods in the afternoon and then met Cohenstein and a group of lawyers from across the world he had assembled for dinner while schmoozing around all day.

30 CDS ON PAKISTANKI DEBT

By Wednesday morning Lohman was back in the office. He did not feel any better educated or smarter, but he had made a contact with a Hong Kong lawyer who needed a law firm for a suit in the United States.

The Wednesday morning schedule started with a conference on Pakistani CDS. The Swifton Bank and Swifton Securities, an investment bank, wanted to get into Pakistani CDS. They thought this was going to be a big deal. Swifty was going to be there as well as the heads of The Bank and Swifton Securities. Swifty was CEO of The Bank, but Denton Choudry, the COO, actually ran it. COO stands for Chief Operating Officer. CEO stands for Chief Executive Officer. Whatever this nomenclature means, Swifty couldn't run a wet dream so Choudry ran The Bank. Pulaski Rhodes headed the Securities Company. As befitted the importance of the matter, St. Charles was there as well as the heads of the firm's corporate, securities and tax departments, John Feepot, Gooster Fileform and Jeffrey Wax. Naturally a lot of junior lawyer lackeys were there to highlight the importance of those present.

CDS are credit default swaps. The market in them had grown to hundreds of trillions of dollars in recent years. Only the largest financial firms, such as The Swifton Bank, were involved. Basically a credit default swap is an insurance contract. It provides in its simplest form that if the debt issued by a particular debtor, be it a company or a government, goes into default then the issuer of the contract will pay the holder of the debt the amount of the reduction in value of the debt by virtue of the default. Many of the buyers of these CDS did not own the debt. They were just speculating on it. Only the biggest banks issued the CDS and they charged sizeable fees for them. Since the issuer of a credit default swap could lose a lot if the debt actually went into default, the issuers of CDS covered themselves by buying protection themselves, often from other banks to which they had issued CDS.

The Dead One Stinks

Rhodes had concluded that CDS on Pakistani debt would be very volatile. That is, they would fluctuate in value a lot due to the rapidly changing news about war and terrorists and its relationship with the US. This would allow someone to make a lot of money by trading the CDS as well as issuing them. All they had to do was create tradable CDS and make a market for them. There was already a market, but it was not widespread and it was private and restricted to only the largest financial firms. Now if they could create an index fund tied to the price of the CDS and sell interests to the general public they might have something. All they would have to do is come up with a method for getting price quotes on the CDS. The details had to be worked out and that is what everyone was meeting for.

In any event, Choudry knew that Swifty knew the President, the Secretary of State and the head of the CIA. Various other Bank people had access to other important figures, both at home and abroad. How difficult would it be to get inside information on the situation in Pakistan? As with all these deals, a major consideration of those present was to set up something they could trade on inside information. If it looked like the U.S. would announce tomorrow that we were going to war with Pakistan unless it did something or other, then today one could buy the CDS, the price of which would go up when people found out that maybe Pakistan would be at war and not able to pay its debt. They would make a bundle. And if they could do this with borrowed money, they wouldn't have to put up any of their own money. And if the whole thing didn't work out, they would have arranged it so they were not personally liable for the money they borrowed to pay for the CDS.

Those present did not discuss their interests in possible insider trading explicitly. It was illegal. They did discuss how others might do it and how it might be done and how they should guard against it. They also discussed the main deal which was issue of the CDS and buying offsetting

CDS. How can anyone make money if they sell for one dollar and then buy the same thing back for one dollar?

Accountants were in the meeting too and they explained how these trillions of obligations to pay if someone's debt went into default were not on the balance sheets of the banks that issued them. In other words, the banks did not show them as debt or a contingent liability. A contingent liability is a something you may have to pay someday.

After all this discussion of these complex matters had gone on for a while St. Charles looked at Swifty and said, "Complicated, isn't it?" Now if I was paying for everyone in that room at what it was costing Swifty's companies, I would think my head lawyer should understand the deal. Not so with Swifty. He and St. Charles owned the joint and in their league when you hired someone for a deal and they came up with something you didn't understand you thought you were getting your money's worth.

Swifty answered, "Great!"

Those present then went into possibly setting up some other entities to issue the CDS and still get The Bank's name on them. CDS could be sold only by the biggest financial firms, but if they could get some other entity to issue them then they could sell interests to the public to pay the costs and get big fees for setting up those entities to boot. Then those entities could borrow money and there would be that much more to invest in the CDS business. After all, one man's debt is another man's asset so the more debt there is the richer everyone is.

Everyone started throwing out their thoughts on these subjects and pointing out defects in the ideas others were advancing. Along the way one of the junior lawyers looked up from his smart phone and said, "How about CDS on Plutonian debt? Not only would you know what is happening there before everyone else does, but you can control the press releases that tell everyone what is happening."

The Dead One Stinks

The room fell silent. Nobody moved. Nobody spoke. Everybody was thinking that someone should tell this kid that insider trading was illegal, but everyone was aghast that what they all wished they could figure out how to do would be openly discussed. Finally Choudry said, "There isn't any Plutonian debt yet. And there probably won't be much of it for some time. There wouldn't be any sizeable market there."

Rhodes spoke up. "We can make a market. Hell, it's a great idea! You don't need to have any of the debt yourself to do a CDS on it. Anybody can borrow money. Maybe not ten thousand bucks. But billions? Yes. Anyone. We pour it out there, we pour out the CDS to protect the investor. Then think of what we could do with the Money! It's like using a country instead of a private company as the investment vehicle. Genius! Look Denton, let's set up a task force to look into this."

Swifty looked at St. Charles. St. Charles looked at Lohman. Lohman rolled his eyes up into his forehead to which he lifted his hand. St. Charles looked back at Swifty. Swifty nodded at Choudry. Choudry said, "Let's."

Lohman thought to himself how easy financial fraud is. You don't have to deliver anything except a promise to pay in the future. In the meantime the victim has to pay cash. Who is to say the promisor actually knows his promise is hogwash? Reputation? A history of coming across with the goods? He wondered how any of the big financial firms could meet those standards. In any event he reminded himself that he was glad he didn't have a mortgage on his house.

Along the way Feepot mentioned that O'Brien had wanted in on the deal. Choudry chimed in to confirm this. They then started discussing whether this was still feasible. Feepot said he knew O'Brien was serious about it and had asked for a report on the deal which The Bank authorized him to give to O'Brien. "I sent it to him that Friday. The day before you found him Bumper," he said. Then he looked at Sean

Featherbottom who he had brought to the meeting. "Did he say anything to you about it Featherbottom?"

Sean said, "No."

Another associate from the tax department said he been in the conference with O'Brien in the Thursday before Lohman fond him in the men's room and he had heard Henry make a comment about Pakistani CDS to O'Brien, but that all O'Brien said was 'Yes' and there was no more discussion. He said there wasn't any more talk about them because Henry was mainly complaining about someone having stolen his pen or possibly having lost it and he was complaining to O'Brien how badly he treated him.

The legal points brought up in the meeting were summarized by Fileform and Feepot and people were assigned to investigate them and come up with legal memoranda on them. The meeting then broke up.

Lohman was walking down the hall behind a small group which included Sean. He spoke up. "Sean." Sean stopped and turned around to face Lohman. "Sean, I want to talk to you. Come with me to my office." They made their way to Lohman's office with a minimum of small talk. Lohman thought Sean would like to talk about fashion or something like that and Lohman realized he didn't know anything about it. Sean thought Lohman would like to talk about football and he realized he didn't know anything about that. He did know about soccer and he asked Lohman if he liked soccer, but Lohman just said he didn't know anything about it. He tried to joke and said, "It's a bunch of foreigners isn't it? Maybe it's a terrorist conspiracy and in the middle of some big game they will all attack us." Sean wasn't sure if this was a joke or more wacko firm stuff so he remained silent. He had heard that you have a right to remain silent.

They got to Lohman's office and got seated. Lohman asked, "Did you go to O'Brien's home that Friday before I found his body? What happened?"

Sean said, "Well, I did. Mr. Feepot told me he had an important report to deliver to Mr. O'Brien and he wanted me to deliver it personally. He told me to take Tambola with me. He said two were necessary for security. He didn't say what security, but he said we should both bill for it. So we went there to deliver the papers. I went in and Tambola stayed outside."

"Tambola who?" asked Lohman.

"Tambola," said Sean. "Tambola Cook. You know her. She's done work for you."

Now Lohman remembered her. Miss Leftwitch. Always walking on the left. Often seen around Sean. Short. Wearing a conical, pointed hat much of the time.

"She drove me up there," continued Sean.

"What happened?" asked Lohman.

Sean said, "I went in. As I was going in a light skinned black lady was coming out. How come we never say a dark skinned white lady? Anyway, I don't know who she was. She nodded at me. I was kind of nervous. I never had anything to do with Mr. O'Brien before. I mean someone so important. I have worked on some of the Champion matters, but I never dealt directly with him. I only actually saw him once before. Last spring I saw him in the hall and I offered to help him. He was outside the men's room. I didn't even know it was him until someone told me later. All he said was – well he didn't like me."

"How do you know?" asked Lohman.

"Because of what he said," said Sean.

"What was that?" asked Lohman.

"Do I have to say?" said Sean.

"Oh crap!" said Lohman. "Tell me what he said."

Sean said, "He said 'Get away from me you little queer.' That's what."

"Oh, I'm sorry," said Lohman. "So what happened the other Friday at his house?"

"Well," said Sean, "Mr. O'Brien himself opened the door. I went in. The maid was there. Mr. O'Brien showed me into a room. I said Hello and he said 'Hello'. Then I said what I was there for and offered him the papers and he motioned to a table he was sitting at and I put them there beside him. Boy did he have a pen! It looked like it had a diamond head. And what a fancy shaft! I'd like to know who designs that. Anyway as he was motioning to me he turned in his chair and made a noise. He wasn't saying anything, but he made some sort of noise. You know, a noise that means 'ouch'. Then he reached under himself and got a stone out of his back pocket he was sitting on. Then he threw it at me. I guess it was hurting him when he shifted his position. I caught it and I handed it back to him and he just waived me off. I just took it and got out of there. It's in my office if you want to see it. It has something set in it. It looks like a gemstone. Should I give it back to someone?"

"I'll find out," said Lohman. "Now what about the day before? Do you remember going into the men's room where I found him? Mr. Allen says he was in there and as he was coming out someone like you came in."

"I remember Mr. Allen coming out. I didn't see Mr. O'Brien," said Sean. "I remember being there. I saw a wheel chair. That must have been his if he was there. Anyway, I did my business and left. I heard someone making noise in the disabled person stall. I went out the way I came in. Then I remembered something I had to get on the other side of the building and I went around the floor and I was in the hall on the other side of the men's room when I saw Tambola come out. When I was going past the reception area I saw that Henry O'Brien fellow. I know who he is. I've done work for him. I didn't think about it, but I guess he was waiting for his father."

"Tambola came out of the men's room?" asked Lohman. "What was she doing in there? Did you see her in there?"

"No," said Sean. "I didn't see her. But she told me she uses the men's rooms if she needs to. She just stays in the stall until everyone is gone. So I don't know if she was in there when I was or not."

Lohman dismissed Sean and spent the rest of the day catching up on his client matters.

31 AT THE CLUB

Thursday evening was one of those busy times for Lohman when he supposedly wasn't working. He was going to meet some of the firm people for dinner at the Pullman Club and later go to the symphony with Glor who he was going to meet there. She had a women's do to attend so she was eating with the girls.

At 5:30 Lohman met St. Charles and Cohenstein in St. Charles' office and then the three headed over to the Club. This was actually St. Charles' only form of exercise so he was no speed ball getting there. The Pullman Club was five blocks away. The three of them chatted about various new clients and prospects as they walked.

At the Club they met Swifty and Biff McCain, one of the old wealth inheritors who nominally ran the family empire. His name to his friends was the Biffster. Actually his real name was Biffster, not Biff. He and Swifty, along with St. Charles, were members of the Club. Outside the Club they were often referred to as the Three Stooges, although that did give them credit for a higher mental level than they actually possessed. Within the Club however, they were known as wealthy and therefore brilliant. Lohman and Cohenstein were allowed in as guests and in order, by contrast, to highlight the superiority of St. Charles and crew.

They all went to the dining room and made themselves comfortable. The waiter came over with the menus and wine list and began his spiel. "Good evening gentlemen," he said as he handed out the menus. Then he began talking about the specials. Finally he got near the end and said, "Tonight's organic special is plated root vegetables with Hyderabadian Deluxe curry sauce and Mongolian accented gerbil wings."

The Biffster asked, "What are gerbil wings? Those are organic? What's the rest of it?"

The waiter said, "Gerbil wings are the chef's version of a strain of Garbanzo beans that have delicate wing like leaves."

They all looked at each other blankly. Then The Biffster said, "Thank you. Sounds delicious."

The waiter then took their drink orders and left.

Then Cohenstein said, "Did you hear that piece on the news about Little Richard?"

"Oh, I love his music!" said The Biffster.

"I mean Little Richard Daley, our past mayor," said Cohenstein.

"Oh his too!" exclaimed The Biffster.

"I didn't know he did music," commented Cohenstein. "They announced today he was joining Lowheimer and Gray. I know he's a lawyer, but I don't think he knows where the court house is. Anyway, he's probably just going to sell and do lobbying. Too bad he doesn't like Bungus. We could have used him. Did any of you hear what kind of deal he got?" None of them did.

The topic changed to O'Brien and what had happened. The Biffster was all ears. He said, "I have been wondering what happened. You know the Thursday before we heard about it on the news. Saturday, that was when the news broke. I was lunching here that Thursday and that Jason O'Brien showed up. He practically ran in. He was by himself. He really looked like Hell. He seemed all flustered about something. I didn't pay much attention to it until Saturday when the news broke. Did what happened have anything to do with Jason's condition?"

No one knew and they got on to other subjects and got their drinks and more drinks and more and then their dinners and wine and more wine. After a while they were quite freely and loudly having a good old time. Graybee started talking about how he was worried about something and then Swifty said, "Good old Graybee. It's too bad your pussy isn't here. Whenever you get upset about anything you grab your pussy and start stroking it."

St. Charles said, "Oh yes! My pussy. How I would like to stoke her now!"

Just then someone from a neighboring table pushed back his chair and threw his napkin down on the table and came over to them. "Sir!" he exclaimed. "Watch your language! I shall have the House Committee on you if this continues."

All at the St. Charles table looked at each other as the fellow left. "Who is he?" asked The Biffster.

"A nobody," said St. Charles. He's Carlington Schweitzer. He doesn't even have a respectable business. He runs scrap yards. $50 million a year at most. So he is of no importance."

"How did we let him in the Club?" asked Swifty.

Cohenstein said, "I don't know how you guys run the place, but he probably got in because his net worth is around $200 million. And he does deals. I heard he is looking for some now."

"Oh Heavens!" said St. Charles. "I'll go over and apologize to him." He did so. And in doing so he actually explained his pussy to Carlington.

When St. Charles got back to the table Swifty was telling everyone about how he went to Windsor Castle for a party the last time he was in England. He explained how few people were invited and how hard it was to get invited. He told of how he sat ten feet away from the Queen at a ceremony after dinner. He described what she was wearing, what she was saying and her every move and facial expression. Everyone was wrapped up in the story. All were making comments, except Lohman and Cohenstein. Who cared what Lohman thought? And he never said anything anyway. But Cohenstein was more fun. Swifty asked him if he ever met the Queen. They wanted to make him admit that he was not at that level. Not that they did not like him. Peasants can be quite nice and their presence is often necessary for contrast.

Cohenstein said, "No, I never met the Queen or went to a palace. However, I was in Hell recently for a burning and I was a mere five feet from the Devil himself. A very impressive figure. Sooo correct in all he does. He was sitting there naked, doing a hit of coke and picking his nose and sticking the boogers behind his ear. On yes! He has such a flair for showmanship. But then he discovered I was there. He knows I'm a Jew. He said, 'We don't allow your kind here,' and he shot me up to Heaven where I belong."

The Biffster took this literally. He asked, "So what are you doing here?"

"I'm on work release," said Cohenstein.

After an awkward silence the conversation changed to other subjects.

32 AT THE CONCERT

After dinner Lohman went over to Orchestra Hall several blocks up Michigan Avenue. Gloria was waiting for him in the lobby. They were going to be guests of Hector and Lucey Ducey who were large benefactors of the Symphony. The Duceys were originally friends of Gloria and they liked Bumper so the Lohmans were often invited to enjoy the performances with them. The Duceys had a choice box near the center of the Orchestra Hall semicircle of boxes. Bumper and Gloria went to the box office and picked up their passes and proceeded to enter the auditorium and walk up to the mezzanine where the boxes were.

Neither of them was up on classical music, but they enjoyed the performances. Lucey Ducey had explained the upcoming performance to Gloria when she had invited her. The legendary Godabella Pinkowski was going to conduct. He was going to lead off with an overture from a Rossini opera and then get into the major attraction which was Beethoven's 12th Symphony. Even Gloria knew this sounded odd and she had asked if Beethoven had written more symphonies that had just recently been discovered. "Pinky Beethoven," Lucey had said. "The avant guard Beethoven. He used to be Pinky Fink, but he changed his name to get known. Thank God he did or else we wouldn't have his wonderful music. After all, how many composers can do variations on a theme of Bach with only five different notes for one hundred twenty bars? Glorious!"

"Well," thought Gloria, "Not all the performances are that great." What she said was, "Fabulous!"

The Lohmans arrived on the mezzanine and went to the Ducey's box. It was an eight person box. The Duceys were already there along with another couple they often invited, John and Cornbletta Putay. They were both professors of music at the Chicago Conservatory of Music and were very popular on the artistic circuit. Cornbletta was a prominent pianist and performed frequently with the major orchestras around the world.

The world of the major orchestra is like a lot of other not-for-profit institutions. These institutions depend on major donors for their support. They do not survive on box office receipts. The donors, on the other hand, are seldom interested in advancing the institutions. They are mainly interested in getting public credit for their donations and getting the opportunity to meet and deal with other people with enough loot to join the game. While the donors use other words to describe their participation, what they are mainly interested in is advertising, public relations and networking with other rich people. There is also a social aspect to the giving. The donors wanted to be in with the donor set.

A lot of ordinary people wanted to support the Orchestra too, but they did not produce major money. As the size of the donations increased, the number of donors decreased. To foster the giving process the Orchestra set up a number of boards. The legal entity for all this was The Symphony Association. It was run by a ruling Board of Directors. The directors were the biggest donors who had been giving the longest. Everyone aspired to this Board. There were also numerous subsidiary boards and committees. These were populated by newer and lesser donors who were hoping to work their way up to the more important boards and committees and the more important people who populated them. All in all, hundreds of people were involved in this process and the competition to move on up was fierce. They liked to pretend that, while anyone could give big gifts, few had the talents to properly administer a major modern symphony orchestra. This was true. It was also true that few of them had the talents. In practice, the bigger the giving, the sooner you moved up. Of course, it took a while for places at the top board to open, but The Association had been known to increase the size of the Board for very sizeable gifts.

The Dead One Stinks

The whole system supporting the Orchestra was one huge pool of social and business networking climbers trying to move on up. The result was that a fantastically expensive group of dilettantes known as the Orchestra existed to perform for people who actually could appreciate the music.

The Lion had been playing this game too. He was a major donor and had been for years. In addition everyone wanted to associate with the richest guy in town so he was on the governing Board of Directors. The Duceys were on some of the subsidiary boards and committees which is how they got access to one of the most attractive boxes. The box was actually assigned to one of the governing Board members, but he rarely attended the performances and he let the Duceys use his box. They knew enough to praise him publicly for this and he got more of what he wanted that way.

The Lohmans entered the box, greeted everyone, and made themselves comfortable. Since they were the last to arrive they sat in the back. The performance started at eight and they were fairly early so those in the box engaged in conversation. In the past one of the major problems with orchestral performances was people who arrived late. They wanted to enter the auditorium during the performance and this interfered with the performance. The ushers no longer allowed them to enter the auditorium during the performance. On the other hand, a new problem had developed with people who arrived early and started conversations. They did not stop when the performance started. They just kept on talking. Nor did they turn off their phones or stop rustling their programs. Some of those phones rang every night. All in all, one was lucky these days to hear more of the music than the audience. The Duceys, being performers themselves, seemed to think they were exempt from all the rules applicable to mere audience members and they often needed help from their box mates to quiet down when the conductor came out.

Lohman was not up on orchestral music, but he knew enough to shut up when the show started and he also knew the Duceys did not. Consequently he was a little uncomfortable waiting for the conductor to emerge. He was wondering what sort of effort would be required to secure quiet this time.

The Duceys wanted to know all about The Lion and what happened to him. They wanted a full report from Bumper, the insider. It soon became clear that he had no more to report than had come out in the media.

Lucey Ducey said, "We were wondering if it had anything to do with Hyman."

"Hyman who?" asked Gloria.

"Hyman Oyveyer," said Lucey. "Do you know him?"

"I've heard of him," said Gloria, "but we don't know him."

Lucey said, "He's quite prominent. Do you know him Bumper? Perhaps you do work for him?"

"Now, now," said Lohman, "we can't say who we work for. All client matters are confidential." He was remembering that he had heard about Oyveyer. The Lion had got adverse information about Oyveyer's company and then sold the stock before the news came out. He remembered being told that Oyveyer thought The Lion had released the bad news on purpose. He wasn't going to say anything about that.

"So what happened with Oyveyer?" asked Gloria.

"Well Dear," said Lucey, "Hyman is on one of our higher level boards and he wanted to move up to the governing Board. He told me he wanted to get close to someone – I won't say who – who was a potential investor in his company who was also on the governing Board." As any good gossiper should, Lucey had planted the seed of curiosity. Who was it? She went on. "Naturally Hyman would have to increase his contributions significantly. Very much so. There weren't any openings except – well you know – old Mrs. Reiner was going to die soon. But there were many ahead of Hyman. And they would all give so it would have been an auction. Who would give the most? Naturally, Dear, the successor would have to have suitable artistic and management credentials as well. But what Ivan did, or so I have heard, is he arranged it so Hyman's minimum contribution level to stay on the board he was already on was raised. And just then something happened to Hymans' company and he couldn't raise the money. Some very bad news about it came out. There was supposedly a terrible ruckus between them. Naturally I do not know these things myself, but we have it on very good authority."

She went on, "I do know that Hyman was accusing Ivan privately of doing something to hurt his company. Then this stopped for some reason. It was just about when he had that unfortunate incident at his estate. Do you remember Hector?" She turned towards her husband.

Hector just shook his head and said, "Terrible."

"What incident?" asked Gloria.

"Someone reportedly started shooting a gun at him from the woods surrounding the estate," said Lucey. "I wonder if that could have anything to do with Ivan."

Just then Pinkowski assumed the stage and Lohman saw an opportunity to quiet things down. "Look!" he exclaimed. "See how everyone quiets down when Pinkowski makes his entrance."

Pinkowski assumed the podium and turned to face the audience and accepted his applause. Then he turned to face the orchestra and raised his baton. Soon the magnificent rush and captivating melodies of the overture to The Pink Lady of Milan filled the auditorium and the performance had begun.

33 MORE LAW FIRM BUSINESS

Friday morning Lohman had reserved one of the downstairs conference rooms for a meeting to discuss the status of the O'Brien estate matters. They were mainly going to discuss some tax matters and the technical details of the probate process. Due to the size of the estate, the details were fairly complex. They also wanted to discuss how they could keep as much information as possible about The Lion's affairs from becoming part of the public record. Lohman had assigned some of his juniors to look into the law applicable to sealing the court record. Since actual work was going to be done, not too many of the senior firm partners were going to be there.

Nuftdone and some people from The Bank's Wealth Management department who were working on the estate were scheduled to be there. Bungus LaRue was also going to be there, mainly so he could get up to speed on some of the estate details to aid him in his nefarious dealings, whatever they were, and you shouldn't ask. Nuftdone had his usual crew of five associates and junior partners there. Lohman had asked Sean Featherbottom to look into some of the corporate issues and he had asked Tambola Cook to work up the memorandum of law on sealing the court record. Legal research and memo writing she was good at. Just don't let her talk to anyone. Sweeney was there because of what he knew about publicity, due to the nature of his clients, and because he knew the family as well as anyone.

Lohman got there first and the others came in one, by one, except for Sean and Tambola who came in together. They all got seated, but Nuftdone still wasn't there. His juniors were though. They were waiting for Bungus too. Lohman was going through his papers and he looked up for a moment. Tambola was sitting next to him. She was fiddling with her smart phone. Lohman looked over her shoulder. She was oblivious to this. He looked at her phone and saw the text. He kept

219

looking as she texted and read replies. She and Sean were texting each other. He stopped his snooping and after a while she stopped.

Those present were engaging in small talk to pass the time until Nuftdone and LaRue got there. One of the associates sitting next to Sean asked him what was new. Sean allowed as how he had got a new bicycle. Sweeney chimed in, "You're the biker, Dude. You still riding to the Lake County office?"

The firm had an office in the northern suburb of Highland Park which was in Lake County, the next county to the north. People from the Chicago office often went up there for specific matters. It was well known that Sean usually rode his bike up there when he went.

"Yes," said Sean, "when I go. Sometimes I just go up north on a ride, even if I'm not working. I usually go up to North Chicago, or even the State line if I have time."

Sweeney said, "You're a bikeomaniac Dude! I'll bet it's one of those $3000 dollar bikes. Right?"

"Twenty five hundred," said Sean. "I've seen your bike. Now that's a $3000 bike. More. You should talk. The colors are great. It's like a designer bike. And the logo! Oh wow, would I like to have that on my bike!"

"Yeah, Man. I got a top dollar one because I need more help from the bike than you do."

Lohman had a bike. He liked to ride it around the city. It cost $175 at Sears. He loved it. He wondered what a $3000 bike was like.

Sweeney was going on. "I go up north sometimes too, but nowhere as far as you go. I go up that North Shore – Green Bay Trail. But going that far takes a lot out of me. And it's getting dangerous. All the other riders seem like they want to kill you. This summer I went up there one Sunday. There I am riding along on this trail through a wooded stretch with trees on each side. It's just wide enough for two bikes to pass. This guy's coming at me. He's coming fast. He's right in the middle of the trail. No room to get around him. Talk about the money bike. He's got the $5000 bike and the $2000 outfit. Big guy. About six foot five and three hundred pounds. He rules. He's looking straight at me. He's God and I better get out of the way. So I lean back and to the left and hit the front brake hard and the rear of my bike swings across the trail. I let it fall right in front of him and step aside. He hits my bike and flies off his bike. He's getting up slow. I run over and kick him in the nuts. Again. He grabs for 'em and keels over. I knee him in the face. He starts screaming like a girl. Beggin' for mercy. 'Fuckin' watch where you're goin' Man', I say. I pick up my bike and take off."

Sean was wide eyed through all this. He said, "You did that?"

"I wish!" said Sweeney. "I had to hit the trees. He didn't even notice."

The conversation continued on about other aspects of biking until Nuftdone and LaRue got there. Lohman then quickly directed everyone's attention to the subjects at hand and the meeting was over in several hours.

He then went back to his office and as he was coming in Tete got his attention. "Look at this Hon," she said. "You know accounting has been reviewing all the billings on the O'Brien matters. So they find out that Sprack fellow in IP is billing a fortune on some matter where there aren't any details. We don't even know what kind of matter he is billing on. Look." She held out some papers to Lohman. "See Hon. It says 'Unspecified' where we usually say what type of matter or what case it is. The time records do not say how the time was spent. Just the time is recorded. Look." She pointed to another page. "See. It just gives his name and the names of the other lawyers on the matter and then the time, the hours and minutes and then for the explanation we have a blank. He's got over $250,000 billed this way. Just this year."

Lohman took the papers and went into his office. He didn't have much time to review them because he had to be in court that afternoon. He went out again and told Tete, "I'm going to the lunch room. I'll be back soon. He left and went for quick lunch. He often met someone who he could shoot the breeze with there, but today there was no one so inclined. He might be inclined, but most of the junior people around a large law firm do not want to sit and talk to the boss. So Lohman occupied himself with looking out the window as he ate some soup and salad.

Lohman soon became aware that someone at a nearby table was talking about O'Brien. He looked over and saw one of the most gorgeous women he had ever seen. He recognized her as one of the secretaries who worked for LaRue. LaRue had three secretaries, whereas most lawyers shared one secretary with another lawyer. LaRue did only the talking parts and there were many scut work parts for his operation so he had more secretaries. This particular secretary was not only Miss Gorgeous, but she had quite a set of bazooms. In fact her nickname around the firm was Miss Jugs. She was talking about meeting O'Brien in the hall on the Friday before Lohman found his body. She apparently knew O'Brien from having worked for LaRue.

Lohman went over to her table and said, "Excuse me. I couldn't help hearing what you were saying about Mr. O'Brien. You say you saw him that Friday?"

"Oh hello Mr. Lohman," she said. "Yes I saw him in the hall. Henry O'Brien was wheeling him down the hall in that wheel chair. I was going down the hall the other way. I said 'Hello', but I got no response."

"That's odd," said Lohman. What he was thinking is that, while The Lion often ignored some people, he never ignored a lovely lady. "He didn't say anything? Not even 'Hello'?"

"No," she said. "Not a word. I just went on down the hall."

Lohman went back to his office and gathered together his papers for court. He had to go argue a motion in a contract dispute between two large companies. He got over to the court room. There were hardly any people there because in the afternoon in that courtroom they had only the more time consuming matters and the crowds of the morning were not there. The judge was not on the bench yet and Lohman entered and checked in with the clerk. The judge was not going to come out until the clerk told him that both sides were there. Lohman went to one of the lawyers' tables and got his papers out of his brief case. He arranged them on the table and waited for the other side. His opponent arrived fifteen minutes late. He had ten other junior lawyers in tow. Lohman offered his hand to the opponent and greeted him. The opposing lawyer ignored him. Then his opponent said, "Where's your team. I don't have all day to wait around here you know."

Lohman said, "I'm the team. Let's tell the judge we're ready."

The opponent said, "You're alone?"

"Yes," said Lohman. "Just me."

The opponent looked at him curiously. "How can you handle a matter of this importance alone? You know, if your client can't afford litigation why don't you just give up. Do you know who you are dealing with?"

Lohman did, but he didn't want to insult the guy. He said, "Most certainly. Your reputation precedes you."

That quieted the twit for a while. The judge came out and they proceeded to argue the motion. Lohman won. After the hearing his opponent said, "You know, there's just going to be more and more of this. You guys can't afford this. Just give up now. You think it over and get in touch with one of my people about how much you are going to pay."

Lohman asked, "I shouldn't talk to you?"

His opponent said, "Not on a matter at this level. Talk to one of my juniors."

"Which one?" asked Lohman.

His opponent just waived his hand at his crew and said, "Oh any one of them." Then he walked out and all his juniors scooped up their papers in a panic and ran after him.

34 MORE ABOUT THE FAMILY AND THE LION

Monday evening was October 31st. The official Halloween. Appropriately, St. Charles had scheduled something he called a "Solidarity Conference" with the family. The basic idea was to see that they were all working together and to encourage them to keep doing so. Most of the day Monday Lohman was conferring with other lawyers getting ready for the dinner and brushing up on the status of the O'Brien affairs which, since he was dead, were confined to his business matters.

The first thing that morning Lohman met with Nuftdone and Sweeney to brush up on the family relationships and their interactions. In short, he wanted to learn more about them personally. It was remarkable how the group included all the ex-wives and not just the children. More remarkable was that this group included the current girlfriend. They all included themselves and each other in the word "family". They often met as a group socially and they were all involved on one or more of the businesses in various ways. None of them considered this unusual. The ex-wives even included their current husbands or boyfriends as part of the group. And so did the other family members. It was just one big happy family, except to any non-family member who might be present among them. An outsider who experienced one of their gatherings would have thought they were in the middle of World War III. There was one exception to all this and that was Ivan's brother Ryan. He was hardly ever included in the family gatherings.

All the ex-wives used their maiden names. The first wife had been Hu Yen Fong. She was mother to Jason and Watta. Her current boyfriend was Fung Goo. The second wife had been Latrina Foxglover. She was mother to Wandrasha and Dwante. Wandrasha had been married to a DeLang and her daughter was Trisha DeLang. The third wife had been Veronica Goldstein. She was mother to Glover and Henry. The girlfriend was Moronika Headpin. Trisha was the only grandkid over ten.

Nuftdone was quite aghast at all this. In the first place there was the racial mix. One mixed marriage is enough to get you kicked out of polite society. Three with assorted mixtures are unheard of. Even in the new society of superior merit and wealth these are demerits. Nuftdone made these ideas very clear to Lohman. Hu Yen was Asian. Latrina was Black. Veronica was White (but the Jewish kind). And Moronika! O'Brien was going through the races. She was half Arapaho!

"What's the other half?" asked Lohman.

"Blondie," said Sweeney. "Half blonde, half Arapaho. Man, I'd like to rap that ho!"

"How did she get a name like that?" asked Lohman. "Was her father the Headpin?"

"I understand he was the Caucasian," sniffed Nuftdone. "And you know how it is with these Indians. They think they own the country. She's very much above her station."

"Fhat the wuck?" exclaimed Sweeney.

"What does that mean?" asked Nuftdone. It was fortunate for Sweeney that he really had no idea what Sweeney had just said.

Lohman did. "Now, now," he cautioned.

"Yeah, yeah, Bumps," said Sweeney, "so let's go on forever about the family and yada, yada, yada."

"What did you say?" asked Nuftdone.

"He wants to tell us more about the family," said Lohman.

Sweeney was fiddling with his smart phone through all this, as he usually did in any meeting. Nuftdone said, "Put that thing down. You associates! You all appear to be in love with those things."

"Yeah Dude," said Sweeney. "I wish I was one big huge smart phone. Then all the pretty young girls would touch me and stroke me and put their lips up against me. Or maybe not. Are there smart phones just for girls? I'll have to find out. I know who to ask. He used to be an engineer working with cellular things before joining the family. Fung Goo."

"Watch your language young man!" said Nuftdone.

Lohman could see they were getting nowhere. Nuftdone and Sweeny did not speak the same language. Nor did they exist on the same planet. Lohman then steered the meeting into the characteristics of each family member and the things they cared about and what they liked and what they did not like. Nuftdone described the bad traits of each and Sweeney told Lohman all about the good traits.

Lohman managed to get them through the meeting without any serious problems just in time for another meeting which included them and other lawyers in the firm. This meeting was going to be about the status of the probate proceeding, seeing how taxes could be reduced and surveying the major pending matters to see that no unusual problems had cropped up. Lohman wanted to be prepared for whatever might come up at the "Solidarity Conference" that evening.

Nuftdone had summoned a lot of associates and younger partners to help him out with this because they had been working on the substantive legal matters. He needed a lot of help on legal issues. LaRue was also involved because one thing being considered was getting Congress to change the estate tax retroactively in a way that would benefit the O'Brien estate. Congress had recently made retroactive changes in the tax, so why not again. The estate and tax lawyers were present to suggest possible ways in which the law could be changed so as to benefit the estate while not being too obvious or damaging to the US revenue in general.

The Dead One Stinks

One thing everyone had not considered was mentioned by Lohman. They were all thinking of eliminating the estate tax again as of some date before The Lion died or reducing it to a very low rate or just adding specific tax breaks that could benefit the O'Brien estate retroactively. Lohman suggested that since they had been exploring the Plutonian Principality as a way of eliminating The Lion's estate tax burden before he died, they should continue that exploration. Lohman explained that the plan had been to have O'Brien become a Plutonian citizen and not subject to US estate tax. Since he had been a citizen here that would have required a change in the law. LaRue had already been working on this and they had a head start. Lohman acknowledged that The Lion could hardly change his citizenship after his death, but he already had many connections to the Principality and these might be utilized to fashion special tax treatment. This would also have the additional benefit of not requiring any change in the basic estate tax.

LaRue liked the idea, but he said, "There are a lot of problems we have to deal with. One, this is going to be expensive. A lot more than I was figuring on. I'll have to figure it out. And we have to see that the money comes from the right sources and then goes to the right places. I'll work on it. But we have people problems too. I was working with a lot of people on this and one was Senator Clagghonk of South Carolina. He had a company with a lot of government contracts. Well, ostensibly it was a public company with a lot of owners. He just had a minor stake. But he took out most of the profits in consulting fees. Now Ivan knew all about this. He wanted the contracts himself and we were working on it. So out of nowhere and without asking me he has one of his papers accuse Clagghonk of supporting the terrorists by selling war goods to them. Was that true? I don't know. Ivan told me he had the goods on the Senator. Anyway it didn't work. Ivan didn't come up with anything besides gossip. The whole thing quieted down and Clagghonk kept the contracts. So Ivan goes and does a hostile takeover of the Senator's company and gets the contracts that way. He terminated the Senator's consulting fees. Now you may ask why I am able to deal with the Senator on Ivan's behalf after all this happened. Well, times change and he was coming around."

Lohman thought nothing had changed. Politicians don't care where the money comes from.

LaRue continued. "There was always something we need Senatorial cooperation on and participation at all other levels of government too. So we were exploring how we could be of aid to the Senator again. He seemed to be interested in helping to eliminate import duties for Plutonian goods and we made a significant contribution to the Foreign Trade Institute which he sponsors to study the issue. At the same time I was consulting with Ivan about something that the Senator could make use of in his own state. Basically Ivan wanted to get into education. Now you know that, what with government backed student loans and all sorts of government grants like Pell grants and VA subsidies, the education business has become quite lucrative. How much more profitable could it be if the schools did not have to pay for the buildings? And if only one school got government subsidized buildings it could charge less and eventually wipe out all the competitors. So how do we do this? Ivan was exploring various ways to get government grants. For instance here in Illinois he was going to do TIFs. Tax increment financing districts. All the tax increases in the district over time go to funding some special project beneficial to the common good. And what is more beneficial than education? Ah, but how do we get the TIF? The usual way of working with and supporting suitable key agents in government. The only cost is the campaign contributions and they are minimal compared to the possible profits."

"Think of it," LaRue continued. "Ivan was going to offer the youth of America careers as film producers and directors and as prominent actors and leading artists, all for free or very little cost. The market is unlimited. Just look at all the other schools that have sprung up. And he was going to have another advantage. To the extent investment capital was necessary, he was going to get it from investors who would be motivated by the tax breaks from the TIFs. Ivan was also exploring ways of issuing tax free municipal bonds to finance part of the capital costs. He had the securities firm and all the elements necessary to reach investors and secure their funds. They would own the buildings, the equipment, everything physical. Ivan would own the schools using the investors' property and equipment. To the extent the property and equipment generated returns, Ivan would participate there too by being a partner in the deals in return for his services in setting them up. He would also siphon off most of the profit in management fees. In these times of low interest rates it doesn't take much to get investor money."

"The Senator," said LaRue, "was interested in all this. Especially in helping us explore how to see that the right people favorable to our scheme would be elected and helping us determine how much their campaigns would need and what sources of funds were available. We hired one of his companies to consult on that too."

At this point one of the junior lawyers present exclaimed, "I can't believe this! Just last month when I was in that meeting with you and Mr. O'Brien he said he was going to kill you. About that consulting company of yours. Now you are talking like ---." He realized he shouldn't have said it as soon as he said it. All eyes turned towards him.

Lohman stepped in. Not many people in the firm knew it, but LaRue had a consulting company that he used to funnel various payments to various sources in a process F, P & C did not want to be connected with. The firm partners who knew about this also suspected he diverted part of the fees that would otherwise accrue to the firm to that consulting company. In keeping with the deliberate lack of inquiry into anything LaRue was doing, the partners did not go into this. Lohman said, "Let's keep focused on our current problems here shall we."

LaRue added, "That was nothing. You may not know it, but Ivan was always getting hostile about everything. He calmed down quickly. He probably threatened to get me or kill me ten times. He was excitable. Remember at the same time he was threatening to disinherit his son Jason. No one even knew why. And also remember he did not do that. He didn't 'even have a will to cut Jason out of. Remember what we were talking about at that meeting. We were not even talking about this subject. We were talking about rezoning of the land next to his shopping center in Lake County. Remember, he was showing us his pen and talking about it. And that stone too. Always with that pen and that stone! And then out of nowhere he says he is going to cut Jason out of his estate and then he says that thing about my company. None of this was serious. You had to know him to know what he really meant."

Lohman thought to himself, "God! Listen to all this. I'm glad we never press Bungus on what he is doing. And look how we can buy off politicians. Kill them one day and buy them the next. Maybe we can find a pig that can fly, but can we ever find an honest politician?"

The discussion at the meeting got into some pretty technical matters and then ended in the early afternoon. Lohman stopped in the lunch room on the way back to his office and picked up a sandwich. When he got back to his office he learned Sprack, the IT partner, wanted to talk to him. Tete had asked Sprack for an explanation of his billings and he had called and said he wanted to explain in person to Lohman.

Sprack came in and explained that he was doing the work at the request of Henry O'Brien. It involved work on patenting a remote control device that does not need any wires or connection to the thing controlled or any prior coordination with the thing controlled. Sprack explained that they were debating whether to patent the invention or just keep the idea secret. A patent requires disclosure of the technology. And it has a limited life. If you can make a device using the technology without revealing the technology to a user you can keep the invention secret and use it forever. In the meantime strange people had been contacting Sprack about the device and technology. Henry had told him to keep everything about it, even the billings, secret. Oddly enough, Henry had told him to talk to the strange people and they had told him to keep everything secret too. These people were not connected with the O'Brien companies that Sprack could tell, but he was told not to ask about them or where they were from.

"So you have no idea who they are?" asked Lohman.

"I do have an idea," said Sprack. "Some secret government branch. CIA, Defense Department, military. Something like that. With this technology we could control North Korean rockets. At least potentially. It hasn't been perfected for that. They are still working on it. So far as I know they haven't got it working yet. It's theoretical still and I'm just working out the legal issues in advance."

"And nobody had been asking about these bills without detail?" asked Lohman. "I did see that they were paid."

"No," said Sprack. "Henry's getting them approved. No problems."

"Did The Lion ever mention them?" asked Lohman.

"No," said Sprack.

"Did he know about them?" asked Lohman.

"I don't know," said Sprack. "They weren't a big thing for someone with his wealth."

"He's gone," said Lohman. "Whether he knew or not, someone else is now going to be in control. Can you hold off on these billings for a while? Whoever takes over could require us to explain."

"I can do that," said Sprack. "There's no work going on with that matter right now."

Lohman and Sprack parted and Lohman got busy preparing for the evening's production number starring St. Charles and the family.

The evening's event was to be in a private set of rooms at the Pullman Club. All the key family members were there and all the firm's people with solid family contacts were too. St. Charles was there, Cohenstein, LaRue and Lohman were too. Lohman was not there because of his crucial family contacts, but because St. Charles and Cohenstein always wanted him present at important gatherings. He was their safety blanket. Sweeney and Winter Goren were there and that was because of their crucial family contacts. Swifty was also there, once again because he carried weight with a lot of the family. The operating officers and directors of the family controlled companies were not there. When push came to shove, they were controlled by the family.

Lohman had been working on another matter when the time to go over to the Pullman Club arrived and he had to interrupt his work. Tambola Cook was working on a legal memo on the matter and she was not yet done with it when Lohman had to go over to the Club. Since he had to have read it by the following morning he had instructed her to deliver it to him at the Club when she had it ready.

Lohman got to the Pullman Club by himself a little late and went up to join the gathering. It was already in progress with what amounted to a large cocktail party before the dinner. St. Charles had just assumed a podium set up at one end of the room to launch into his endless outpouring of malarkey when Lohman came in. St. Charles motioned Lohman up to the podium and called everyone's attention to him and gave out with ten minutes of what a great guy he was. Just at the end of this Tambola came in to hand an envelope with the memorandum to Lohman. She was a little, short, plump young thing with a black floor length outer coat on. It was more a shroud than a coat. She had on her black conical hat. She rushed up to the podium and handed the envelope to Lohman and turned and left as quickly as she came. Most of the family thought this was some kind of prearranged Halloween entertainment and they broke out in applause. This just caused Tambola to scurry out faster.

Lohman took the envelope and came down from the podium to join the crowd. St. Charles started in to the rest of his verbose introductory comments with repeated calls for solidarity and sticking together. Finally he ran out of gas and the cocktail party resumed. Lohman found himself next to Moronika and they started talking.

"He's really impressive," she said.

"Yes indeed," said Lohman. Neither one of them mentioned what it was St. Charles was impressive at. Moronika then started talking about what a strange relationship the family had. They were all talking to O'Brien on their own and trying to curry favor with him. They all had keys to his house and went there often to butter him up without the others present. Some often had to be there to consult with him on business matters too and they also used these occasions to get on his good side. She related several instances when she came across Ryan or Henry or Jason talking to Ivan about some business matters and hearing them get into bad mouthing other family members and informing O'Brien of their stellar accomplishments of the moment. Then Moronika started talking about the all the bickering amongst family members when they were together. She also talked about how it was probably inevitable. She mentioned that she had to put up with a lot of comments from the others that indicated that they resented her status as the current girlfriend, but they all understood that none of the ex-wives would have been able to put up with O'Brien even if they were still married to him. And she did not make any bones about the fact that they were all in it for the money. She even said, "I don't think I could have taken it much more if it wasn't for the money. Anyway, in the end we all know that we are better off working together than going to war with each other. And some of them like the bitching too, so while they might sound like they are having a tough time of it, they are actually enjoying it."

As Moronika went on Hu Yen Fong came by, chasing a waiter for another glass of wine. Moronika said, "Anyway, I had to take care of him and be with him and it was getting harder and harder. He was getting more and more difficult. Maybe Ryan was right. Maybe he was losing it."

At this stage Hu Yen got her wine and joined Moronika and Lohman. Her boyfriend soon came up beside her. Hu Yen had heard the conversation and said, "You're right. He was gone. But, you know, now that I think of it, he was always gone or difficult or whatever you call it. So maybe he wasn't, as you might say, legally gone."

Her boyfriend said, "Oh face facts. He was gone, or a long way there."

"Oh Fung Goo, he was not," said Hu Yen.

Moronika said, "Well, I was taking care of him and I think he was at a little off, even if it wasn't all the way."

"You never took care of him!" said Hu Yen. "You cared more for yourself than him. Face it, you were just after his money."

Moronika ignored this and started talking about the things she did for The Lion.

Hu Yen interrupted, "Moronika! Can't you hear? I just insulted you. Maybe what they say about blondes is true."

Moronika responded, "Oh, was that an insult? How would I know? After all when a crocodile turd says something that could be construed as derogatory, you do not take offense. Instead you are amazed that it can speak."

Hu Yen asked, "Did you just insult me?"

"Certainly not," said Moronika, "I merely described you."

"Have you no consideration or thought for my feelings?" said HuYen.

"Look," said Moronika, "If I had to pay a dollar for each time I thought of you, you'd owe me money."

Hu Yen and Fung Goo stomped off. Moronika turned to Lohman and said, "See what I mean? We understand each other. And you can see that I am one of those who enjoy the bickering. In my case though, I am aware of the fact that I get off on it. Most of them aren't. That's sick."

Moronika noticed someone else she wanted to talk to and she took her leave of Lohman. Lohman started moving around the room looking for waitresses with appealing appetizers on their trays. He found what he wanted on the tray of a waitress who was holding it out to Henry and Glover. They were both making a selection while Henry was saying to Glover, "So I found it again. Here, look" He held out a pen to Glover. It was a diamond headed pen, just like O'Brien's.

Lohman said, "That's the one that looks just like your father's pen."

"Yes," said Henry. "Remember I told you we had identical pens. I got two and gave him one. Then somehow I lost mine or misplaced it."

"Oh?" asked Lohman. "Where did you lose it? When did you find it?"

Henry looked at him for a while. Then he said, "Well naturally I don't know how I lost it. If I did I would have got it back right away."

"So how did you get it back," asked Lohman.

The Dead One Stinks

Henry looked at him again. Then he answered, "I can't remember the details. All I know is, I reached for it the other day and there it was. Right in my pocket. Maybe I put it in the wrong pocket and forgot it. Who cares? I have it now."

As they were going in to dinner, Sweeney came by and said to Lohman, "Hey Bumpy! Great show! How'd you get Cookie to do that? I didn't even know she existed outside the office."

"Tambola?" asked Lohman.

"Yeah," said Sweeney. "Miss Leftwitch. The little wicked witch of Chicago. Great show! The Halloween touch. Trisha wants to use her in one of her videos."

"It wasn't a show," said Lohman. "She was just delivering something to me I have to go through for a meeting tomorrow."

After everyone was seated at the dinner tables St. Charles arose and delivered further evidence of his being very impressive at something no one could exactly define. Most of those in attendance then ate, boozed some more and went home. Lohman was not a boozer on a working night or hardly ever. He left early and for once, thought he would take a cab home. While he was looking for a cab he was thinking to himself that if he had a brain like most of the people at the dinner he could clean every carpet in sight real quick. Then he saw a teenager walking by with an adult who appeared to be his father. The kid had pants that were about to fall off and the father was telling him to pull up his pants. This reminded Lohman that he had been told by Cohenstein that Confucius once said, "If want son to wear pants up, wear pants down."

Once Lohman got home he went through Tambola's memorandum which was mercifully short. He had a little free time so he joined Gloria in watching a TV program. Once in a while they did this and got through a whole program without trying to molest each other. They called watching TV moronocide.

35 WHAT WIGGY FOUND OUT

Tuesday morning Lohman assigned some junior lawyers to tasks based on what he had learned from Tambola's memorandum. Then he met with Wiggy Rodriguez.

Lohman wanted to know what Wiggy thought of the Medical Examiner's conclusion that O'Brien died on Thursday, instead of Friday. Wiggy said that he wasn't up on homicide, but he would ask some of his police contacts what they might know about the matter. Then Lohman wanted to know if Wiggy had found out anything more.

"Some rumors," said Wiggy. "You know I look up all sorts of public records and I know a lot of investigators with public agencies. And I looked over what we have going on with the O'Brien interests. I saw from our firm time sheets the SEC was after him. So I know a guy at the Illinois Securities Department who used to be with the SEC. Unusual. Normally they go up the ladder. So this guy goes from a federal agency to a state agency. A demotion you could say. And he gets paid less. But, in Illinois, you know, there are other opportunities. One involves selling information. So I ask him about O'Brien and I ask him if he knows about the SEC matter. He has an insurance agency on the side and he asks if I know anyone who wants insurance. So I talk to Mr. LaRue and he tells me he knows someone who wants insurance and he tells me that unidentified someone also wants to find out something. So I tell Mr. LaRue who the guy in the Securities Department is. A little later Mr. LaRue calls me in and tells me maybe a guy called Oyveyer told the SEC about Champion Foods pumping up its numbers. I call the guy at the Securites Department about it and he says he never heard of Mr. LaRue or talked to him and he doesn't know anything about O'Brien or Oyveyer."

"That sounds like our Mr. LaRue," said Lohman. "Do you know anything about Oyveyer?"

239

"No," said Wiggy. "I haven't had time to a thorough job on him yet."

"There are rumors about him and The Lion," said Lohman. "There is a rumor that O'Brien knew him and got adverse information about Oyveyer's company out of him and then sold the company short just before releasing the information. When you sell short you don't own the stock you are selling. You buy it later. So supposedly The Lion sold the stock and then let the adverse information out. When it got out to the public that sent the stock price down. Supposedly O'Brien sold the stock at the higher price and then bought it later at the lower price and made a killing. And then I heard that the two of them got into a dispute at the Orchestra about Oyveyer moving up to a higher position and getting a better box."

"Well, maybe there's something to it," said Wiggy. "It can take all sorts of time and money to get the truth out of rumors though. On the other hand some of them you can tell right off probably have some substance to them. Now, you know there's quite a lot of – sexual activity – around here. Maybe you don't. Anyway, there is a lot of talk about it and a lot of rumors. Whenever I have to go into it I find out about half the rumors aren't true or at least don't name the right people. On the other hand, I find half are true and accurate."

"What does this have to do with The Lion?" asked Lohman.

"You sure you want to know?" asked Wiggy.

"If it involves O'Brien I do," said Lohman.

"Well," said Wiggy hesitantly, "it seems he could still get it up. He was talking those testosterone shots and he had that 22 year old girlfriend. Rumor is that wasn't enough. Rumor is that he was doing some partner's wife. And she was doing one of the accountants working for some of our clients."

"Who?" asked Lohman.

"It's only rumors," said Wiggy.

"Half of which you say are true around here," said Lohman.

Wiggy went on, "I don't know if this is one of the true ones. I haven't followed up on it."

"So tell me," said Lohman. "I'll remember it may not be so."

"Mr. Nuftdone," said Wiggy. "The rumor is that his wife was doing O'Brien and then she was doing some accountant who represents some of our clients too. But this accountant didn't have anything to do with O'Brien."

"Do you think this is actually happening?" asked Lohman. "Is this one of the accurate rumors?"

"As I said," Wiggy responded, "I don't know. But around here if you pick any two or three people or even three or four, chances are fifty-fifty they have done it or are going to. If you want to know this kind of thing just ask your secretary."

"Tete?" asked Lohman.

"She knows all the rumors," said Wiggy. "Don't you ever talk to her?"

"Not about that," said Lohman. "Christ! Anyway, what else did you find out besides getting the dirt on everyone?"

"I did get something solid," said Wiggy. "Mr. Henry O'Brien. You said he went to Omaha on October sixth. Not that I can find out. I had to go out to Omaha recently to interview a potential witness in a case and I looked into his stay there. I found his flight and his hotel. October seven. Not six."

The Dead One Stinks

"How did you find that out?" asked Lohman.

Wiggy made a motion with his hand, rubbing his fingers together, indicating money was involved. Or maybe indicating that his finger-tips itched. "I'll tell you Mr. Lohman," he said, "it's getting harder and harder to get around. That TSA! They supposedly protect me from terrorists, but who is going to protect me from them? What if I have the wrong brand of shoes? Or underwear? All our clothing is made somewhere else. What if I am wearing some shoes that say 'Made in Afghanistan'? Do I go straight to Guantanamo? And look at this." He lifted his wig off his head. "They make me take this off."

Lohman recalled his own experiences at the airports. He sympathized with Wiggy. Wiggy went on, "So there I am at O'Hare and the TSA wants to do a special search on me. Right in front of everyone. The guy reaches for my crotch. With his rubber gloves on. So I say, 'When pigs fly you can feel my nuts'. He looks around and says, 'See all the pigs who are going to fly?' For Christ's sake! Then he turns me around to feel my buns. He did this to all the women too. They should call it the Tits and Ass Administration. They want to feel all the tits and asses. You remember they had security before the 9/11 attacks. That didn't stop anything and this won't either. Or maybe it'll stop people from flying. And I think this whole flying thing will be over soon. They have drone planes now. So why not drone passengers? You know, if God wanted us to fly he would have given us wings – or at least tickets. If the Devil wanted us to fly he would have given us exactly what we have now."

Lohman commiserated with Wiggy for a while. Then Wiggy said, "Oh, I forgot to tell you. I was wrong. I did check out that Oyveyer in our records. I went to Henner Pigman in IT and he ran a search and came up with something in the time records for Mr. LaRue that mentioned an Oyveyer. It was for the Thursday before O'Brien died. Or maybe he died on that Thursday. And I checked the building log and he was checked in to see Mr. LaRue that morning. Have you heard about this?"

"No," said Lohman. "I'll check it out with Mr. LaRue."

"And another thing," said Wiggy. "You told me Henry O'Brien said he went to meet people on the West coast on Friday. I called that company, Hen Fen I think. I told them I was working for Champion and for him and asked if he left his iPad there. I said he couldn't find it after he came back. They put me on to some guy with a name I can't pronounce who said he met with Henry out there. He said Henry didn't leave anything, but along the way he let me know Henry was there Saturday, not Friday."

Then Lohman asked, "What about Friday – did you find anyone who saw The Lion after Mr. Nuftdone did?"

"Only reception," said Wiggy. "On 40. She saw him get on the elevator. I haven't been able to find anyone else who saw him."

"Did you find out anything about what the building did about the temperature in Allen's office?" asked Lohman.

"Just that they didn't do anything," said Wiggy. "That's probably why Ms. Goblat got a second complaint from Mr. Allen."

The two engaged in small talk for a while and then Wiggy took his leave.

36 IT'S CONFIDENTIAL

Later in the day Lohman managed to find Bungus LaRue and meet with him. They exchanged greetings and some small talk and then Lohman got to the point. "So Bungus. I see from our records that you met with an Oyveyer on the Thursday before I found The Lion's body. What was that about?"

"Confidential," said Bungus. "You know what I deal with is all confidential." If you had asked Bungus where he was when he was sitting right in front of you and talking to you he would have told you that was confidential.

"Yes, yes," said Lohman. "But you well know that while we must keep client matters confidential, that does not mean they are confidential within the firm. The whole firm represents the clients so lawyers within the firm can share information about clients. Your confidentiality stems from other considerations." Here Lohman felt the need to mimic a bull at stool. "We all know that the sensitive matters you handle in your particular field require that you be left without interference or second guessing in order that your expertise is not diluted. However, in this case perhaps some outside input is needed. It has come to my attention that The Lion and a Hyman Oyveyer might have had a feud going on. Now I find that Oyveyer came in here to talk to you and it is The Lion we represented. So you can see that Oyveyer is a natural subject of inquiry."

"I see," said Bungus. "It was about that. The feud, as you call it. Evidently his lawyer had called Graybee to complain about Ivan. They wanted an immediate conference and you know how Graybee is. He's always occupied with something like stroking his pussy. Anyway he can't be bothered with anything on short notice so he told them to come on in and then he got ahold of me. I think he was looking for anyone who was free. I was so he sent them to me. I never heard of Oyveyer before. So he and his lawyer came in and I didn't know anything about what was going on. They basically said Ivan had released bad information about Oyveyer's company and the SEC was investigating and they wanted big bucks or they were going to sue. They also hinted that a settlement could influence what kind of cooperation they would give the SEC. Like big pay, no talk. So they came in, they talked, I played dumb, and that was that. I told Graybee about it."

"What did he say?" asked Lohman.

"Not much," said LaRue. "He said he'd talk to Zenon about it."

"I understand this was on Thursday," said Lohman. "The day before The Lion died. Or maybe the day he died. There is still some doubt about the day he died."

"Yes, I think it was on a Thursday," said LaRue.

"So what else happened?" asked Lohman.

"Not much," answered LaRue. "We talked. They were nasty. I was nice. Then they left. I walked them down the hall. We had been using a conference room down on 43. I wanted to go, so I left them at the john. Or I thought I would. Oyveyer wanted to go too, so he came in with me. His lawyer said he would wait for Oyveyer in the reception room. I peed, Oyveyer went into a stall. I left. That's it."

"Did you see The Lion?" asked Lohman. "That's where he died. Whether he died that day or the next, he was in there on Thursday. But, then, Friday too according to witnesses. Anyway, alive or dead, he was in there on Thursday."

"No, I didn't see him," said LaRue

"Did you see his wheel chair? What time of day was this?" asked Lohman.

"About, oh, after twelve. After noon," said LaRue. I remember, because I was going to be late for a lunch meeting with the Governor at twelve thirty. I didn't see any wheelchair."

Lohman wanted to know what LaRue was talking to the Governor about, but he knew enough not to ask. And he knew that, while in one sense he wanted to know, in another sense he knew he didn't want to know. Instead he asked, "Was Oyveyer still in there?"

"So far as I know," said LaRue.

Lohman then left and went back to his office and looked at the building log. He saw Oyveyer checked in around ten thirty. While Lohman was at it he looked to see if O'Brien checked back in after noontime on Friday. He did not see any entry for that. Then he went down to the receptionist on 40 and asked her what she remembered about the matter. She told Lohman that she remembered what happened on Friday pretty well because the police had been over it with her on that Saturday. They came to her home to interview her. Later they interviewed her in the office about the events of that day again, but this time they had asked her about what happened on Thursday as well. She did remember a guy leaving in a wheel chair who had come in earlier. He had checked in as O'Brien. Then, as she was about to leave for her lunch break two men left. She remembered one because he was so friendly. He had been friendly when they came in too and she checked the log. He had logged in as Oyveyer. She remembered the guy in the wheelchair leaving on Friday too. She saw him get in the elevator.

Lohman thanked her and went back to his office. When he got there he told Tete to tell Wiggy what he had found out about Oyveyer and to do a thorough check on the guy. Tete said, "Wiggy. The guy with the bush on his head. That guy! He's always asking me about all sorts of gossip around here. I think he's more of a gossip collector than an investigator."

Lohman said, "He says you know all the gossip."

"I do Hon," she said.

Lohman decided to let the matter rest before he heard more things he didn't want to hear and he went on into his office. When he got into his office Lohman reviewed his notes on what he had to do and noticed that he wanted to hear from Sean and Tambola about a matter he had assigned both of them to. He told Tete to round them up in Sean's office for a meeting the next morning and he got to work on some of his client matters.

37 TAMBOLA AND THE CHAMBER OF DEATH

Wednesday morning Lohman met with Sean and Tambola in Sean's office. They were waiting for him when he arrived. Unlike most junior lawyers, Sean paid a lot of attention to the interior design of his office. One of the features was a set of shelves along one wall that had all sorts of little art objects on them. There were a lot of small china pieces, some small pictures, some jewelry items and other assorted knickknacks. Lohman always gave it a look see when he came in. This time he noticed a stone with a piece of glass or gem in it. "What's this?" he asked.

Sean said, "That's Mr. O'Brien's. Remember I told you he threw it at me that day I went to his house to deliver papers. He sat on it or something and it hurt him and he threw it at me. I caught it and held it out to him and he waived me away. I just left. I didn't know what to do. He was like Attila the Hun."

Tambola said, "You're a Hon, Sean."

Sean started turning red. Redder and redder. Lohman thought he was going to turn into a beet. He said, "OK, OK. Enough of that. Let's get down to business."

The three of them reviewed the matter Lohman came there to discuss. Then Lohman and Tambola left together. As they were walking down the hall she asked Lohman out of nowhere, "Did Sean do it?"

"Do what?" asked Lohman.

"You know," she said. "Kill Mr. O'Brien. Did he?"

"Why on earth would you ask me that?" said Lohman. "What makes you think that?"

"Well," she said, "you remember last spring when Mr. Kirkland was killed in our Lake County office. You were thinking Sean did it because he was up there that night and he had Mr. Kirkland's prize tea cup in his office on the shelves. So now he has Mr. O'Brien's stone and he was in the men's room with him."

Lohman just said, "Let's not talk about this in the hall. Let's go to your office."

When they got to Tambola's office Lohman had to clear files off a chair before he could sit down. Like many of the associates' offices, there were files everywhere. They did the scut-work and they had the files. More and more of them tried to work with files on the computer and they had somewhat less paper in their offices, but they still very often needed the paper files. Of course, some were neater than others. Tambola was one of the others.

Lohman was holding the files he took off the chair. "Where do you want to put these?" he asked.

She held out her hands and said, "Here. Give them to me." She took them and placed them neatly next to other files on the floor.

"The reason I want to talk to you is personal," said Lohman. "Nothing about the matters you are working on. Anyway, it is one of those delicate matters that no one wants to talk about, but – well – what were you doing in the men's room on 43 the Thursday before The Lion died? I understand you use our men's rooms a lot or at least more than just that time."

Tambola didn't answer. She just looked at him.

"I'm asking what you are doing in our men's room," said Lohman.

"What?" said Tambola.

"Oh crap what!" said Lohman. "You heard me."

"Who told you that?" asked Tambola.

"When you won't answer my question, why should I answer yours?" said Lohman. "Now try hard and answer my question."

"Well, sometimes I have to go," she said.

"And you can't make it to the ladies' room?" asked Lohman. "We have them on every floor."

"Well, sometimes I gotta go and I use whatever is nearest," she said.

Lohman said, "That's not a good idea. Now, I could care less, but many people around here would put up a big stink if they found you there. What if Mr.St. Charles found you there?"

She replied, "I doubt he would. He has his own."

"You know that?" asked Lohman.

"Yes," she said, "I've used it. I couldn't hold it once."

"Oh crap!" said Lohman. "Look, just stay out of the men's rooms. Please. Before someone finds out about it. It's your job. You understand. If some of our more prudish people find out about it you're gone."

"I'll try," she said.

"Christ!" said Lohman. "Don't just try. Succeed. Run to the ladies' if you have to."

"Well I do go fast down the halls, but everyone keeps running in to me," she said.

"Try walking on the right. Your right," said Lohman.

251

Tambola looked at him like he was crazy.

"Anyhow," said Lohman, "Were you in there on 43 that Thursday."

"I guess so," Tambola conceded.

"So who else was in there?" asked Lohman.

"Well," she said, "when I came in there was a wheel chair there and someone in the disabled stall. He was making noise. I guess that was Mr. O'Brien. Then - who was it – our bald headed partner – he came in and blew his nose. Then Sean came in. I heard him go. I could see them through the crack. Then I left. The wheel chair was still there, but I didn't hear any more noise from the disabled stall."

Lohman asked, "Did you see Mr. LaRue or someone else? Do you know who Hyman Oyveyer is?"

"I don't know who he is," Tambola said. "Anyway, I didn't see anyone else."

"OK," said Lohman. "Just remember to stay out of the men's rooms. And never, ever go near Mr. St. Charles'."

Tambola responded with a pout and Lohman took his leave and went back to his office.

When he got there Tete said, "Pigman's looking for you. He wants you to call." So Lohman went into his office and called him.

Pigman wanted to talk about a new system for checking people in and out of the firm at the reception desks. IT people love security and Pigman thought the recent events demonstrated that the firm needed a better system, especially one that could tell them when people who had checked in checked out. He wanted to get Lohman's OK to start looking into such a system.

"I was talking to someone at a party," said Pigman. "This guy works in one of the Champion companies and does database work for them. So he told me that Mr. O'Brien – he called him The Chair – he said The Chair was having a dispute with his son Henry about the cost of IT and help systems. The Chair had some cost figures, like $10,000 per computer terminal per year for IT support, and he was saying Henry was wasting his money. Henry was of course trying to explain how modern systems work – I always have that trouble too – you guys who aren't tech savvy don't understand these things. So this guy goes on and on about it. He said Mr. O'Brien was going to fire Henry."

"Then," continued Pigman, "I got to talking to Henry about this at a meeting we had about some software we got from one of his companies. That's where he told me about this new device and software he is working on at his house. He works on this stuff at home. He has his own workshop. So this system will let us check people in and out with minimal interruption of the traffic flow. It's great. Let's make a time and come down and I'll show it to you. So we get to talking and I ask him about the rumor that Mr. O'Brien was going to fire him. Henry said that was just a plan that didn't pan out. Mr. O'Brien was going to spread a rumor that he was going to fire Henry over cost issues and then do it. Then Henry would get a job with a certain competitor. The idea was that Champion could get all the competitor's information in their database and confidential information about a certain chemical formula they used. But Henry said they decided not to do it. They couldn't be sure it was going to work he said. They're something else, huh?"

"Yes," said Lohman. "I certainly hope you are not something else."

Then they made an appointment for Lohman to meet with Pigman about the system and Lohman hung up.

38 TRISHA DELANG

Thursday, Lohman had to be up in the Highland Park, or Lake County office, as it was called. A meeting was scheduled there to discuss the terms of a new movie deal with Trisha DeLang. She was staying at a hotel up there and rehearsing for a concert she was giving Friday evening at Ravine Park which was in Highland Park. This was used as the summer home of the Symphony and a lot of other types of performances were held there too. It was called Ravine Park because there were a lot of ravines in the area. Lohman was not Trisha's lawyer. Sweeney was, but Lohman often attended meetings about her legal affairs so a partner would be present.

Those present at the meeting were Trisha, Sweeney, Lohman, Eben Gohr, who was Trisha's agent, and Monahan O'Reilley, one of the firm's semi-retired partners, referred to as "of counsel". O'Reilley was there because he had done a lot of movie deals in his time. He was one of the lawyers resident in the Lake County office. Sean Featherbottom was there too because he often helped Sweeny out. Trisha was still a minor and she had a guardian who was her mother, but her mother never attended the business discussions. Sweeney just filled her in later and she signed whatever was necessary.

O'Reilley was a drunk. Not the only one in the firm, but perhaps the most colorful. Now, a good old drunk is a handy thing to have these days. Many modern lawyers are high on crystal or cocaine or some other exotic things that don't smell. Booze does, and you can always tell when a drunk is corked. Not so with the more modern and higher class "supplements". O'Reilley often was seen carrying a vase around with him especially on his way to the bathroom. He kept this in his office and used it to puke in. Lohman was one of the few people who knew this and he was relieved to see that O'Reilley had not brought his vase to the meeting. O'Reilley was not only a drunk, but he was drunk. Not too much, but he had enough in him to kill most ordinary people. For him it just made him functional. And it made him smell like booze.

The meeting started at ten in the conference room. Everyone was there except Trisha. They were waiting for her. Soon she came in. She looked around the room and said, "Hi ya'll. Sorry I'm late." Sean was quite impressed by Trisha's celebrity. He sort of gapped at her with a slightly open mouth. She looked at him and said, "You're a cutie, a hottie. Oh Yes! I'm gonna like this meet!"

Sean started turning red again. Lohman thought he would stop breathing soon so Lohman said, "Us too! You're our favorite client. So let's get to work." He turned to Gohr who started explaining things.

The discussion centered around what terms they should ask for in negotiations about the deal coming up the next month and what strategies they should use and who should be licensed to do what. The movie was going to use Trisha's songs and a script she had supposedly written. Actually The Lion had had it ghost written for her. Anyway, she was going to collect the license fees for its use in the movie. They discussed what they thought they could get, what they were going to ask for, and what they thought they would get. They decided on a strategy and then started shooting the breeze and talking about where they should go for lunch or whether they should go at all or just order in. The other stuff was insignificant compared to this. They decided just to order something in and they engaged in small talk until the food came.

Along the way the subject of The Lion's demise came up. Lohman reviewed what he knew with them and allowed as how he thought The Lion was probably murdered. Certainly the police seemed to think so or they would have dropped the matter. He explained that the circumstances would indicate murder. He explained about the two syringes and the lack of finger prints on the one in the neck.

Trisha spoke up, "We all think he was offed. After all, he didn't have too big a fan club."

"Not like yours," Sweeney interjected.

Sean was taking all this in with wide open eyes and a slightly open mouth. He was just looking at one after another as they spoke.

"Thanks," said Trisha. "Hell, I wasn't even too fond of him myself. Even when I was a kid he used to bounce me on his lap and try to get me to feel his crotch. He tried to feel mine too. No,no,no,no – I wouldn't let him. You'd think he was a producer. What a family! Everyone is doing everyone else. Gramps told me he was doing some other women besides Moronika. One was that Nuftdone's wife. Then one day Gramps tells me he knew Cooper, the chauffeur, was doing Moronika. Then he tells me he was doing Cooper's wife. Now, don't tell anyone, but I did Cooper once in a while too. He's good sex. I don't know if Gramps knew that. The whole family's doing it everywhere too. Except Henry. All he does is stay home and fiddle in his workshop. His 'Lab' he calls it. He's strange. I don't even think he knows what sex is. Or maybe he made himself a sex machine. Anyhow, I think in the terms you guys use, we're all a bunch of perverts and sex maniacs. In show business we call this promotional activity. It's just sex."

O'Reilley chimed in. "Oh, I'll say! I used to screw your mother Trisha. Did she tell you?"

Trisha looked at him with a dagger or two. "You couldn't screw a cork Bozo! You need a squirrel on crack climbing up your butt!"

O'Reilley looked at her and said, "Feisty! I like that!"

Sweeney chimed in. "Now Trish, don't get all itchy bitchy. Save it for the concert."

Lohman couldn't help asking, "She's supposed to bring this up in the concert?"

Sweeney said, "No Dude. Not explicitly. If she thinks about it then it'll just make her mad and motivate her. She'll have better delivery."

O'Reilley wasn't done. "My! In all my years with show biz clients! Someone like you Trisha is usually completely well behaved and disciplined at one end even if they are completely depraved and wanton at the other end. One only has to guess which end is up and when. You, on the other hand - you little doll – with you both ends are the naughty part."

Trisha didn't even flinch. She just said, without looking at him, "Go rape yourself!"

Sean was just completely open eyed and open mouthed and amazed. He would have paid big bucks to see this all on stage. And here he was, right in the show! Right on the stage!

Well, did they all walk off in a huff? No. The food arrived and they had an enjoyable lunch. Then they all took pleasant leave of each other.

39 THE CELEBRATION

Nuftdone had been working on opening the probate estate for The Lion and LaRue and others had been working behind the scenes to encourage the court to grant the family's request to seal the record. By Friday both had been accomplished. Everyone involved had anticipated success on both matters and St. Charles and Arty had been working on what they called a victory celebration. Presumably the family could celebrate the fact that someone suitable had taken charge and the fact that their affairs were to remain private. What was really being celebrated so far as St. Charles and Swifty were concerned was the fact that the Swifton Bank was in charge and they both had a lock on keeping the business.

They had arranged the celebration for the next Friday evening, November 11, at the Swifton Palace Hotel in downtown Chicago. This was one of the Swifton family hotels. The Lion never did like the hotel business and he had only a handful of hotels, none of which were in Chicago.

Lohman was looking forward to getting some of his non-O'Brien client matters done and spent the whole week before the celebration doing so, except for a brief meeting with Detective Bongwad and Sargent Gilbert on Tuesday morning.

They met in the conference room next to Lohman's office and compared notes. They updated Lohman on what they had found out, which was not much. Then Lohman updated them on what he had learned.

When Lohman had finished Bongwad and Gilbert exchanged significant looks and Bongwad said, "That explains a lot. That may just wrap it up."

"You know who did it?" asked Lohman.

"Maybe," said Bongwad. "We'll have to check it out. We'll let you know."

"So who do you think it was?" asked Lohman.

"It's pretty simple," said Bongwad. "It's a rule of thumb in murder. The last guy to see the victim alive did it." As he was saying this he and Gilbert got up to go.

Lohman got up too and walked them down the hall asking Bongwad, "So who was the last one to see him? And when? When did he die?"

"It's pretty clear," said Bongwad. "You can't see it?"

"No," said Lohman.

Bongwad and Gilbert both looked at each other. "We'll let you know when we have checked it out," Bongwad said.

Lohman got to the elevator with them. The elevator came and they said goodbye and left.

Lohman spent an unremarkable few days for once and by the next Friday he was ready for the party. Gloria was going to meet him in the office and they were going to go over to the hotel together.

St. Charles and Swifty had planned a fairly big event with all the family members, some of the top officers of Champion companies, the top officers of The Bank and the Wealth Management officers who were going to handle the estate. There were also a variety of F, P & C people there and some of the outside accountants and various other advisers and sycophants. Included also were some of the top politicians, namely several congressmen, both Illinois Senators, Senator Clagghonk, the governor, the mayor and Branda Coulter, the mayoral candidate.

Pansy and her latest boy toy were there as well as many of the socially prominent Chicagoans who were eager to mingle with the even more socially prominent. This element included a contingent of people from the Symphony. There were several from the top board and some from the lower level boards. The Duceys were there and also Hyman Oyveyer and his wife. This may have disturbed The Lion, were he there, but he wasn't and his family had no particular quarrel with Oyveyer.

To bless the whole event The Prophet Andy and the Cardinal had been invited. The Prophet was going to bless the opening and the Cardinal was going to bless the end. St. Charles and Swifty had made it very clear to both that this order had been determined by flipping a coin. At first the Cardinal was very pleased at the opportunity to have the final word, but this feeling disappeared when he realized that The Prophet had no power to keep The Devil away and thus the Dark Prince might appear and disrupt the proceedings before the Cardinal could clean them up. In other words, by the time the Cardinal was to perform a lot of people might have left and the rest might be drunk.

The firm encouraged as many of its people to be there as could attend and a lot of firm partners and associates who had any connection at all with O'Brien or his affairs were there. Many of them were billing for their attendance. Naturally Sweeney was there. He had brought Sean along and when Tambola had learned that Sean was going she demanded to go. Morton Wharton, Nuftdone, Cohenstein, LaRue, Sprack, Feepot, Fileform, Wax, Winter Goren and a lot of other firm partners were there. Monica Platt came along with Lohman and Gloria, just for the social event.

The celebration occupied two ballrooms adjacent to each other. One was set up for cocktails and dinner with a raised stage at one end. St.

Charles, Cohenstein, Lohman, Swifty, The Prophet, The Cardinal and a few of the highest Bank and Champion officers were to sit there at a table facing the audience with a podium for speakers in the middle. Their wives sat with them, except for The Cardinal and the Prophet. Those two were to be seated at opposite ends of the table to forestall any awkwardness.

The evening began with cocktails and socializing which went on until St. Charles assumed the podium and called for everyone's attention. Once everyone was seated The Prophet gave the opening prayer and then St. Charles went back to the podium and started into his imitation of a moron. Or perhaps it wasn't an imitation.

After half an hour of St. Charles, Cohenstein got up and told everyone what he claimed St. Charles had told them. It took five minutes. He had just finished and was going to tell everyone to enjoy their dinner when every door to the room suddenly burst open and a horde of police officers rushed in and surrounded everyone. Behind them Bongwad and Gilbert ran in with five officers dressed in riot gear and automatic rifles at the ready. They paused as they entered and looked around. Gilbert saw something and pointed. "Get that blonde kid!" he commanded. "The little blonde poof! That's him. And that little witch next to him."

The officers rushed over to Sean Featherbottom and Tambola Cook and grabbed both of them and hauled them out of their chairs. By now Bongwad and Gilbert had approached the stage and were going up to talk to Lohman. Bongwad called out his name. "Lohman," he said, "We told you we'd let you know. Here he is. And her. They were in on it together." He motioned to the uniformed storm troopers to bring Sean and Tambola up to the stage. "Here they are," said Bongwad and the uniformed officers brought them up on the stage. "The last ones to see O'Brien alive. He did it. O'Brien called him a queer. So he killed O'Brien. She was in on it too. She was there. We found out about her. She'll do anything he says."

Gilbert added, "Used to be the other way around. It used to be the queers who got killed."

Sean was handcuffed and being held by two of the biggest officers. One had a rope around his neck. He just looked from one to the other. He thought he was going to die. He hoped he didn't pee. Not right in front of everyone. Tambola was struggling with two of the other officers who were restraining her.

Lohman threw down his napkin and arose. He went over to the podium where the microphone was and said to Bongwad, "Stop! If there is one person who did not kill The Lion it was Sean Featherbottom!"

"Oh yeah?" said Gilbert. "So who did?'

"Not him," said Lohman. But he then thought to himself, "Yes. Who did?" He knew he better figure it out quick or Sean and Tambola were gone. This was the second time Sean had been accused of murder within the year. He probably wouldn't even get bail set.

"Just listen to me," said Lohman. "All will be made clear. All will be revealed." Then he said, not because he knew what had happened, but because he wanted to keep the cops from disposing of Sean and Tambola, "It is all very obvious. I will explain it to you." He licked his lips and got to work.

Lohman started in. "First, was The Lion murdered at all? He died from an overdose of heroin. That by itself does not indicate murder. But I will grant you that the other details indicate murder. Under all that covering he wore there were two syringes that had the drug in them. One in his arm and one in his neck. The one in his arm had his prints on it. It was labeled to contain testosterone and that is a drug he took regularly. He probably injected it himself. There is no indication he was an addict. The Medical Examiner concluded this. So why did he have the drug? Maybe it was suicide. On the other hand, this is not likely since the other details indicate someone else was involved. For one thing, all the syringes in his wheel chair bag had heroin in them. Their labels indicated they contained testosterone. If he wanted to fill one with heroin and kill himself with it he didn't need that many. However, if someone wanted him to take the drug by mistake, that is what they would do. Fill all the syringes with the heroin and leave it to him to take the drug himself, not knowing it was heroin. Then we see that the syringe in his neck had no prints on it. Nor the unused syringes in his bag. Additionally the syringe in his neck was in a vein. Could he have done this after taking the dose in his arm? Both were fatal. If he did the neck first, could he have then done the arm shot? But perhaps the most telling thing is that both syringes were covered up. After taking both fatal doses, could he have brought his shirt down over his arm and put on his jacket and put his scarf back around his neck? He also had gloves on. Since his prints were on one of the syringes, he would have had to put gloves on after the first injection. This could explain why the syringe in the neck had no prints, but once again, could he have done this after taking the first injection? And why do one without gloves and then one with gloves? Someone else did this."

"The next question that comes to the fore is, when was he murdered? When did he die?" Lohman looked at the officers and paused. "You know yourself there is some question here. Your Medical Examiner says he died no later than Thursday. How is this possible? Numerous people saw The Lion after Thursday. Sean himself says he did. On Friday morning at The Lion's house. But of course we must discount this, at least for purposes of determining what happened. Others saw him at home that morning too. Wandrasha, his daughter for one. Then our Mr. Nuftdone and numerous others were in a conference in our offices with him on Friday. His son Henry was there with him. Numerous others were too. Henry left the conference room with him. They went down the hall and Henry took him in to the washroom. Then Mr. Nuftdone saw him leaving the firm offices. The receptionist did too. She saw him get on the elevator. And his wheel chair was found later at his home. So how could he have been murdered on Thursday?"

Lohman paused and then continued. "Now no one saw him after he left our offices on Friday afternoon. He was supposed to meet with our Mr. LaRue and our Mr. St. Charles Friday afternoon and he never appeared. This makes it seem that he died on Friday afternoon."

"On the other hand," continued Lohman, "there are some troubling questions that remain unresolved about this conclusion. For one thing, how did he or his body get back into our offices? He was not checked in again in the lobby. Our receptionist does not recall him coming back. He was hard to miss. Then, while he missed a meeting on Friday afternoon, he also missed a meeting with The Prophet Andy on Thursday afternoon. Missing meetings and not getting in touch with the other participants to reschedule in advance was not like him."

"And speaking of things that were unusual for him, let's look at his behavior with the ladies. Whatever he was doing, and whatever mood he was in, an attractive young lady got his full attention and conversation. Yet in two instances he ignored two attractive young ladies. No one who knew him ever saw him do that. When he came up the elevator to our offices on Friday he was with a client of ours who, believe me, is stunningly beautiful, and who is someone who he had met casually before. She greeted him. He ignored her. And again, once in our offices, he ignored a lovely lady he passed in our halls. The secretary to Mr. LaRue who is also a beauty."

"And then we have the conclusion of the Medical Examiner. It is hard to disagree with the conclusions of the experts. In this case one thing I could say right at the outset when I found the body is that the dead one stinks. If you put a piece of meat out on your counter and let it sit I don't think it would smell like that in one day. Of course the meat we buy has been cleaned up and is not attached to the innards of the animal which I am told is where the stink develops, but at any rate I am assured that bodies do not begin to smell that bad in one day. I am also told there is no easy way to speed up the process of decomposition to speed up the time of producing such odors."

"So," said Lohman. "So when did he die? The Medical Examiner gives us an opinion. A conclusion based on certain facts. But the Medical Examiner did not see the murder take place. On the other hand we have the eye witnesses. They saw The Lion Friday. But did they see the murder? No. they did not see it either. What did they see? They saw The Lion. But did they? The way The Lion was usually dressed you could not really see him. Almost his entire face was covered. But they heard him speak. Did they? Remember he spoke through an electro larynx. It made a sound like a machine speaking. Furthermore, when he was in our offices, he said very little on Friday. For one thing he had been advised not to say anything because the other side was there. And to the extent he did say anything, from what I have heard from those in the conference, he said mostly 'yes' and 'no'."

Lohman paused again. "So what does all this mean? Who everyone could have seen was an imposter. No one saw who was under all that covering. So I will grant you that if an imposter was involved, Sean and Tambola are still not ruled out. However, that would mean they had an accomplice."

Sean and Tambola exchanged glances. Sean looked like he was going to die from woe. Tambola looked like she was very interested in what Lohman had to say. She also looked like she was quite happy with two big storm troopers restraining her.

Lohman continued. "Who did it? That is really the question. The question is not when he died, other than as how that helps us determine who did it. So let's review what we know about who did what. There are several people of interest here."

The Dead One Stinks

"Let's look at Hyman Oyveyer for one. He was here that Thursday morning. He had a fight with The Lion going on. He thought The Lion had released adverse information about his company causing the stock to go down. He also supposedly had a disagreement with The Lion about matters at the Symphony. He wanted to get on the top level board with the best prospects for networking and The Lion, who was powerful there, prevented this. There is also a rumor that Mr. Oyveyer was adamantly complaining about these things in various circles and that he had informed on The Lion to the SEC about certain matters. The rumor is that these complaints stopped when some started shooting at Mr. Oyveyer from the woods around his home. That Thursday morning he was here to complain about these things to Mr. LaRue of our firm. They both went to the men's room on 43 later. That is where I found The Lion's body on Saturday. He was wheeled in there on Thursday, by his son Jason. "

"So let us look at what happened on Thursday in the wash room," said Lohman. "Oddly enough there was a witness. Who? Miss Cook." Lohman nodded at Tambola. "Now we do not want to base things on what the accused persons say, unless they are admissions. She admits she was in there. So does Sean." Just then Lohman remembered what this sounded like. "Well – she was. Some sort of mistake. She was using the facilities by mistake."

Lohman was vaguely thinking he had said she had thought it was the ladies' room, but at any rate he knew he should get on with it before anyone got to thinking about just what she was doing there. "Naturally Miss Cook was in one of the stalls. She tells us who was there and she does not mention Mr. Oyveyer or Mr. LaRue. On the other hand they both admit being there. The important thing here is that Ms. Cook and Sean both tell us the wheel chair was there when they were there. Both Mr. Oyveyer and Mr. LaRue say there was no wheel chair there."

"So did The Lion leave? The impostor? Did the impostor come in and assume The Lion's identity and leave in the wheel chair? I guess that is where this leads. But that would mean leaving the body in the stall where I found it. The cleaning person says the stall was occupied Thursday night when she was cleaning the room. One thing we know is that the body was not there on Friday. Mr. Sweeney used that stall on Friday. Was the body moved to another stall? How and by who? Were all the other stalls used before then? Usually most of the other stalls are used each day from my experience. When I found the body it was in the disabled stall, so if it had been moved from there we also have to ask who moved it back."

"So now," said Lohman, "by the time Mr. Oyveyer and Mr. LaRue got there it would seem that Elvis had left the building, so to speak. Of course that leaves Sean and Tambola as having been the last to see The Lion or be with him. And one of them could have been the impostor. Or is this realistic? Let us remember that Sean did have The Lion's stone. This is another thing we all remember about The Lion. He always had the stone with the glass or gem stone in it. Sean says The Lion had this on Friday morning and threw it at him and wouldn't take it back. Now is that realistic? We all know how The Lion was attached to that stone and took it out to fondle at the slightest sign of distress. Note also that The Lion had the stone at the Thursday meeting, but not at the Friday meeting."

At this one of the officers holding Sean tightened the noose around his neck.

Lohman went on. "Who else was there on Thursday? Jason O'Brien. He wheeled The Lion into the men's room to begin with. However, our Mr. Allen says he saw Jason leaving as he, Mr. Allen, was going in. Our Miss Cook confirms this. What about Henry O'Brien? On Thursday he went down the hall with Jason and The Lion. But he did not go into the wash room with them. He went on down the hall."

Lohman looked around and then said, "Let's get back to Mr. Allen. After all these events of Thursday through Saturday he had a pen like The Lion's. We all know about the pen. It was always sticking out of his jacket pocket displaying the diamond on its end. How did he get The Lion's pen? The Lion had it in the meeting on Friday and Thursday. Should I say the impostor had it on Friday? And there is something I have noticed about Mr. Allen. When I found the body I noticed that the toilet paper in the stall had one corner folded under. I have seen this in our washrooms before. Who does this? Curiously, when I talked to Mr. Allen about the pen, he started doing this with pieces of paper on his desk. Does this mean he was in the stall? After all, when I found the body, the toilet did not appear to have been used and The Lion's pants had not been taken down. There was no indication he had used the toilet in any way except to sit on. And we remember that he may have gone in there just to take an injection of his medicine, not to relieve himself. "

"So who else might have wanted to kill The Lion?" asked Lohman. Here Lohman considered ways to soften what he was about to say and came up with, "He was a man of great prominence. He had an effect on the lives of many people. And in business there are winners and losers. Some of the losers do not take it well and The Lion was usually the winner. I have heard many rumors about people like this, but none seems to have had contact with The Lion during the times at issue here."

"So where does this leave us?" said Lohman. He paused.

St.Charles could be heard saying, "Confused." But then, he always was.

Swifty could be heard saying, "This is exciting!" Well, it certainly beats banking and meat packing.

Lohman started up again. "Let's look at this pen of The Lion's. Actually there were two identical pens. Henry found them and bought them and gave one to his father. He kept the other pen for himself. What happened to his pen? On Thursday he was complaining that he had lost his pen. The Lion had his and he signed papers with it. Mr. Nuftdone confirmed his signature by having it checked with prior known signatures of his. And Friday The Lion, or whoever it was, had the pen sticking out of his pocket. Yet by Saturday when I found the body there was no pen or stone. After that day we find there are still two pens. Henry found his and Mr. Allen left one of them in my office. Now these pens are very distinctive in ways other than having a diamond on the end. One was the color of ink. Since I am responsible for the day to day business of the firm and since Mr. Allen is an interested and active partner, he leaves my secretary notes from time to time about things he thinks need attention. The color of his notes changed dramatically to the color of the diamond headed pen between October 3rd and the 5th. The Monday and Wednesday before October 6th, the Thursday when the Medical Examiner says The Lion died. So does this mean that Mr. Allen is the killer? Probably not. He is – well he shares a characteristic in common with many men of prominence in that he is forgetful about things like pens."

St. Charles could have flipped out these words without any thought or effort at all. Even if he would have been incapable of the brevity. However, for Lohman, this kind of malarkey was a conscious effort. He paused and then continued. "We have found out that Mr. Allen and Henry were in a conference with Mr. Sprack of our firm on October 3rd. It is not hard to suppose that Mr. Allen picked up Henry's pen at that time. That would account for Henry's comments about missing his pen on Thursday."

Lohman went on. "At this point a very interesting fact must be noted. Mr. Allen left the pen in my office. And Henry found his pen again. Was this his own pen he found or his father's? They were identical. Remember, the pen was not found on the body. So if Mr. Allen got Henry's pen then Henry got his father's pen. How did this happen? Did Henry kill his father and then take The Lion's pen to replace his? Ridiculous, it seems. The very next day Henry was in a conference at our offices with his father, or the imposter, I should say. And the pen was on the imposter. So if Henry had anything to do with it, who was the imposter? This does not make sense."

Lohman thought for a moment. Then he went on. "What if we are not talking about an imposter? Or at least not all the time. While all the covering kept us from seeing that the person in the chair was an imposter, it could also have kept us from seeing that the person was The Lion. The dead Lion. This could explain a lot. He could have been killed on Thursday and left in the men's room. He was seen leaving by himself so that could have been the imposter. That would explain why there was no wheel chair left in the wash room. The imposter could have gone to The Lion's home. Jason saw him there Thursday afternoon. Sean and Wandrasha saw him there the next day. He didn't say much to any of them. Then he comes back to our office for the Friday meeting. This is the imposter. He then goes to the men's room and gets the real Lion from the stall and puts him in the wheel chair. The wheel chair then contains the dead body all wrapped up and in that condition it attends the meeting. This would explain why the stall was empty later, during the meeting, when Mr. Sweeney used it. After the meeting the body was left in the stall and the imposter took over again and that is why The Lion was seen leaving our offices, but never again. This also answers the question of how The Lion's body got back in our offices. It never left."

"So," Lohman said, "what is the significance of Henry having his father's pen? Once again, did he get it when he killed his father? Why would he do such a thing anyway? It may not be the best motive and I may be barking up a tree, but The Lion was always criticizing Henry. He was quite vocal about it and did it in front of others. He threatened to fire Henry. And who else did he fire? Was it a believable threat? He did fire his own brother Ryan. And he did fire the whole Champion Screw & Bolt Board of Directors, apart from his daughter. And that was over an IT issue which is what he was always criticizing Henry for."

"But this is all pretty far out. People heard The Lion speaking Friday. How does a corpse speak? They saw him propelling his own wheel chair. How does a corpse do that? Both were electronically controlled, that's how. And Henry was working on a device which could control other devices. Something that could take over control of anything that depended on electrical impulses for its control. This is how the wheel chair and the electro larynx were controlled. This would also account for the restricted nature of The Lion's speech in the meeting. And at that Friday meeting Henry had a different smart phone which he kept using. Using a smart phone was usual for him in any meeting, of course, but he said this one was experimental. And when he discussed his invention with us at another meeting and turned things on and off he did so with his smart phone."

Then Lohman remembered. "Now we ask, who was the imposter who left the building on Thursday as The Lion? And who then went to The Lion's home and spoke later in the day with Jason and the next morning with Sean and Wandrasha? Henry tells us he went to Omaha Thursday and did not come back to Chicago until the next day. Then he said he went to Los Angeles Friday. We checked. He did go to Omaha, but it was on Friday. Not Thursday. Apparently he was here to impersonate his father on Thursday. Why would he tell us this, except to supply an alibi? Maybe he was just mistaken. But about both days? We found out he did go to L.A. too, but that was Saturday."

"Another significant fact is this. Jason took his father into the men's room on Thursday. He left his father there. Then we hear about Mr. Allen, Sean and Tambola being there. They all saw the wheel chair. Tambola was there all along. She heard noise from the disabled stall. Then nothing. If The Lion had injected himself with the first syringe, that would have quieted him down at least. Then she left. Later Mr. Oyveyer and Mr. LaRue came in and the wheel chair was not there. Sean came out a little before Tambola. He went around the floor to the other side. The wash room has entrances on both sides of the building. While he was over on the other side from where he had exited he saw Miss Cook come out. But he saw something else. He saw Henry in the 43rd floor waiting area. Henry was still there. So while no one saw Henry being that last one to see The Lion alive, he had access. The next witnesses we have say the wheel chair was no longer there, which it wouldn't be if Henry had gone in and given his father another shot in the neck just to make sure and then dressed up as his father and taken off in the wheel chair. Remember that he always had that big bag with him and he could have had an outfit similar to his father's in there."

Lohman then said, "Now who came in when on Friday? Henry came in at a different time than his father or the imposter. The building records show Henry came in about twenty minutes, I think, after his father. Does that clear him? Not if he came in dressed as his father and then went to the men's room took off the disguise and dressed as himself and then left the building and then checked back in again as himself. Remember, we don't have any record of who left the building and when. He probably left the wheel chair in his father's stall. After coming back in he went to the stall and got his father and came into the meeting with him. After the meeting he took his father back to the men's room and left him in the stall. He dressed as his father again and left the building in the wheel chair. Apparently he took the wheelchair to The Lion's home. He was not risking too much if he was seen doing this since he had succeeded at it on Thursday afternoon and Friday morning. Nor was he risking anything if he was seen as himself at The Lion's home because he was there often. After going there as The Lion he took off for Omaha."

Lohman continued, "We do not have to wonder too much about where Henry got the heroin either. It came from Champion Pharmaceuticals which is also where The Lion got his testosterone and it should not have been too hard for the owner's son to get both."

The Dead One Stinks

"Numerous small questions present themselves, but none are of much importance. For instance, how did Henry get into the stall on Thursday? To begin with, someone did. If The Lion let someone in it would more probably have been one of his sons rather than a stranger. And if The Lion was out of it or dead from the first dose of the drug then he did not let anyone in. Instead the person could have stepped up on the wheel chair and reached over to undo the latch or the person could have got down on the floor and slipped under the door and unlatched it."

In the background Swifty could be heard saying, "Just like when we were kids at the airport."

Lohman continued. "Obviously they did not take these steps on leaving. Whoever it was just placed a paper wedge in the door to keep it shut."

Lohman then said, "This scenario would also explain why The Lion did not appear at the Thursday and Friday afternoon meetings. His being dead would explain it, but the scenario also explains why there was no cancellation. Henry did not know about the meetings. That's why, even as an imposter, he did not call to cancel."

Then Lohman looked around the room and saw Henry. He pointed at Henry and said, "So it was you Henry. But you forgot that after a while the dead one stinks. And you took the pen."

At this Henry shot up, pulled out his smart phone and pointed it at the podium and shut off the microphone. He started running for the doors and raised his smart phone again and the lights went out. At this point Tete was just coming in through the same doors with something she had to deliver to Lohman. She had no idea what was going on, but she did know some maniac was trying to run her down. She decked him and the police ran up and restrained his writhing body on the floor. Tete just kept walking in and looking for Lohman. Up front Monica Platt had come forward from the audience and was hugging Lohman and telling him what a performance he had put on.

Tete turned to the nearest table and said, "See! Look at that will you!"